CW01262958

WITHIN THE SHADOWS SERIES
BOOK TWO

TOOTH AND CLAW

AMY NEVILLS

This novel is entirely a work of fiction. The names, characters and incidents portrayed in it are the work of the author's imagination. Any resemblance to actual persons, living or dead, events or localities is entirely coincidental.

Copyright © by Amy Nevills 2025.
Cover art by: Miblart

All rights reserved. No part of this publication may be reproduced, stored or transmitted in any form or by any means, electronic, mechanical, photocopying, recording, scanning, or otherwise without written permission from the publisher. It is illegal to copy this book, post it to a website, or distribute it by any other means without permission.

ISBN 979-8-990-9525-3-9

CHAPTER ONE

Once upon a darkened night

"Stop googling yourself," the bored, flat voice ordered, as if she could do nothing but immediately obey his demands. "Wallowing and pouting is beneath you and, frankly, pretty unappealing."

"Stop telling me what to do," she shot back sharply, her guilty fingers freezing from their soundless tapping on her phone. "Besides, who says I'm even doing that?"

Years ago, when she first got into the business, her agent had told her to never, ever set up alerts for her own name on her phone. Better for her peace of mind. If the media said something she needed to know, her agency would be sure to convey the message. But sometimes the temptation to search herself was too great and she succumbed. An actress out of the public eye was forgotten like last week's trash unless, of course, her disappearance was due to scandal. The press and public ate that shit up. Unfortunately.

"You get a sneaky look in your eyes, and then you curl up away from everyone, so we can't see what you're doing." An exasperated sigh escaped him, followed by the soft thud of his foot hitting the floor as he rearranged himself.

The bored sound echoing through the room made her want to throw her phone at him. Who was he to sigh at her as if she were the problem?

"But we're not idiots. We all know what you're doing." *We* referred to her 24/7 security team. None of them were quite as underfoot as this one, though.

Snorting, Ravyn mumbled, "Debatable." Out of the corner of her eye, the outline of another eye appeared on her dark phone, watching her, before slowly blinking closed and going dark once again.

Damn. She *had* seen that, right?

Refraining from simply crushing her phone in her hand, she flipped the phone over without giving herself a chance to find out if the reflection was her own eye, a figment of her imagination—or something more sinister.

Not enough, Ravyn decided immediately. Shoving her phone under the throw pillow she lay curled against as if trying to resist temptation, she nonchalantly eased her legs down so she wasn't quite so turned away from the rest of the room. There. It could no longer see her if, in fact, *it* even looked at her. After centuries of living, she despised this helpless feeling, this feeling that someone or *something* could be watching her unaware. How could you battle something you couldn't even see? That, apparently, was the question of this century.

Sitting in a chair across from her, still hidden by a newspaper and not even bothering to look over or around the paper, he dryly informed her, "Your fans will hardly forget you within a few weeks." One foot crossed over a knee again; he didn't even deign to meet her eyes when he issued this particular proclamation as he flipped a page in the thin paper.

She knew from observing him over the past few months that the paper came from some place in Missouri that she'd never heard of but arrived weekly no matter what their current address was. Perhaps it was picked up on a weekly run, one that included picking up her subsistence. Didn't he know he could read the news online? Anything of importance anyway.

This time, she was unable to resist the urge to throw something at him. The pillow flattened the newspaper against his still hidden face, and Ravyn smiled in satisfaction when she heard another tiny sigh escape him. This was followed by the unsettled jostling of his crossed foot before it abruptly cut off movement. Knowing that he knew her irritation at least briefly brought her a childish sense of satisfaction that Ravyn knew she should be well above. Removing the pillow and tossing it next to his chair, he folded the newspaper in half and then half again and again with crisply executed motions, before tossing the mess of wrinkled paper onto the floor next to the pillow. Setting both feet firmly on the floor, he leaned forward, placing an elbow on each knee as he leaned toward her.

His face, smooth and devoid of emotion, settled on her. "You have my attention now. Is there something you need to say or tell me? Otherwise, I might misunderstand such childishness. So please"—he waved a hand outward— "please continue. What might I possibly do for you, Princess?"

He wasn't as unaffected as he attempted to appear, though. After weeks with him, she knew his shifter heartbeat better than her own slow thumping. It was always fast, but right now its siren song thumped through her head even faster than normal.

"I don't think Oliver pays you to call me names," Ravyn said, knowing she was behaving childishly and hating herself for it. Never in all her many, many years had she been stuck in one place for so long. She was just so incredibly bored. And a bored vampire was a dangerous vampire, or at least that was what her captors—er, guards—should consider. Staring up at the wall, she strained her eyes to count the points on the patterned border around the room.

"First, Oliver doesn't pay me at all; we're partners. Second, I'm not calling you names; I'm stating a few facts." Sebastian stared at her as if he could figure her out. "Besides, you call me names all the time."

"Thor? Isn't that your name?" Ravyn smiled, losing count of the points on the wall, even though she'd counted them many times over the past few months. Needling the wolf shifter was better than counting. Knowing and hating how silly she was acting; she was unable to stop. So, he did notice she called him that; she'd been doing so for months now and he acted as if she was saying his name correctly the entire time. But come on; tall, super build, a jawline that could cut glass and curly, blond hair? His mother should have just named him Thor at birth.

That sharp jawline clenched tightly; she'd been doing that a lot to him lately. "You know as well as I do that the threats out there mean we need to hang tight for a while. Unless, of course, you want me to call Oliver and get approval for something else." Sebastien let that threat simmer in the air for a second. "Besides, you have plenty to do here, or I can get the pup to come play a card game with you or run some lines here in your gilded cage."

"You wouldn't dare call Oliver," Ravyn hissed, feeling her fangs threaten to descend at the wolf shifter's blasphemy. Her progeny was finally out of his office and taking a well-deserved trip with his new girlfriend. They weren't disturbing the two unless someone died.

How funny that sounded. Oliver's girlfriend.

Ollie's special friend? Partner? No, Sebastian was Oliver's business partner, and it seemed wrong to rank his relationship with Eva that as well.

Oliver's lover? No. Gross.

"Besides, I think he's turned his phone off while they're out of the country." Traveling, enjoying life, having adventures went without saying, she thought with more than a smidgen of jealousy. "Besides you're *partners*. Why would you ask his permission to let me out of my cage? Do you really want to tell him how bad it's gotten?" Goddess, she was grouchy. Childish and grouchy... What a combination for a vampire.

"Nothing has gotten *bad*. The only thing bad right now is this waiting game. I won't call Oliver," Sebastian admitted with a growl deep from his chest, as if his wolf gave its agreement as well. "As if I don't know he needs the break. And as if I wouldn't know how to get a hold of my partner even with his phone off. How could I disturb him during this time with his new mate?"

Ravyn considered his words. Yes, Eva could be called Oliver's mate. That seemed more acceptable than "girlfriend." The confirmed bachelor had settled down quite nicely into domestic bliss. Hell, he even had part-time custody of an unpredictable, headstrong hellhound pup thanks to his new mate, Eva.

Yes, *mate* rolled off the tongue. She silently mouthed the word, trying it out. It fit. *Mate*, she purred in her head. Did Bash have a mate? Of course he didn't, or he wouldn't be here with her for weeks on end away from a beloved mate. Her throat rumbled in a low growl at the thought of him having someone else out there waiting for him. Damn, she'd been locked up here too long when she considered mate and the wolf in the same thought.

Despite having his hair pulled back in a smooth bun, Bash attempted to run a frustrated hand through it.

Frustration, brought on by yours truly, Ravyn thought guiltily.

He muttered a curse. "Fenrir! Princess, you try my patience." Pushing up from his chair, Sebastian paced the room, pausing at the windows that overlooked the cityscape, most likely his own animal begging to be let out. He wasn't the picture of calmness that he appeared. The waiting game was playing on him as well.

For a moment, Ravyn felt a bit of guilt. She was better than this juvenile facade, and she knew better than anyone what was at stake. *At stake?* Eva would like that one. Although an overused vampire pun, it had come out naturally enough. But for Thor to use the name of his wolf creator as a curse meant that he wasn't happy with the current situation either. Or perhaps it was a prayer to him? Either way, it didn't bode well for the current situation. Knowing she wasn't alone in this frustrating waiting game helped her a bit— not much, but a bit.

Being trapped in a 6,000-square-foot apartment floor with every amenity possible was hardly a chore and despite the complaints she made, she did know if was for her own safety. Her boredom didn't compare to the ennui of the man's wolf, which certainly chaffed to be let out to run. Sebastian had spent all his time in the city the last few months since the threats had escalated. That couldn't be good for an animal that needed to run and hunt. His sacrifice was more than hers, she reluctantly admitted to herself.

Maybe. Probably. Instead of staying in her apartment, perhaps it was time to move homes for a bit again. Shake things up. Maybe they could find a house in suburbia with a small yard? Even if the wolf couldn't come out there, the man could feel the grass and dirt beneath his feet. Although more than likely it would be turf and sand; probably not a feasible way to ground oneself.

"There are no lines to run or practice." He was referring to his earlier suggestion.

No scripts meant no lines.

"I'm worried they'll forget me." Ravyn said the words softly, almost hoping he wouldn't hear her or the vulnerability in her voice, especially considering it was mostly a lie. Worry about being forgotten was a fear, but Ravyn knew the ambiguity of her statement meant "they" could be interpreted as her fans and co-workers when, in fact, she hated being left behind by Oliver, even if she complained about his constant meddling in her life.

"As if..." Sebastian humphed, glancing back as he

paced from wall to window, stretching his arms overhead, exposing a tiny bit of his tanned skin above his hips for a moment before twisting his neck back and forth, easing out the kinks that came from too much time spent in one position. A Celtic tattoo peeked out from his collarbone as he stretched, then he rearranged his simple white tee before she could focus on it for too long.

Snap. A bird rammed into the window grabbing both of their attention before it fluttered away stunned. The building was a magnet for confused birds.

"You don't know that. This industry—the fans, the directors, the paparazzi—all of them are fickle. If you aren't in their face, they forget you for the next up and coming thing. I'm not ready to be forgotten this lifetime. Even if I were in the news for being missing from the public eye, it's better than nothing." It wasn't a lie that she was focused on the public attention; however, it was a lie or, as she liked to tell herself, an exaggeration that she cared much about it. Focusing on that unimportant drivel allowed her to occupy her mind with things other than what was truly bothering her.

Silence.

Her supernatural stalker had been silent in the weeks following Eva's rescue from his warlock minions. It was assumed that he needed to regroup since he'd lost the powerful mage who more than likely was behind most, if not all, of the ward breaches. And whatever secondary magic had soured and boosted the deranged mage had been quiet as well. Regrouping or giving up? After all that had occurred, it seemed impossible that the stalker was giving up.

The hellhounds he'd forced to track and terrorize Eva were gone, free to return with their pup to the underworld. The minor witches who had been killed alongside their leader might not have been too much of a threat, but they were still bodies and servants gone from his service, hopefully leaving him weak, vulnerable, exposed.

Goddess knew that Ravyn herself was sick of feeling this way and wished he received tenfold the suffering. Then, and only then, would she gleefully rip his throat out and bathe in his blood. Shuddering a little in anticipation of that moment, Ravyn hardly noticed when Sebastian turned away from the window to watch her.

When had he opened the drapes? She'd closed them earlier when she first came in despite the tint allowing just a trickle of the fall sunlight to filter through, something she normally enjoyed. But she'd closed them against the reflection, the possibility of a face looking back at her that wasn't her own. The light filtered through in one, two, three, four, five, six spots. Ravyn wanted to maim and kill whoever had broken through her sanctuary, threatening her well-earned peace.

"They'll wait for you," he murmured, breaking her

Tooth and Claw

mental revelry of ripping apart the faceless, nameless entity who stalked and threatened her. "If not this lifetime, then the next."

Wordlessly, Bash handed her a spiced wine-and-blood mixture, which she took with a small nod and grateful smile. Apparently, it was meal time again, but the day had gotten away from her as she mindlessly scrolled the internet. "They'll wait," he ascertained firmly before he released the glass.

For a moment, Ravyn had forgotten who he was talking about. Oh yes, her public. The public whose adoration she claimed to want and need. Her mind was adrift, but she needed to keep her focus if she expected her deviations from the truth to remain believable.

"Not that you're worried about them." Scrunching his face, Sebastian considered her words and actions. He examined her so intently she feared he read her mind. Perhaps he did; nothing about this damn wolf surprised her anymore.

"Don't presume to tell me my mind, Thor," Ravyn retorted sharply, raising her chin in a futile attempt to look down her nose at the wolf looming above her as she settled her meal against her lips.

"As if," muttered Sebastian, brown eyes gazing toward the heavens as if pleading to his own gods for mercy. "Princess, do you think I've not noticed you've either covered or broken every mirror in this place? Or that you cover any reflective surface the minute you enter a room?" A pointed look at the window confirmed that he'd opened the blinds on purpose. "You don't even hold your wine glass between sips, probably because you're either afraid of your own reflection or of what you might see there."

This wolf was observant, clearly one reason why Oliver trusted him with half his business as well as her safety. However, if Oliver knew the elicit thoughts she'd been having about Bash, he definitely would have pulled him from the detail, partners or not.

The silence grew heavy between the two, and Ravyn looked away from Sebastian's dark, inquisitive eyes, afraid he might see the truth in hers. Couldn't he just leave her in peace? But no, nothing could be kept secret. The air between them grew as thick and heavy as the silence for several moments, while Ravyn studied a throw pillow on the end of the sofa, refusing to respond at all.

"Ah, I see. Why did it take this long to put it together? You're not afraid of what you'll see, but what might see you?" The air nearly snapped as the anger and heat sizzled off him with his realization.

"Ravyn, gods above! Has the bastard found another way in already? We've been sitting on our asses watching and waiting and you've not said anything. We can't do our jobs if you aren't honest with us. I... I can't even begin to know or guess what you're thinking. Why wouldn't you tell us immediately? And why in all the hells isn't the over-the-top, expensive-as-hell, magical security system that is supposed to be so great keeping him out?"

The three scrunched wrinkles between his eyes only appeared when he was angry or frustrated. Ravyn nearly had them memorized. One, two, three. He would probably snap if she touched them, yet they still called to her to smooth them away.

It took Ravyn a moment to recognize the feeling building in the pit of her stomach and moving up through her chest.

The uncomfortable sensation of guilt.

She'd known that the team would want to know, and should know, about the vexatious feelings of being watched through the mirrors. The eye or eyes that would stare at her unblinking through the reflective area of a serving tray or the darkness that swam through the windows, searching and following her every movement. But a small part of her thought the feelings were the result of paranoia, that the glimpses out of the corner of an eye were her fears and imagination coming to life. She just hadn't been *sure.*

Pulling her knees to her chin, Ravyn wrapped her arms around her legs, trying to find a way to articulate what she'd felt and sensed and why she hadn't told them yet. Yes, she'd planned to tell them soon, once she knew for sure. Her only excuse for not telling them was that after a few millennia, she was just used to taking care of herself. Despite Ollie's constant need to offer her protection, it was entirely unnecessary; or at least in the past it had been.

Her fingers tapped one at a time against her thumb. One, two, three, four. Other hand. Five, six, seven, eight. Repeat.

Ravyn allowed Oliver's security because it simply made things easier. But ease made one inattentive, and in this world letting your guard down was akin to being killed—or worse, discovered. She hadn't lived this long due to the protection of others. During the times she and Oliver had traveled together, they'd trusted and relied on each other to remain hidden in plain sight, but as the times changed, Oliver considered sentinels the same level of protection, if not better than friends and comrades. He'd apparently forgotten that for years she'd relied on no one, and that he was neither the first nor the last companion with whom she would travel. Obviously, she'd let him win the battle, but at what cost? Her edge had softened, and someone obviously considered her weak enough to stalk, kidnap, and torture her friends. Maybe it was easier to simply pack up and start over with a new name and identity somewhere far, far away.

The ten years that Oliver's security detail had been attached to her in Hollywood was a blink of an eye for her. In public, his security remained hidden from all prying eyes, but she knew they were there. They allowed the facade of human security to push her past the crowds, open doors for her, and be the face of protection. But her real security was a mixture of vampires and wolf shifters who blended into the shadows in public and took up residence in whatever building she made her accommodations in.

Shrugging a slender shoulder at the enraged wolf who fought to keep his anger controlled wasn't answer enough. She knew that such a disrespectful answer would enrage her if she herself had received that as an answer. Ravyn waited a breath as Sebastian smoothed his blond hair back, pausing to compose himself and consider her non-response. Mesmerized, she watched as he removed his ponytail, letting down what she mentally called his Thor locks.

He meticulously smoothed the unruly waves into submission before twisting them back into a bun. Delay. He delayed before responding. Ravyn recognized the technique used to lull a mark into thinking things were going differently than they were. She used it a lot.

Sebastian's hooded eyes never left Ravyn's as he completed his task, ending with smoothing the already smooth tresses once again. Lips tightly smashed together; his jawline clicked as he refrained from speaking to her. If she were a gambling woman, she would bet he was holding back from throttling her. She wasn't, of course; what a waste of time.

She sipped cautiously from her wine mixture—and yes, he'd correctly ascertained that she didn't once look into the glass and also set it down an arm's length away from her. It didn't occur every time;

in fact, seldom did an eye stare back at her, but it did happen.

"Thor, it's just glances, hints, if you may, over the past few days." Ravyn felt herself faltering and forced the words to come forward; this was the price she'd promised if she were to remain in Hollywood. Years ago, Oliver had agreed to this separation. A farce, really, but she had to agree to his own security detail, and she *had* promised. A woman's word was nothing if she couldn't keep a promise to an old, dear friend. "I've not been sure. Sometimes, I feel like I'm being watched, but nothing like the attack on opening night earlier this year. I just haven't been certain, and it seemed ridiculous to alarm anyone just because…"

Earlier in the year, Ravyn had attended the opening night of her newest movie, and to be honest, she'd already forgotten which movie it was. She loved acting and throwing herself headfirst into new roles, but by the time a new one came along, the last was all but forgotten as she repeated the cycle. But that particular night, she'd been physically and mentally assaulted by whatever creature had been leaving her "gifts." This stalker had broken past human and paranormal security to leave her trinkets such as jewelry and flowers until it escalated into small dead animals and finally to human body parts! Then the night of the premiere, a full out assault on her senses occurred under everyone's watchful eye.

Everything had changed that night. That was the

Tooth and Claw

night she met Sebastian Moldover face to face. She had, of course, exchanged emails with the head of Oliver's security teams and even phone calls with him as needed, but he'd largely remained hidden and out of sight. In fact, Ravyn had assumed he could be anywhere in the world managing his teams while they protected their clients. But that night, he'd been there.

Immediately, Sebastian had seen her distress when the entity had taunted and touched her while whispering dark threats in her ear. Caressing her intimately and unseen in front of the public as well as the cameras, he'd caused her to panic, to stumble. And like a white knight, Sebastian had swooped in, giving her an arm to lean on and leading her to safety while maintaining her dignity. Despite all the chaos, visible to no one and felt only by her, her first thought had been of her perfectly honed career. Falling or falling apart in public was akin to career suicide.

Headlines would flash: "Diva Does Drugs" or "Drunk Diva Diving in Public" or some other horrible lie that would spin her as an out of control and soon to be out of work actress. She could compel a few people to forget lies and even go as far as print a retraction, but the public... the public perception was a different beast. No matter how much good one did, they would much rather see a train wreck and then glory in the carnage.

At first, she'd thought Sebastian a Viking from days gone by. A large warrior with golden locks stepping out of time to swoop down on her, protecting her from this unseen threat.

A whispered code word brought her out of that state of confusion, reminding her that her hidden security surrounded her and as always stood at the ready to head off any dangers. Raising her chin high as she straightened up to the entirety of her five feet three, she'd taken the offered arm as support. Managing to regally enter the theater where her human security kept others at arm's reach, she'd silently regained her composure before Sebastian led her to her seat, taking the one nearest her and leaving her "date" to find another spot. Sebastian had kept most others away, except for the bravest, by staring them down whenever they dared to approach her throughout the evening. Only those she wished to speak to approached her.

After that evening, her former boy band "date" hadn't called to ask for another date, or at least her people hadn't passed on that his people had reached out. But Sebastian had stayed, and stayed, and stayed, moving out of the shadows and becoming a permanent fixture in her life. From unseen to always seen and always underfoot. During the early weeks when she still left her apartment, paparazzi had snapped pictures of the two, hinting at some sort of secret romance with a bodyguard. But as time passed, aside from the one night, the arm's length propriety had snapped firmly in place, leaving that particular bit of gossip to dry up.

Now it appeared that all gossip pertaining to her had dried up as soon as her appearances stopped. Her last movie had wrapped up filming weeks ago, and Ravyn was taking what she called a well-earned break, but deep down she knew she was simply hiding out. At one time she might have been considered the greatest horror of all time; now she was a coward.

A coward.

"You're not a coward," Sebastian spat at her. "You're anything but that. Reckless, headstrong, careless, but not a coward."

Ravyn shut her eyes briefly. Had she said that out loud? "Thor, you flatter me with your words. Careful, or it may all go to my pretty little head."

Bash shook his head gently at her, as if he saw right through her cheapened words. Pulling up his phone, he called an offsite team member and with short, terse words ordered another sweep of Ravyn's building as well as another ward reinforcement.

As if it will help, Ravyn thought bitterly, knowing that once more they were on the offense…

And she was prey.

Chapter Two

Noah sent out the raven

*M*oving his hands behind his back, Sebastian fisted them in an attempt to push his claws back into place, determined to bring the simmering wolf under control. He drew a deep breath once, twice before relaxing his grip so as not to draw blood. Ravyn would know if he spilled as much as a drop, and he was determined not to let the ancient seductress know how close he constantly was to losing control around her. She could already monitor his breathing and heart rate if she chose to, and even if he couldn't control those parts of him, he refused to show a complete lack of control.

Calling her a seductress, even in his mind, was a cheap shot—especially since the raven-haired beauty had made no such attempt on him; not really anyway. She teased and tormented, but it was an act used to deflect from the real problems they faced, as well as her fears.

It wasn't her fault he was drawn to her in an

inexplicable way. It wasn't her fault that his wolf had grown confused over the course of watching over her. His wolf guarded her with the ferociousness reserved for a mate. He'd pretty much given up explaining to the beast that watching Ravyn was a job. It had led to an already confined wolf straining against the constraints placed upon them in the city and suburbs. Both parts of him were happy to bask in her presence; just being in a room with her kept the dual sides of him content. Mostly.

In fact, if he were being honest, most of the time it seemed like she either picked on him as one might a little pup or attempted to drive him away. Which, if he were still being honest, didn't bother him half as much as he led her to believe. It secretly made him smile inside when she called him Thor.

Of course, at first it had confused him. Sebastian had thought her feeble minded and kept repeating his name to her in case her memory actually was the problem. Before they met in person, she'd never seemed to have a problem remembering his name; she often purred it over the line in a way that made his wolf chuff happily. After an embarrassing length of time, it finally clicked that she was teasing him about his size and unruly blond curls. The realization had brought a warmth through him despite how unusual it seemed coming from an ancient vampire.

Before he met Ravyn, Sebastian had assumed she would be stoic and boring like the old vampires in

Europe whom their security team usually catered to. Even though those vamps were half her age, they embraced acting aloof and above damn near everything; unless, of course, they were in the thralls of blood lust. During blood lust all bets were off. At those times, he and his team were literally locking them into place and running damage control. Most of these jobs required them to protect their charges from danger as well as protect humans from their charges. It was a fine line to walk, but Bash liked to think they'd been able to balance it well for the past several decades.

Ravyn wasn't like that, though. He found her habit of refocusing or thinking while counting adorable. She acted as if no one noticed it, so they all pretended not to notice her affinity toward counting and organizing items. Her control impeccable, never had she as much as bared her teeth at a human since they'd taken to patrolling her. Not that she would need to; her beauty would draw any man or woman to her like a beacon. No need for mind control when all she needed to do was crook her finger and smile. Like moths to a flame.

Sebastian shuddered to think that if she decided to use her power for evil or against them, there would be no taking her down. His wolf huffed at the thought, and Bash swore that when this was over, he would take a long vacation back home to get their heads on straight.

Typically, each security team consisted of two

wolves and two vampires on all shifts except for the hours when the vampire weakened. A few wolves were typically stronger than a single vampire, but if a powerful enough vampire were able to maim or destroy the wolves, a few vamps might be the only way to either restrain or cut down a weakened creature. The balance worked, creating teams that melded strengths and filled in weaknesses. Typically, Ravyn's security details were a cakewalk. For ten years, they'd followed her on set and to parties, living with her and around her, occasionally redirecting an overzealous human fan turned stalker or clearing a path smoothly to make her travels easier. Sometimes they did a deep background check on those who were in her inner circle or trying to be.

Ravyn liked her blood warmed with spiced wine or occasionally with black coffee. Admittedly, she'd very occasionally drunk from the source of a well-rewarded lover. A lover who generally left the bed satisfied albeit unusually tired but sent safely on their way well fed, with a nice gift waiting for them when they least expected it. An unclaimed check made its way to them from some unknown source, an unexpected win, or a special assignment on a different movie set were a few that had been reported, but Bash was certain there were more, none of which could be traced back to Ravyn. She was clever that way.

And although the reports had spoken of it, during his short tenure he had yet to see her take a lover.

Thankfully. He feared such a thing might put his confused wolf over the edge. His wolf had taken to forcing Bash to keep her well fed and her glass filled during her mealtimes. Ravyn had yet to realize he was doing so, but she always thanked him with a smile of appreciation and as time went by, it was less his wolf reminding him of her needs than him anticipating them.

This job was a cinch compared to so many others. His employees who got this assignment usually didn't choose to leave. Babysitting a vampire actress who had impeccable self-control and no natural or supernatural enemies, based in California, along with travel and parties with other famous people? Simply put, it was a dream assignment. Until it wasn't. Until the threats started. Still, they would lay down their lives to protect their client or their queen as needed.

Of course, the gifts didn't openly appear to be threats, especially not at first. Some flowers delivered inside a locked and guarded dressing room. Beautiful blood red and golden yellow roses which instead of having traditional baby's breath had an accent of gold mustard seed flowers. Unusual for sure, but annoying for a vampire. Written off as a lark, an unusual coincidence. They were followed by a bouquet of fresh and fragrant purple wolfsbane accented with its even deadlier cousin, pale purple vervain. No longer a lark or a coincidence, but a threat. A poison to werewolves and vampires alike, and a weapon often utilized by witches.

The rose of Jericho appeared, a dead-looking resurrection plant left in her secure apartment, waiting for life to be given back to it. And after careful examination, it was discovered the resurrection plant had been previously fed blood and magic, not water, by its sender. Water no longer revived the plant; it thirsted for the blood that it had grown accustomed to. These *gifts* hinted at much more than a human fan's obsession.

Then things escalated A dead mouse. A vile of unidentified blood that when opened caused the lone vampire in the room to go temporarily feral at its scent. No one had yet to determine why or how.

Two dead rats.

"Gifts" continued until a pile of unrecognizable road kill found its way into Ravyn's bed inside her very secure, top-floor apartment, past human security, past his own security as well as the cyber security that Oliver had insisted be installed.

But it hadn't stopped there. That would have led them to believe their countermeasures were effective. A courier arrived with a half-dried ear, a tiny hoop attached to its decaying edges, blood long dried from whatever poor soul it had belonged to. The delivery woman's mind had been wiped clean, no idea who arranged the delivery or where it had been picked up from.

Then came a puffy, gray bloated finger with a

diamond-encrusted gold band shoved firmly up to its knuckle, securing it in place. Again, flecks of blackened dried blood crusted the sparkling diamonds, working their way deep into the grooves of the ring. This item had found Ravyn in her freshly warded and reinforced apartment, the one security had just cleared and led her into. It lay almost reverently on a crisp white napkin in the center of the cherry dining table. The same table that had been empty merely minutes before was now adorned with a grotesque parody of a macabre marriage proposal.

Sebastian had been present for the grand finale. Having flown in hours before, he insinuated himself as a door opener at the movie premiere, giving him a firsthand look at the first of the attacks on Ravyn, as well as the first time he laid eyes on her in person. The pictures and even the movies didn't do her justice. They didn't capture the wildness that lay just beneath her skin or the kindness that embodied her simple touches. She constantly touched people. Service people were granted a tiny caress on the hand along with a "thank you"; others she might lay a hand on a bare arm when she spoke to them, listening intently with her bright green eyes as well as her ears.

His wolf had howled sharply in his mind when she stepped out of the car, followed by a roar when the pompous has-been rocker had placed a possessive arm around her waist for pictures. And even though the jackass removed it nearly immediately after the pictures had been taken, it hadn't been quick enough to calm the beast that paced inside him.

A punch to the gut nearly brought him to his knees when she turned to begin a slow walk toward the door he was to open for her. For the seconds before she turned to face the paparazzi again, he almost choked on the desire that she walk straight to him. *"Mate,"* his wolf snarled at him, and he fought the beast down, firmly denying the claim.

If he'd had to speak at that moment, he wouldn't have been able to form a coherent word. But then a silent chaos erupted and the screams of the crowd dimmed in his mind as his wolf panicked, sending garbled thoughts of both danger and mate to him.

When the unseen entity attacked her and she faltered, he immediately went into protective mode, strong-arming her ridiculous date out of the way and whispering the code that marked him as one of her hidden detail. "Fenrir sends his regards."

Glued to her side for the evening, he pretended that his employment forced him to stay when, in fact, his wolf refused to let him stand more than a step away the entire night. The evening was marked with him constantly scanning for danger and keeping his wolf from ripping apart anyone who ventured close to her or even those she approached. Despite his outwardly calm facade, he was on edge all evening, with his wolf ready to step in and take over at a moment's notice.

The attack in Oliver's home had almost ended him. His wolf simply couldn't allow Oliver to place anyone's safety over hers, and the two men nearly came to blows. Forgiveness came easily enough when Bash realized that Oliver fought for his mate, but forgetting still didn't.

Dead end after dead end, it seemed. They simply couldn't catch a break. Whoever this was, they were equally powerful and smart—not qualities anyone wanted in an enemy.

Striking down the band of witches who had kidnapped Eva, who had inadvertently been caught up in the crossfire, had given Ravyn a reprieve from the offensive gifts being left behind in securely warded areas. Clearly the main source of these gifts had been the old mage, who carried his secrets to the grave and beyond. But before his death, he'd revealed to Eva that he served a higher master and that Ravyn was meant for another. Despite the blow to the group the mastermind, the one the mage called "Master," was still hidden from sight.

Decapitation of the revolting creature hadn't stopped Oliver from having a necromancer revive him, but despite his decaying mess of a physical form, he'd been powerful enough to protect his secrets even after death. Muttering gibberish about a master and his queen, he melted into a hideous, laughing pile of goo. The old mage was just a servant; a powerful, magical source carrying out tricks for yet another master. He may have been the one somehow breaking through their every ward to deliver the tormenting gifts, but he wasn't the one actually gifting them.

Apparently, this blasted stalker had now acquired the ability to scry either by honing the skill himself or by acquiring yet another witch or mage to work for him. None of these were cheap options, so at this point what they knew about the stalker was sparse.

The work-up they'd made was short, but at the same time specific. "This confirms, yet again, that he's wealthy," Sebastian muttered as he warily eyed the reflective surface of the windows before reluctantly drawing the drapes closed. "No one in my tax bracket could afford the skills he's hiring out for."

"I'm assuming the $250,000 ring he sent me with a finger still attached might have been the first clue," Ravyn bit back at him, angry, as if he'd been the one hiding events from her. As if he wasn't the one being kept in the dark about things.

Bash knew better than to take her anger personally; she was angry at the situation and herself. In the few months since he'd attached himself to her, she'd showed time and time again that she cared deeply for those around her and took any infraction as a reflection of herself. She was unlike any vampire he'd ever met before, and he'd met many over the years. Most of them were careless and self-involved. But not Ravyn. She'd been devastated and blamed herself when Eva was abducted. Even Oliver could be a bit standoffish and careless with those around him. Eva had certainly softened him, but that didn't extend to everyone her vampire progeny met.

They'd traced the ring. It had been purchased in Beverly Hills by a young woman who, despite the heat, covered herself head to toe with layers, sunglasses, and a scarf. Maybe that wasn't so unusual in a land where plastic surgeons marked every corner. The woman had also been careful to angle away from the in-store cameras, keeping her head tilted down or away, appearing casual to the service associate, but clearly avoiding the cameras. Filling out the buyer information for an abandoned building and a fake name hadn't raised any suspicions. Nor did paying with a cashier's check that had already been created to include the exact sales tax. The cashier's check had been purchased by a street kid who hadn't been seen since the transaction. The teen had excitedly told his friends he'd scored a big deal and, as so many deals went, they were unsurprised when he hadn't returned to them. Just another day in the streets... His few possessions were divided up and his spot filled by another runaway who may or may not be there in a week.

In short, dead end after dead end.

"Of course it was," Sebastian said evenly, "but that could have been a one-off. And having a mage of that caliber on staff could have been a debt owed. But also having a scryer? Serious money, unless he collects debts and calls them in all at one time just for the singular purpose of—"

"What? Singular purpose of what? Stalking me? Torturing my friends? *Al'ama*, so many better uses of money." She swore softly, biting off the edges of her words as she spat them out. Damn.

Bash checked the background of every assignment that came across his desk. He knew Oliver had high expectations for the type of people to whom he offered cyber security or in-person security protection. It was one of the things that had first attracted him to the company. They were choosy about who they represented and who they protected. While no one was perfect and they'd been on missions with downright narcissistic clients, none of them were truly evil. Despite the fact that Ravyn was fast-tracked through the process as a close personal friend of Oliver's, he'd still sifted through what he could find on her. And ultimately, she was a good person. That wasn't a farce or a front.

"The hunt may be as important or more important than the actual capture," Sebastian repeated, knowing full well that as a natural predator she understood that more than most; at least as much as him. "He's enjoying the physical part as much as anything."

Bash could imagine the psychopath gleefully envisioning the reactions he was getting to the gifts he was leaving as well as basking in the upheaval he caused every time he broke through a physical or magical barrier. A rich, powerful, absolutely bat-shit crazy psychopath who was obsessed with Ravyn.

"All we've done over and over is react to what he's done." Anger flickered through him. "We've been on the run, and that's got to be encouraging him in some sick fashion."

At one time, it had seemed like a good idea, moving from place to place, but even that didn't matter. Ravyn had been found in every location they moved to, until they decided to just stay in her apartments, hoping he would make a mistake. The unsettling peace that they'd enjoyed after the death of his mage was now gone.

Constantly moving made them prey. Bash could vomit with disgust. Prey. Prey was weak, and weakness was toyed with until the predator got tired of the game and ended it. Better to stand and face them, if only the bastard would come out of the shadows.

"We need a witch in here to track him again." He spoke the words out loud, but mostly to himself. The last attempt had been a simple track and search spell. They needed more, though; they needed to trace this magic. He wasn't sure if the witch they had on staff had the capability to follow that type of magic back to its source. Tracing magic was a dangerous sport and numerous safeguards needed to be put in place, safeguards that Bash didn't understand but knew offered some protection against traps hidden within the magic. There could be a magical backlash if the originator knew they were being tracked and decided to attack a vulnerable witch on their tail. Very specialized training, rare, but surely with their resources they could find a suitable witch.

"Delta has already touched the magic, and she can't trace it. It's unrecognizable to her and she's the best," Ravyn reminded him, referring to Oliver's powerful in-house witch back in Chicagoland. "Bash, I just want to feel normal again." She sounded weary, tired of this game of cat and mouse. It had gotten them nowhere.

Despite the solemness of the situation, Sebastian's wolf hummed, reminding him of the pleasure of hearing his nickname for the first time from her lips. Too bad he couldn't just enjoy the moment.

"I know you do, Princess. I wish it were as easy as that." He focused on the curt nickname he called her that he knew she hated, just to remind himself that theirs was a relationship built from business. They weren't friends or anything more despite what his wolf wanted.

Bash blocked out the low growl in the back of his mind as the wolf denied the facts of the situation. He was a paid protector, a bodyguard to a princess. *No*, he reminded himself, *to a queen*.

CHAPTER THREE

And thou art wild

*S*anctuary.

If one word could describe Ravyn's home, it was "sanctuary." Every inch had been designed and created with her and her every need in mind. Automatic tinted windows, blackout blinds, furniture for lounging on, seating that invited someone to stay awhile. And most importantly, an endless wine closet that was on the verge of becoming a wine room.

The security system had been designed and put in place by Oliver solely with the intent to keep out all uninvited guests. Wards, designed and placed by his team of magic users, ensured that no one would unintentionally be hurt but by design should also annihilate any supernatural being intent on causing harm to Ravyn. The magical backlash alone was enough to kill a mortal and possibly most supernatural creatures as well. The few neighbors in the building had been through a vetting process so thorough that the team knew more about each of them than their own mothers did. Anyone questionable was bought out with terms they couldn't refuse and were replaced.

Several apartments scattered throughout the building housed the security team members who opted to remain on site even while off duty.

Ultimately, they were the best of the best but apparently, she was still very much prey despite remaining inside the walls of her apartment. She despised being prey. Still, it felt better to be home than bouncing between safe houses, hotels, and apartments in an attempt to stay one step ahead of her hunter.

The young wolf who had accompanied Sebastian for the last few months apparently felt the same way as he kicked back on her sofa with a freshly made cup of coffee.

"It's good to be home." Toby had been back and forth across the country with them when they visited Ollie and met Eva, the half-demon Ravyn had unintentionally tied herself to nearly two decades ago. He'd remained behind at Ollie's home for a few weeks, before rejoining them last night.

His mop of brown hair fell in front of his eyes as he made this proclamation and Ravyn smiled in agreement, pleased that he felt the comfort of her home even if it was no longer the sanctuary she'd built.

The youth's hair had grown out since he'd joined the group. When Toby first arrived, his hair had been shorn high and tight, close on the sides with only a bit of length on top. Now it was curly, slightly past his neck and the front, more often than not, dipped in front of his eyes. It was darker than Sebastian's hair, but the same unruly waves and curls marked a connection between them.

"Tobias Franklin, get your feet off the furniture," Sebastian growled. "In fact, why don't you get yourself down to *our* rooms and settle yourself in there, if there's nothing for you to do here."

Toby let out a groan but began drawing his still lanky teen body off the sofa. "Uncle Bash, please. I'm begging you, call me Toby... sir," he added in a quick afterthought.

"Stay," Ravyn ordered. She felt a certain amount of satisfaction when he immediately obeyed. She liked the boy being around, although she wasn't certain why he was or what his relationship was to her head of security. He did call Sebastian "uncle," but was that a true blood relation or an honorary title? Despite calling him by his full name, Bash hadn't slipped and used a last name for the youth yet. No one had told her, and she hadn't asked, but that didn't stop her from wondering. The teen had just shown up with Bash after his mandatory three days off several months ago.

Most of the month, Sebastian didn't as much as take an hour off from her employ, but the three days a month surrounding the full moon were non-negotiable. His wolf had to run. It was already cruel to make it remain in the city or its suburbs the other twenty-seven or twenty-eight days, but the wolf had to be let out when the moon called.

TOOTH AND CLAW

Ravyn wasn't sure where he went to run, only that all the wolves did, leaving around-the-clock security filled with vamps instead of wolf shifters. They all came back looking a combination of refreshed and exhausted. A strange combination for sure, but it kept them from becoming surly. The other wolves took a day or two off during the week, and most likely used the time to roam in wolf form in a national park, but not her Bash. He only ever took the mandatory leave.

Toby grunted as he dropped back onto the sofa, holding his coffee up high so as not to spill it. As he began to lower his cup, Sebastian smoothly swooped down, removing the cup from the youth's grasp.

"You drink too much of this stuff," he stated as he sipped the coffee, watching the teen over the top of the cup as if daring him to complain. "Damn, that's good. Almost as good as Eva's; you've been holding out on me." Nodding and clearly pleased with the idea that apparently formed in his head, he went on, "Yes, you've just got a promotion. You can be my official barista now. Not so sweet next time, though. I'm sweet enough."

Ravyn hid her smile at the banter but couldn't stop her eye roll. She didn't care for the sweetened coffee concoctions; red wine had been and always would be her drink of choice, but after spending time at Ollie's, she'd seen how much the guards there had enjoyed Eva's creations. Ordering the setup as well as all the goodies had been a small price to pay to give the staff a daily treat.

Clearly, Toby had been spending his time at Oliver's perfecting his coffee-making skills under Eva's tutelage. Even if Toby complained, he would be happy that someone appreciated his efforts. Ravyn watched the two, trying to figure out why the boy had joined her security detail but still refusing to ask. Honestly, it gave her something to think about outside of a crazed stalker. Brushing her hair, she began to plait the long, dark strands away from her face.

"Sir." The boy nodded and stood up to make himself another frothy concoction before settling back down on the sofa, where once again his hair flopped in front of his face.

Bash eyed him with a hint of annoyance while Ravyn continued to silently watch the exchange.

Bash sighed and began, "Toby, you need..." His voice cut out as Ravyn shook her head sharply, eyes widened. For a leader of wolves and men, sometimes he could be completely dim.

Standing up, Ravyn moved behind the boy on the couch. As he leaned forward to track what she was doing, she gently pulled his shoulders back against the sofa. "Hold still, let me fix it." Running her fingers gently through his soft hair, she began using the same brush to comb through his unruly tresses, gently releasing the snarled knots near the nape of his neck as she counted out each stroke in her mind.

One, two, three, four, five, six...

Tooth and Claw

At twenty-seven, she stopped brushing and used her hands to measure the length. Considering the mass of hair, she finally pulled and smoothed the front and sides into a short pony tail on the top of his head while the extras curled around his neck. "Not quite as long as your"—she paused, considering—"as your uncle's, but you can fix it this way to keep it out of your face. And it looks good too."

She continued to smooth it before wrapping a hair tie around the hair. "Go check it out and let me know what you think," she ordered, and the boy nearly leaped from his seat to stride down the hall.

"Thanks!" he shouted as he went to find a mirror.

"Make sure you cover the mirror back when you've finished," Bash shouted gruffly after him, before fixing an almost embarrassed gaze at Ravyn. He quietly told her, "Thanks, I didn't think."

Ravyn waved her hand at him before settling back down on the sofa. "It's nothing. Clearly, he looks up to you and your Thor look for whatever reason. It would have hurt his feelings for you to tell him to cut it." Men were dense creatures. No wonder the gods had created women.

"Well, thank you. Sometimes I don't know exactly what to say to him, and too often I seem to mess it up when I do open my mouth." Bash looked down at the cup in his hands while admitting his lack of knowledge.

"Just be yourself; that's who he likes." Ravyn

didn't care for the way Sebastian was scrutinizing her, watching her through those dark predator's eyes as if attempting to figure out if she was being nice or if it was a trick. Why couldn't he continue staring into his coffee cup? Refusing to meet his eyes, she picked up the mail that had been forwarded from her agent's office, where it had been sitting for a few weeks, by her guess. As far as her agency knew, she'd been on a rest due to exhaustion. Unfortunately, in the business this generally meant rehab, but at least it ensured that no one bothered her during her period of "rest."

Junk, junk, junk.

She tossed piece after piece aside before stopping at a fancy, hand-addressed envelope with flowery script and a small symbol in the lower right-hand corner of the envelope. It was so small it looked as if someone had just set a pen down briefly and the ink spread ever so slightly in random directions with a tiny dot nearly indiscernible to the side. The ink splotch was anything but random. For Ravyn, it meant much more than that.

It was a symbol most often written in the dust of a field or the walls of a temple with a damp fingerprint that meant "let's get together" or even simply "come." This small symbol would call the giggling young girls together late in the evening after chores and prayers were complete for a night of just being young and free again, away from the prying, judging temple eyes.

"Holy goddess," she murmured. After all this time

it couldn't possibly be. Chills ran down her arms and through her legs as the seemingly innocent letter stared up at her.

Setting the letter on the table, watching it warily as if it might bite her, set Bash immediately on edge.

"What is it?" he demanded, the coffee all but forgotten as he leaned down to examine the letter without touching it.

"I think it's from my sister," admitted Ravyn, sitting back on the sofa, gulping her wine, refusing to touch the letter again even as it called her to. "*A* sister," she corrected, not willing nor able to take her eyes off the letter.

After all these years? Was it even possible? She couldn't move her limbs. A feeling—a mixture of fear and hope or excitement—spread through her paralyzed limbs as she looked at the letter as though it might disappear in a blink of an eye or perhaps, she'd misunderstood the symbol. She allowed herself to blink before once again staring wide-eyed at the envelope.

Quickly flipping the envelope over, snatching her fingers back as soon as it hit the table, she saw the same small and barely discernible mark on the back. The sender wanted it clear that the mark wasn't an accident, a pooling of a pen set too long to paper. The mark was intentional and the message clear.

It's time to come together.

Ravyn closed her eyes, breathing in and out and

focusing on each breath before reopening her eyes. The mark was still there, marring the backside of the otherwise white envelope.

Sebastian's face crunched slightly in puzzlement as he looked from the letter to her and then back again, mouth slightly agape as he considered. Then he questioned with a tilt of his head. "You have a sister?"

Clearly, his background check didn't show him that, she thought haughtily, as if she didn't know the research he'd done on her. This secret life was so long ago, before history even recorded such things. Who would care about an unknown girl from an unknown village brought to serve a temple for a few short years before the temple fell?

"Yes, several. Six who lived, to be exact."

The seven sisters, Ravyn fondly thought, the memory enough to make her blink back the tears forming in her eyes.

"Your parents had seven girls?" Bash continued, puzzled.

She hadn't spoken of them ever, not even to Oliver, and Eva hadn't seen or written about them in her novels. Or perhaps she'd seen them but decided the story worked better with just one girl undergoing the transformation from human to demon.

"No." Ravyn chuckled softly, feeling the absolute irony and recognizing the horror of the situation. "No, my parents just had me. At one time, though, I was one of twelve, but then there were seven." She knew she made no sense, but the thoughts and words didn't seem to want to connect between her brain and her tongue. After all these damned, blessed years.

The white envelope with the blue script stared mockingly at her, seemingly innocent, but at the same time perhaps a snare set to entrap her if she so much as touched it. All these years, she'd all but given up hope to ever know what had happened to any of them. *Well*, she thought guiltily, *most of them anyway*. Perhaps some secrets were best left secret.

"Do you need a witch to check it?" asked Bash, still clearly puzzling over this revelation. "Or want me to?"

"No, no…" Ravyn watched the letter as if it might rearrange itself. "It's not spelled. I'm just…" *Considering*. "I'm just thinking." Yes, that was the best answer. Thinking on it. Why now? After two millennia, why now?

Hesitantly, she reached out and poked the envelope with a finger, pushing it an inch along the table before an outraged Sebastian could stop her. Waving her hand at him, she shut off his indignation. "I know a witch has already checked them over. You already insisted on that for all my mail, so it's not really necessary to do it again. And you really should consider having them throw away my junk mail while they're rifling through it. Save me a step. And I'm just thinking. Let me think for a bit."

Surprisingly enough, he did. The shifter settled

down, sipping his sweetened coffee while alternating between watching her and the wall. This lasted for a few moments, before agitation settled over Ravyn.

"Stop watching me or leave the room. I need to think in peace."

And he did that as well. Picking up a magazine, he silently began flipping through it, not sparing a single glance at her, so engrossed was he in the women's high-end fashion magazine.

The silence settled over the two of them while she pondered and considered. A minute turned to two, then three, while she considered the scenario.

Ravyn stood up abruptly and walked into the kitchen, returning with a hand full of coffee beans, which she scattered on the table. She began sorting them into first piles of ten, counting each one off as she slid it into its place.

One, two, three, four, five, six, seven, eight, nine, ten. Repeat. Six piles with seven left over. Next, piles of twenty-five. And then she simply counted them all, relaxing as the numbers settled over her while she slid each dark bean across the table. She gently blew the dust away from the beans as it settled on the table, calming her mind as she considered where a missive from a sister could have come from.

After all this time… What could it mean?

Chapter Four

Death upon her eyes

After half an hour or more had passed, Ravyn spoke without looking at Sebastian. "I was born an ordinary girl about two thousand years ago, by my best estimate." Feeling more than seeing him startle, she let out another small, uneasy laugh. "Yes, Eva's books weren't exaggerating that—assuming you've read them and remember those details. But she did take some creative liberties. I wasn't born a princess, or royalty, or even to any sort of nobility. I was born in a small village, dirt floors and everything. I played along the river delta; I imagine it was perhaps the Nile although I didn't have the knowledge or even the memories to be certain. I don't even remember the name I was born with.

"Sometime by or around my tenth year, I was taken from them—my parents—to live in a temple. I don't remember having any siblings, and perhaps after I was taken, they went on to have more. I don't know. I just know the day I was taken was the last time I saw the people who gave me life." Even that memory had faded over the years. Instead of a clear recollection, what remained was a more visceral feeling, fear and tears, but also a hint of excitement.

The beans slid on the glass tabletop as she bent over them, silently counting as they left streaks of blackened dust in their wake. As each count finished, she deftly swooped the beans back into a pile to resort and count, once again blowing away the residual dust.

"For years, I wasn't sure why I was chosen to serve the goddess Nephthys in her temple on the perhaps Nile." The goddess of twilight and death, a deity who embodied death, decay, and destruction.

"Later, I learned that they visited every village across the land every few years, testing the blood. I went on a two such trips as service to the goddess. The priest would prick the finger of every girl entering her tenth year or greater, stealing a drop of her blood to taste."

Shuddering, Ravyn recalled the grotesque priest suckling up each bit of blood offered to him, rolling it across his tongue as he pondered its taste, its essence, before rendering a verdict. Her face, as well as the faces of the others who accompanied him, remained stoic and impassioned while he conducted his trials, mostly sending the scared, crying girls back to their families. Rarely in the two years she traveled with him did a girl pass whatever test he administered in the name of the goddess and join them on their journey

Tooth and Claw

back to the temple. It became Ravyn's job to soothe the tears of a crying young girl who was leaving her entire life and family behind in service to a goddess that she'd never seen and most likely never would.

"We were acolytes in the temple for Nephthys, a temple hidden away from others. We grew much of our own food, drank and swam in what I still assume was the Nile, but to be honest we could have been anywhere; it could have been a lake or a small pond even. The world was so large and we were so small. But there we learned her ways, offering worship and sacrificial offerings to the goddess of death. We were divided mostly by the years we were found. Twelve in my group; some groups were only two or three and we were by far the largest. We were all about the same age, some a few years older and some a few years younger. I always assumed I was the youngest in our group; I was the smallest, so it seemed possible. We didn't have a way to gauge time and mostly our minds couldn't grasp the counting of time. We could count items we could see, but the passage of time? Not comprehensible to a bunch of girls from small villages. Seasons came and went as did the girls. Groups would age out, and younger girls would join us. It was a cycle, and eventually I was among the oldest."

As far as Ravyn could determine, they'd been in service of the goddess of darkness and decay for well over a decade, more than half their young lives. But despite the sounds of it, their days were filled with endless sunshine and warmth. Eventually, as with all little girls, they grew and evolved into young women, filling in and out with the curves of women everywhere. Worldly as she was now, Ravyn would have had other fears as a young girl serving a handful of old priests in a temple, but their bodies and virtues had been safe and, in fact, uninteresting to the residents of the temple. Mostly their day in and day out remained unchanged. Occasionally their fingers would be pricked again, and the single drop of blood would roll around on the old priest's tongue as he considered each morsel, before roughly shoving them to be on their way. Chores, prayers, meals, chores, prayers, meals, prayers, rest, and repeat. Unless the symbol had been drawn out.

The symbol. Really, none of them knew what it meant. None of them could read; at best they could decipher a bit of the hieroglyphics that surrounded them in their temple life. But on a rare special occasion, someone in their group would silently draw out the symbol—a slash of a few lines, really—passing along the invite to all the young women within their grouping. That night, they would gather. The location varied and wasn't spoken out loud; somehow it was just known and they would all show up, wandering in after their day was done and the temple had fallen quiet. It was a time and place to let their hair down and laugh aloud and freely among themselves.

Sometimes a brave girl would swipe an offering for the goddess: a bottle of watered-down wine for their meeting. Stealing from the altar made it all the sweeter. They passed it around, each taking tiny swigs and, as the hours passed, pulling longer drinks as their courage grew alongside their raucous laughter. For a time, they could be young and imagine a bit of freedom to laugh and dream.

"Suddenly we were the oldest group remaining. We assumed the others had finished their training and were set loose in the world to share the teachings of the goddess or sent to other temples to serve the order. The end was surely in sight for us. Exciting times." Ravyn's tone said the exact opposite was to happen and even without looking, she knew that Bash listened to every word she spoke.

"The priests prepared a feast for us. A graduation ceremony of sorts, I suppose. Younger acolytes waited on us, just as we had to previous groups. Ah, the food! The food was nothing like any of us had ever tasted. A last marvelous feast for us to partake in. And the watered-down wine we'd secretly stolen away over the years was nothing like what we were served. Deep reds, full-bodied, and the flavor just rolled around your tongue before warming you through. After serving us, the younger ones left, just as we had over the years. Off to sleep soundly through the night, unaware and most likely drugged, waking up late in the day to yet another group of girls gone."

Ravyn took a deep breath, pausing in her ruminating before continuing, "We stuffed ourselves with foods the likes of which none of us had seen before, and drank deeply from the offered wine. After one cup, we were dancing between the tables and after two, we were *on* the tables. My sisters and I were nearly identical to each other if you didn't know us. Beautiful, really; long, black hair that had been oiled and brushed to perfection for the evening's celebration. We'd used blackened bits of charcoal from the fire to darken around our already dark eyes. The priests had been generous with the oil that night and encouraged us to rub our bronze skin with it, letting it soak into our skin. We were things of beauty that night."

The drink, along with the deep, rhythmic beating of hidden drums, coaxed them into more frenzied movement. First, they tapped their fingers, then a foot, and before long, their shadows twisted and floated around the flickering fireplaces as they found themselves throwing their bodies to the mercy of the music, losing control as the music took hold. It was hazy and blurry, but Ravyn could still recall the freedom she felt as her body swayed while the music ran through her.

The food had been drugged—or the wine, or both—to ensure their compliance, ironically, more than likely with her beloved blue lotus. Despite suspecting that, Ravyn couldn't blame the beautiful flower for what happened next. It only eased what was to come.

When each group of young women reached the age of maturity, they weren't sprinted off to the corners of the known world to worship and share the stories of Nephthys. No, the priests of Nephthys had an agenda that no one knew about, not the village parents from whom they procured the young girls, not the girls themselves, and most likely, none of the various temples that surely knew of their existence. They didn't want to worship the revered Nephthys; their goals were much more sinister. They wished to conquer the goddess; they wished to conquer death.

"To them, we were experiments, 'lab rats,' they might call us today. We were disposable. Who would miss a bunch of poor girls sent off to serve a goddess? Most thought it was a blessing and it was, of course, it was. Until it wasn't."

Ravyn turned her focus on Bash, who looked at her with a combination of horror and pity. She understood the horror, but she despised the pity.

"Don't." She shook her head in warning at him, sending a flash of fang to remind him that she wasn't a weakling to be pitied. Whatever had been done to her, she'd survived.

"What did they do to you?" Sebastian's gentle tone was laced with his horror. "What did they do to all those girls?"

All those girls. Yes, generations gathered, trained

in compliance, and then had their souls ripped from them. *One, two, three, four, five, six, seven, eight, nine, ten, eleven, twelve.* Twelve went in.

"The priests were special too. Mages or witches or warlocks, whatever you wish to call them. Those special, special men." Disdain dripped from her voice. Those terrible times she never spoke of, and now that she'd begun, it was a like a dam burst and Ravyn found herself unable to stop.

"They tested, tasted our blood," she amended, "to check our humanity, but more importantly to see if it contained any traces of demon blood. They were gathering the girls who had any sort of demon blood in their veins. Some had a little, some had more, but they weren't picky. They were happy to take any who did."

Puzzled, Bash asked, "Only the girls? Why no males?"

"I wondered that myself for many years. What made us, but not our brothers, so important? It was, in fact, Oliver's friend Malthazar who explained it to me. Accidentally, of course; as far as I know, he has no idea about my creation, my heritage, so to speak." She took a long, slow sip on her wine again, before pulling her legs up into the sofa and leaning back to stare at the ceiling for another moment.

"As you know, Malth is half demon, half human. In a nutshell, most demon-human hybrids are male. Not sure of the percentage; obviously, no one is really tracking that stuff. So, when a girl is born, like Eva,

TOOTH AND CLAW

for example, they mostly go unnoticed, because they're not expected. But sad story short is that the male babies, the boys, are collected and taken to the demon plane to live out horrible lives there. Malth is one such hybrid and until Eva, he'd never even seen a female hybrid, especially a first generation.

"The birth of a girl could be from an overlooked male hybrid several generations removed or a rare female demon birth that went unnoticed. I could have one percent, ten percent demon blood, or even more. But we all had something. I'm sure I had a decent enough amount, since I survived the… process… but I don't care enough to find out or even know if it's possible to find out after I transitioned to basically another demon variant."

"Are you saying all vampires are made from demons?" A hint of disbelief entered Sebastian's voice, so slight he probably didn't even notice the invocation in his voice, but Ravyn did.

"Originals, yes. A mix of demon blood, witch's magic, and some very heinous men who did horrible things to children are what created the originals, the night walkers, the creatures of the dark. The undead." Ravyn didn't even try to hide the sarcastic anger in her voice. She reminded herself that the story truly was unbelievable. The legend made it sound as if vampires chose and embraced their evil, their creation, but the truth was much worse. It wasn't their fault that they'd never been told the truth. The truth had been buried, much like all the bodies of the young women who were the unsuccessful experiments of evil men who wanted to cheat death. "They didn't truly worship the goddess; they wanted to defeat her. They wanted to defeat death on the backs of children."

Ravyn had no idea if any of the past trials had been deemed successful, but she always assumed some earlier experiments somewhere were or that other temples carried out the same horrifying experimentations. What she did know was that one moment, she'd been filled with laughter, gorging on a feast of food and wine the likes of which she'd never imagined in her wildest dreams. Dancing while linked hand and hand with her sisters, overcome with what they thought was joy for their mother goddess. Moving through corridors deeper into the temple with flashes of candlelight flickering in and out while the music slowly faded.

Another flash of memory, floating in and out of darkness and light deep under the ground, surrounded by the cold earth, while the priests chanted incantations in unknown tongues. Grasping hands with one of her dear sisters, while darkness shot in and around them, the priests touching and tasting their skin before something cut through her body like a blade. It cut through one side and exited the other, stabbing in her torso, her arms and thighs, before blasting through. The shadows swirled faster, punching through her body, piercing her eyes, harder and harder as the incantations grew fevered.

The screams. Dear goddess, the screams. Ravyn hadn't been sure where her screams began and the others' ended. Their throats grew raw and then their screams grew silent because they couldn't make any more sounds. Barely a breath could be drawn before they collapsed one by one onto the floor, while the circle of dispassionate priests continued their chants.

Then Ravyn rose from the blood-slick floor, blood barely flowing from her wounds so empty was her body. She looked down at the girl next to her, blood-splattered and so pale, so very pale, before the girl's eyes began to flutter and finally open with a strange glow to them. Six other girls stood, while five lay still on the floor. The body nearest her stared up with unseeing open eyes, a scream still lit upon them, but Ravyn found she no longer cared. She had an awareness of who stood around her, the ones who'd survived—if you could call it that. The names of those who stood were etched in her mind and the ones who had fallen etched in her heart. But that was later. In those first minutes and hours, she could only focus on one thing.

Hunger.

The sweet, sweet smell of the last of their human blood filled the air, and hesitantly at first, then with renewed vigor, she licked the blood from her hand. The taste. Oh, the taste. Ravyn didn't think she could ever find the words to describe the explosion in her mouth or the feeling of satiation as it coated her throat. It was like the stars had exploded in her mouth. Moaning with both pain and pleasure and nearly mad with the change, she barely noticed the other girls around her as they suckled from those who lay on the floor or dipped their hands greedily in the puddles of their own blood. The more they drank of it, the more they wanted.

"Then almost like it was the first time, I noticed the priests. It had gotten so quiet except for a strange thumping that echoed in my head. The looks on their faces was a combination of fascination, excitement, and then horror. Had they not expected this? Was this not what they wanted? The drumming in my head was their heartbeat, faster and faster. I could hear their withered hearts beating under their decadent fancy robes, the special robes they wore while they killed us."

Thump, thump, thump, thump echoed through the cave of horror. Ravyn could still remember hearing the blood run through their veins as it called its siren song to them.

"And gradually it got all of our attention, the seven of us who still stood, who lived in this manner. We watched them, some standing upright, some on all fours, dripping and covered in our own blood as well as the blood of our sisters." *Thump, thump...* The sounded echoed in her head, the beats rattling faster, louder even than the earlier drums as the men gradually noticed the predatory eyes settled on them. No longer were they priests of a temple, but prey.

It was over within minutes, the priests ripped apart and their blood filling the gluttonous bellies of the former acolytes. No conversations, no cares for the begging or pleading, just one need. The women didn't speak to one another yet they worked together, silently trapping and herding the men to their ends before snarling and fighting over the bodies. Moving like a flash while the flames of the fire flickered around them. One second a dozen cubits away and in a heartbeat, ripping out a throat with growls and cackles. The damned had defeated death, but not their own.

"We broke free from underneath the temple and slaughtered every single child we could find within the temple walls. It wasn't until later, much later, that I even felt a shred of regret for what we'd done. Those first days were filled only with darkness, rage, and blood. Then we all ran—different ways, of course—along the rivers, through the deserts, or hid in the trees. The seven of us, the survivors, I suppose you could call us." Ravyn covered her mouth when a sharp harsh laugh barked out. "And by the time my mind had settled, I'd wiped out countless small settlements, traveled miles upon miles, and that was the end of our sisterhood."

So much death. The death of the priests she had no qualms about, but the others? The others would haunt her always. The chosen girls hadn't been given a choice to be there, but that didn't change the fact that in the thralls of hunger they'd been slaughtered and left for the carrion eaters to pick apart. Despite the fact that Ravyn barely remembered the minutes, hours, and days after the change, she'd never been able to deny the flashes of memories that rose up unexpected in the calm moments.

Finally touching the letter, she picked it up and turned it over slowly in her hands, examining it as if perhaps the message might be seen without even opening it. Tapping the symbol in the lower front corner with a long nail, she said, "Until now, I didn't know for sure if any of them had survived the years."

Ravyn could feel Bash's warmth easing toward her. How she wished she could turn to him and forget the horrors the letter represented. Fall into his warmth, his embrace, and forget the last few moments. How easy it would be to fall into him.

Chapter Five

Upon the raven's wing the halls of Valhalla are met

"Can you hold me, please? Just for a bit. I feel so cold." Ravyn carefully kept the space between them, as if giving him a chance to deny her quiet request. Back rigid and green eyes sharp, she wouldn't allow herself to appear too vulnerable in spite of her words and was clearly preparing to flee if need be. But he knew her. He saw her.

Bash's wolf had already been pressing against his mind, and her small, vulnerable request had nearly let it push through to take control. Thankfully, the wolf calmed itself when Bash pulled Ravyn into his arms, tucking her head under his chin and wrapping his arms around her, pulling her close to his warmth.

Closing his eyes, he selfishly soaked up the moment, enjoying the feeling of her against him and allowing himself to briefly imagine "what if." She was so tiny, a fact that he knew, but holding her like this, feeling her smallness in his grip, while she let herself for a single moment be vulnerable…

"Mine," his wolf growled contently and for once, Sebastian didn't argue with his animal. It should be

permitted this moment as well.

Tentatively, he brought one hand up to her head and let it settle just briefly before relaxing it and petting down the side of her head, allowing her hair to slide beneath it. Then again, this time taking a few strands to smooth between his thumb and forefinger, trying to bring her a bit of comfort the best he knew how. Bash wasn't good at this stuff, but he wanted to be. The faint, still unrecognizable floral that he came to know as her signature scent filled his nose. Normally, his sensitive nostrils rejected any number of perfumed scents, but this woody, green floral scent specific to Ravyn smelled like home.

Ravyn snuggled closer to him, burrowing in as she murmured something so softly that even his enhanced hearing couldn't quite pick it up. In the end, he went with the assumption that she found contentment with his feeble attempts to comfort her, so he continued stroking her head, enjoying the feeling of her soft, sleek hair beneath his hand. Peace wafted over him, enveloping him in a serenity he hadn't felt in years. The scent that anointed Ravyn caressed his own skin. His wolf preened at the marking. Not that he should be thinking that way, not at all; Ravyn was a job, a vampire, and one of his partner's dearest friends. The list could go on and on but right now, for this moment, he was in complete agreement with his wolf.

Just shut up and enjoy it.

"Thank you, Thor," she whispered, her words

TOOTH AND CLAW

clear this time and the softness, the vulnerability in her voice, hit him low and hard. It took every ounce of strength to not pull her even closer and offer to take every bit of fear and pain from her.

Heart pounding faster than just a few minutes ago, he knew she could hear it and feel it speed up, but right now it didn't matter. A soft embrace was all he could safely offer.

"Not a problem, Princess." The words came out more gruffly than he'd intended. In a moment of weakness, he allowed his lips to lie upon the side of her head, deeply inhaling the scent of her, embracing the closeness even as he pulled her tighter into his embrace. It took all of his strength not to grind his face against her, marking her with his own scent.

"All part of the full-security package?" She hesitated as she said the words, and even a big dumb wolf like himself knew that it wasn't just a simple, off-the-cuff question. They'd been dancing around each other for weeks. But Bash wasn't the wolf. He wasn't one to confuse sexual attraction and the innate desire to protect the woman with a lifelong mating bond. No, a mate wasn't a part of his future.

"No, this is a perk reserved especially for you." Pausing a beat, he admitted, "Besides, I do like you a bit."

"I knew it, Thor," she whispered back, before holding still in his embrace as they both—he liked to imagine—savored this moment. Ravyn was strong, stronger than any woman he knew and not just because she was a vampire, and it felt like home offering her a touch of his own strength just for a moment.

"I sort of like you a bit too. Even if you still won't tell me your kinkiest fantasy." She referred to the last question she'd tormented him with at Oliver's home before the entity had struck her down and attempted to force a connection. If the moment hadn't been potentially deadly, he would have thanked Fenrir for the intervention.

Hesitantly at first, then growing bolder, Sebastian allowed his fingers to rub the tension from her hands and lower arms. A small moan escaped her and, embodied with a bit more confidence, Bash shifted his position to allow access to her shoulders and neck, massaging the tension spots with gentle but firm pressure.

"Oh, you're so warm." Ravyn seemed to shiver with delight under his ministrations. Eyes closed, she continued, seemingly unaware of the effect she had on him in return. "Your hands are like magic." Her whisper and the feel of her under his hands did things to his own body that he would rather keep hidden. Shifting in his seat to ease the pressure, he reminded himself and his wolf that this moment was for her. He imagined his wolf rolling its eyes at him.

Bash wanted to tell her that under his hands her skin felt like a cool, refreshing brook in the springtime colliding with the full winter moon. But he remained mute even as his wolf huffed at him, *"Coward."*

All too soon Ravyn pulled away, easing away almost reluctantly from his touch even as his fingers lingered before he removed them from her and set them back on his thighs.

Slowly picking up the envelope as if it might be a viper, she deliberately turned it over in her hands, warily examining the envelope holding the past and future.

"Like a bandage, let's just rip it off." She slid one long nail under the envelope flap, pulling it open while quickly sliding the letter out before anything else could even be suggested. "And it's fancy stationary." Pale yellow paper with tiny blue lotus flowers hand drawn around the border, filled with tiny, precise script elegantly penned in blue ink, as if the writer had much to say but was determined to keep it to a single page.

"As if you would send a letter on school notebook paper. Can't say I would expect less from any sister of yours," Bash grumbled as he shifted himself uncomfortably on the sofa, immediately feeling the loss of her body against his.

Ravyn held the letter in both hands as she leaned back against him as if it were the most normal thing in the world.

As she brushed a finger lightly against the blue lotus flowers, he could feel her happiness.

"She remembered my favorite flower," Ravyn

whispered in awe.

Blue lotus. That made sense. She had tiny, hand-blown glass flowers in her private chambers; he'd chanced upon them one day when he'd popped in to check on her during her quiet time of day. Even her throw pillows had a border of the floating flowers dancing on their edges. Her scent was the blue lotus.

Having never smelled it before he couldn't be sure, but now, as he inhaled her lovely scent, he couldn't help but feel he'd stumbled upon the answer to a question he hadn't known to ask. It was most likely the same flower that had drugged her years ago to gain her compliance in a demonic change she hadn't asked for. Despite that, she clearly didn't hold the delicate flower responsible.

Bash stared straight ahead as Ravyn silently read the words in the letter, not feeling prepared to intrude upon this moment, but not wanting to pull away either. From the corner of his eye, he could see her eyes moving rapidly as she scanned the words. He felt a tinge of relief when her small, mysterious smile passed her lips, showing the hint of white from her teeth. A real smile, not one of those fake plastic smiles she saved for the cameras.

"It's Ibis," Ravyn told him, as if he would know which sister this was, but he nodded and smiled, pleased at her happiness. "She goes by Anya now. When we entered the temple, we were given new names. Animal names, given to each of us that we shared also with the girls from other groups. I suppose recycling the names and giving everyone an animal pendant made it simple for the old fools to know who we each were. Goddess knows we shouldn't be allowed any individuality or any link to our old lives." The scowl across her face was replaced yet again with a smile. "She wants to meet with me."

Bash immediately went on edge, his body only tensing slightly, but he knew that Ravyn would immediately know his thoughts. This could be a trap. It could be that this Anya or Ibis was Ravyn's stalker, and she was either impersonating her sister to gain her trust or had been driven insane over the years and was now planning Ravyn's demise. So many options, and none of them good.

After all these years, a letter drops out of the sky at the same time that a supernatural stalker is taunting Ravyn? There were no such things as coincidences, as far as Sebastian was concerned.

Drawing herself away from him, Ravyn's green eyes went dark before flashing a hint of red at him. The air between them snapped with electricity and if Bash dared take a breath, open his mouth, he knew that he would instantly taste the bite of anger that consumed her.

Spitting out the words, Ravyn instructed him, "You forget yourself, Thor. You forget who and what I am." Holding up the letter, she reminded him as if he could ever forget, "I am thousands of years old and have survived alone for nearly as long. You, you and your men, are here simply because I allow it. You may trick yourself into believing that Oliver controls this situation, but you would be gravely mistaken. I and I alone. Allow. You. Here."

It was almost like the few moments earlier had ceased to exist. His suspicious thoughts had wiped them away, turned a precious moment ugly.

Sometimes it was easy to forget that the tiny woman held more power than all of his men and him combined, including the vampires on the team. As an actress, Ravyn was more than used to allowing people to see what she wanted them to see, portraying the woman they wanted to see. But she was always a predator, a manipulator, and if she chose to embrace that, none of them could stop her. Sure, the stalker had shaken her, but even without them or Oliver to intervene once the initial shock passed, she would handle the situation. Even if by handling it meant she went on the run.

Bash's wolf flared at the challenge but immediately backed down in deference, and he recognized that it was best he follow suit. "My apologies, Ravyn. I wish I could blame the wolf in me." In the back of his mind, the wolf growled lowly at him. "But…"

His brain whirled. *But what?* That a part of him would give his very life to protect her and it had nothing to do with it being a job? That every day with her brought both the highest and lowest of every emotion? That when she left the room, his very breath went with her?

"But I'm an idiot and I apologize. I know absolutely you can more than take care of yourself, but I'm… we're… here to share that load, so you don't have to. Unless of course you want to," he quickly amended. Worst apology ever, but much better than admitting the truth to both the greatest thorn in his side and the reason he woke up each day. The last few months had been hell.

The blackness in Ravyn's eyes slowly drained away, leaving behind the deep green. "Of course." Nodding regally, she agreed. "Apology accepted."

Sighing, she admitted, "Yes, it could be a trap. I'm lazy as of late, but not a fool. It is very convincingly Ibis. She was always the gentlest of us all, full of laughter and love and a bit mischievous." Another hint of a smile as a memory crossed that she didn't share. "But this change might have made her a different woman. Or if she shared her truth with someone else, they might attempt to manipulate me. And after all these years, at the same time as a stalker, it could be a coincidence or something more."

By habit, Ravyn smoothed her hair and began braiding it along the side of her neck while Bash watched, waiting for her to decide how to proceed. He was mesmerized as always by her every move, so graceful even as she smoothed her hair. Hair so black it almost shone blue under the lights. Then she pulled the plait free and began again.

Bash knew that Ravyn counted the movements in her mind even if her lips weren't moving. Over the past few months, he'd come to understand that this habit of hers occurred while she thought things through, considered the outcomes and possibilities. Criss cross, back and forth, one, two, three, and so forth before her fingers pulled the weave free, smoothing out the strands before beginning again. While she pondered, he waited, caught in the thrall of the quick work her long, thin fingers made of the hair.

"Have Oliver's office run a background check on this person." Ravyn twisted the hair up into a bun, allowing a few pieces to sneak free. "It needs to be done fast but thoroughly, of course, though I don't want them to know who she is to me. There may not be anything on her, depending on the life she has chosen this century, but these days, it's difficult to stay hidden. After that, I wish to have a meeting at a secure location with double our detail and you by my side. She claims she currently isn't far from us or at least, from my agent's address."

Flipping the envelope back and forth, she silently examined the return postmark once again. It had been sent weeks ago, but only from across the state. California was large, but not so large that it should keep her from her sister.

Looking up at him through her dark, sooty lashes,

Tooth and Claw

Ravyn pleaded, "I can't miss a chance if this is my sister. I've looked and waited for years."

Bash understood. He would do anything to see his own brother again. "We can make it work. We *will* make it work. But Ravyn"—he hesitated—"this could all be a trap. It may not even be her, or it could be your stalker using her as a lure. Or even this could be your stalker. Maybe the years haven't been as kind to her as this letter would lead you to believe."

Always elegant, with grace and smoothness, Ravyn extracted herself from the sofa, drawing herself up as tall as her petite stature would allow barefoot. "I think I'd like to rest now; I'm going to my rooms. The sun is high." She handed him the envelope with the name and return address but kept the letter half crumpled in her hand.

Cordially, she added with a hint of ice in her tone, "And you… you need to do your job now."

"Let me know if you need anything," Bash offered. His heart sank at her harsh words, but he knew she needed time alone. At Ravyn's age, rest was vital, but even a big dumb wolf like him who barely spoke to women aside from his ma and sister-in-law, Sara, knew what was left unsaid. "I'll get the background check started." He mentally added, *and a background check on every single person this Ibis/Anya person has crossed paths with.*

Oliver's firm was both thorough and discreet. By the end of the day, Sebastian hoped to know everything about this sister down to her favorite blood type and *her* favorite flower.

Glancing at his phone, he saw that the building had once again been scanned and deemed clear of threats. Two more birds had hit the glass during the exam. A witch was on her way and was begrudgingly repeating her ward work despite her claim that it was already impenetrable.

Impossible! Bash thought as he looked at the corner of the window whose blinds he'd opened earlier to scan the city below. In the upper right-hand corner of the high window, a deep crack had formed, nearly six inches long. Rubbing his eyes in frustration, he hoped that when he looked back the weakness would be gone, but if anything, it already appeared larger.

Punching the buttons of his phone, he demanded that the witch bring another to complete her reinforcements, and to triple check the glass.

Would this ever end?

Chapter Six

With a raven's hope at her side

Sebastian was hanging up yet another call as his nephew wandered into the apartment as if he were an invited guest. The building sweep had gone as he feared it would: nothing out of place, no hints of how anyone or anything could be peering in at Ravyn.

With a frown, he saw that the crack in the window had grown. Despite the witch's assurance that it wasn't supernatural, he found it difficult to believe. Standing on a chair, he examined it as closely as he could, which wasn't very well with the tall ceilings. A ladder needed to be brought in; surely there was one around this place somewhere. For a second as he examined it, Bash thought he saw an eye wink into existence inside the reflection of the shatter. It was gone so quickly that he might have imagined it and for a moment, he understood Ravyn's uncertainty in coming forward with what she thought she saw or what she might have seen.

Toby was in and out of all the apartments and seemed to know when to disappear as well as reappear.

Admittedly, Bash wasn't doing well at keeping tabs on the teen like he'd promised his sister-in-law. He'd tried to explain to her that his job meant that Toby would be on his own a lot, but she didn't care. She wanted him away from Missouri for a while.

Sighing, Bash hoped that a half-ass male figure in his life was better than none at all, and surely better than roaming with the other half-feral teenage troublemakers in the pack. Thankfully, the other wolves on his team had semi-adopted the youth and filled in in all the ways Bash didn't. It seemed like time and time again, life wanted to remind him that he wasn't his brother James; that the gods had taken the wrong son.

"Dude, did Ravyn go out?" Toby lounged back in a chair, propping his feet up on the table in front of him. "You finally letting her out of this place?"

Sebastian looked at him sharply... This kid! Letting out a warning growl, he held himself back from knocking the pup's feet to the floor. "Ms. Sinclair," he warned, not for the first time. He deeply regretted the day Ravyn had told his nephew to make himself at home and call her Ravyn.

"Sorry, sorry." Toby held up his free hand in apology as he removed his feet from the table. "Uncle Bash, did Ms. Sinclair go out?" His enunciation on "Ms. Sinclair" teetered on disrespectful, but Bash had learned to pick his battles.

"Ms. Sinclair is resting. And is all you drink

coffee? That will stunt your growth." Hardly; the lanky "boy" was nearly as tall as him and might even beat him by an inch or two in a few years, just as his father had before him. Sebastian wasn't a small wolf, but James... James had seemed like a giant. His heart tightened; damn, he missed his older brother. With a flash of guilt, it was easy enough to remind himself that his loss was overshadowed by the loss that James's mate and children had felt at his death.

"Well, you don't keep soda at our place, so yes."

Sebastian had bought a twelve-pack once, and it had been drunk in one day. And the food... dear gods, the food. How had his mother kept two teenage wolves fed? How had Sara kept Tobias, as well as the twins, so well fed? Just a few weeks after having Toby in his household, he'd added to the already generous amount he deposited into the family's account. Growing pups weren't cheap!

"Try water sometime." Bash smiled at the appalled look that filled Toby's face, but the boy kept quiet. Damn, he looked so much like his brother that Bash's heart squeezed tightly and painfully when he looked at the youth. He wondered, not for the first time, if perhaps that was why Sara had sent her son to him. It had only been a few years since her mate had died, and it had to hurt looking at his replica each and every day. Despite the trouble the boy had gotten in to there were plenty of men within the pack who could keep the pup in line. His heart twinged a little as he thought of

James. If anyone deserved to live a long and happy life it was James, but unfortunately the gods often called their favorites home first. If James watched them now, he surely was disappointed in the lack of parental guidance Bash had been offering his son. He could do better—and he would.

"What have you been up to?" Bash cringed at his own words, but surely it was better than the awkward quiet that so often hung above them. Next, he would be talking about the weather.

"Just talking to the guys back home. Discord." Toby grunted, suddenly very interested in his coffee.

Something was up. But what trouble could he be getting into half a country apart from the other troublemakers? "And what are 'the boys' up to?" Sebastian watched him intently, noticing the rise in his heart rate and breathing.

Sighing, Toby admitted, "There's video… of… you know."

Video. Of course there was video. In this day and age, you couldn't go around scaring campers and hikers without assuming they had a phone on them prepared to record any infraction, any emergency. After all the jump scares the boys had committed and rumors running wild, of course a tourist would come prepared to capture proof of Bigfoot, werewolves, or whatever.

Cringing, Bash pressed on. "How bad and who?"

Toby gulped. "Bad. We were half turned, and all

of us, but especially me."

"Do you have a copy?"

Reluctantly, Toby nodded, finally looking Bash in the eyes. "I'm really sorry, sir. I know I've let everyone down, especially Mom, after…"

Bash nodded and brusquely replied, "Just do better." Coddling him wouldn't help him, and after his father's death, he knew how important it was to keep a low profile near the trails and campgrounds of the national park in Missouri where the wolves liked to roam. Their own land was vast enough, but something about the park called to their wolves.

"Send me the video link and I'll have it scoured." This much was simple enough. He couldn't replace Toby's father, but his job required the ability to wipe away everything, anywhere.

"You can do that?" A hopeful note entered Toby's voice. He was still so young.

"I can do that. Next time, don't wait to tell me, so it can be taken care of sooner," Bash added gruffly, but he was secretly pleased that he could help his nephew. "We can fix this, but we can't stop people from talking once they've seen it."

Admittedly, the video was bad. Sebastian cringed while he watched it, making Tobias sit across from him while he did. He had some time to kill while Ravyn's background checks were run and he had others considering possible meet-up locations, assuming the background checks were acceptable.

The accompanying article surrounding the videos were ridiculous, and Bash flinched as he read the headlines: "Strange Reports of 'Hellhounds' in Missouri's Mark Twain Forest," "Campers Stalked by Beast with Red Eyes in the Forest," and "Sasquatch or Something More Sinister?"

Scanning the articles, he saw that they pretty much all repeated the same talking points. Hikers and campers reported strange creatures stalking them throughout the Mark Twain Forest—the same area his family had run on for a century, out of sight and, mostly, unheard miles from civilization on private acreage. Except, of course, when foolhardy teenage boys decided to prank the humans and on public land, no less. Basically, the same sort of thing that James, himself, and their friends had done at that age without the technology to capture them. Turning half wolf, standing on back legs to give a drunk local a bit of a fright wasn't so much a problem fifty-plus years ago as it was now.

Quite the laugh. Of course, until proof in the way of a video was given. Or someone died.

The video started out dark and hazy, with excited voices in the background whispering about the screams they'd just heard. Sure enough, shortly after the video began, a blood-curdling shriek sounded, followed by the shaky recording of claw marks on a nearby tree with a whispered explanation about how the marks were too big to be a bear. Instead of running away from the shrieks, the group ran toward the sounds, fueled by adrenaline, half excited and half afraid. Humans had no sense of self-preservation, Bash thought with disgust.

Despite the jumpy video, flashes of lights and panicked voices, sure enough there was a group of three half-turned werewolves on the screen. The lighting made it difficult to discern their identities but if Toby said it was him, then it was him. Beasts bigger then bears stood upright on elongated back legs, with pointed snouts and red eyes. As expected, hair covered their appendages, long and bushy and, ending on their outstretched "arms," claws as long as a man's hand extended from them.

Bash didn't watch it all; he didn't need to. He scrolled to the comments and shares. So many shares, and that was just the single app. The comments argued whether it was Bigfoot, werewolves, or simply a fake. Others chimed in, claiming to have seen large, black doglike creatures during their overnight forays, with others retelling stories of similar sightings passed down from their grandparents.

Several commentators argued that the video was completely CGI or AI crap, pointing out their "proof" and disbelief that anyone would believe such an obviously "fake" video. Sebastian wondered how many of the comments actually came from the boys or other wolves trying to cover their literal tracks. Of course it was real, though. Unfortunately.

Bash forwarded the video, as well as instructions, to Oliver's office. He was the muscle and Oliver's side was the tech, but within a day or two, each and every copy of the video would be scrubbed from the Internet, including copies held on any device that at any point in time had connected to the Internet. The proof would be gone.

Of course, that wouldn't stop the true believers, the zealots. These sorts of events brought them out into the forest in droves. They didn't need proof to believe. Faith fueled the fanatic's hunt.

"You need to tell your friends to hang low for a while." *A long while,* he amended in his head. "I'll be honest: we all did stupid things like this growing up. But it's different these days."

Toby nodded glumly. He knew he'd screwed up. He'd put himself, his siblings, his mom, and his pack all in danger.

"All traces of this video will be gone very soon." Toby lit up a bit as Bash assured him of this. "But," Sebastian reminded him, holding up a hand, "people don't forget, especially the fanatics. They'll still be out there hunting and looking for any little proof or slip-up. Times are different, and we have to rise to the challenge of them."

This time, there was more hope in Toby's eyes as he nodded his agreement. "Thank you, thank you. I won't go messing around with tricks like that anymore," he promised. "We're such idiots. It was fun…" Toby trailed off once again, not quite able to meet Bash's eyes.

"Until it wasn't," Bash finished for him. "Until you realized that this put everyone you know in danger." It remained unsaid, but heavy between them both, that this very thing had caused the death of Toby's father a few years ago. Federal land that should have been safe for James to roam on became too much of a temptation for overzealous monster hunters illegally hunting and trapping there. Sure, the hunters got a fine and a short length of jail time for illegally killing a wolf, but they had done much more.

With a lighter step and yet another refill of coffee, Toby took his lanky body back downstairs, probably to let his friends know of this newest development.

"You're good with him." Ravyn's whisper came from directly behind him; another second and her light scent would have given her away. A fragrance almost cherry and almond, but different, tickled his nose after her words. *Blue Lotus.*

Bash rubbed his head, dropping his shoulders. "I try, but I should try harder. These are different times we live in, and it's a battle between letting them find their way and protecting the crap out of them. He's often foolish."

"Ah, to be so young. Better than a fool, at least one can recover from foolishness. We've all been young and we've all made poor choices. Thankfully, it sounds like his are still fixable. It's nice that he has you to guide him. Having that safety net is much better than being alone." Ravyn silently moved farther into the room. "What happened to the boy's father, if I may inquire?"

Tilting his head, Bash considered his words, but he still spoke brashly. "Dead. My brother is dead. Illegally killed by hunters, as if it should ever be legal to hunt down a creature that isn't bothering anyone or anything deep in the forest with no one to help him. Tobias has been hanging out with a few other boys—good boys, sure—but when they're together, their choices are less than ideal. His mom figured some time away with a good role model might help him out." Sarcasm laced his voice. What sort of role model had he been? Bury yourself in work? Hide your true feelings?

Looking back at her, he observed, "You didn't rest long." The reports said she couldn't function for most of the daylight hours, but after working closely alongside her for months, he knew that wasn't true. For whatever reason, she didn't portray her true strength; yet another secret she held close. Others might not notice, but he did. He noticed everything about her.

Letting out a low laugh, she said, "You know I wasn't really resting, and thank you for that. But it has been a few hours. You've been busy, I assume," she added as she ran a hand along the back of the sofa across from him. "I owe you an apology for my harshness earlier."

Ravyn met his eyes and pressed on even as he shook his head no. "I do, and I apologize. You're only doing what you're supposed to do, what you're paid to do. My anger isn't at you, it's at myself." Sighing, she continued, "I'd like to imagine that I'm all powerful, omnipotent, but these last few months have shown how vulnerable I can be and it makes me… it makes me angry and ashamed to feel any sort of helplessness."

Bash could understand that, but being a part of a pack meant not being alone. "There is nothing that says you have to face everything alone. A pack is stronger together," he replied gruffly as his wolf pushed forward, frustrated by the weakness of her words.

"But I'm not in a pack," Ravyn whispered as she closed the distance between the two of them. Laying a cool hand on his chest that he could feel even through his thick tee, she looked up at him, breaking his heart with the seriousness of her words.

His wolf howled inside his head and before Sebastian could even realize what he was doing, he closed the distance between his mouth and hers. Her hand gripped his shirt and pulled him toward her at the same time. He crushed his lips against hers while his hands wrapped around her waist.

Ravyn's lips were at first immobile, but they soon relaxed against his as she leaned her entire body against him. He might have instigated the kiss, but she immediately took control and he was helpless to do anything but try to keep up.

She nipped his lip hard enough that he could feel the blood swell before she licked it clean with a soft velvet tongue. Ravyn pulled back to examine him. His lower extremities swelled at the sight of her licking her own swollen lips and her dilated eyes. His wolf remained strangely quiet, the first time in days whenever they were around Ravyn.

"Took you long enough," drawled Ravyn, looking up at him with heavy eyes that promised the world. But even as he reached back for her, she stepped back, smoothly sidestepping his reaching arms. "You need to be sure. I won't have you looking at me with sad, guilty puppy dog eyes, after."

She swished from the room so quickly that he could almost make himself believe he'd imagined the encounter. Only the soft, exotic scent of blue lotus proved that she'd been in his arms; well, that and his own frustrations.

Still, Bash found a half-dazed smile crossing his face. Even if it were a mistake… But it wasn't a mistake.

Chapter Seven

My heart is light enough to fly

Ravyn returned from her rest with her shield back in place, hiding every expression like she'd done in the early days when he'd joined the team, daring Bash to even hint at what had happened earlier. Following her lead, he stuck with business.

They didn't mention the kiss.

Ravyn intently examined the crack in the window from every angle before murmuring, "Bigger." Letting out a soft sigh of frustration, she picked out a jigsaw puzzle from the dozen or so that were packed away in the apartment.

Ravyn and Toby silently worked on the puzzle, quickly sliding the pieces together while her eyes scanned for the next piece. It was a wonder to watch how quickly the 2000-piece puzzle came together. Bash remained quiet as they all waited for what was to come. He continued to steal glances at Ravyn, uncertain if this changed things in any way. A small smile settled on her face while she worked, but Bash couldn't bring himself to ask what it meant before her mask smoothed down her face once again.

She was right. As much as he hated to admit it, they were stuck in place. The closer they came to the full moon, the surlier his shifters got, and even the vampires hissed in anger if they walked too close to one another. They were all tired of the same walls and even with regular trips outside for the crew, it didn't help Ravyn that she hadn't been permitted to leave at all. If the stalker was hoping to wait them out, he was winning.

The hours ticked lazily by while the background checks cleared and Bash set up a meeting with Anya in an apartment below Ravyn's. The furnishings would allow them to meet comfortably, and they wouldn't be opening her door straight to any potential enemies. As hesitant as he was to bring a virtual stranger into the building, in the end it was the most secure way to do it, and moving from one location to another left Ravyn vulnerable out in the open. Although he couldn't pinpoint it, he felt it in his gut that if Ravyn left the safety of her home, things would happen—bad things out of his control.

Ravyn's home was already compromised if a witch were still spying among the reflections, but still more wards had been placed and they continued to cover every reflective surface in the rooms while watching the crack in the glass continue to expand ever so slightly.

Sebastian had taken over the arrangements,

offering to send Oliver's private plane to accommodate her, which Anya had graciously declined. Apparently, she enjoyed driving, and she wasn't far. Her letter had suggested she spent part of her time in California and part of her time in the Midwest. Despite being an ancient, original vampire, she'd already proven herself different than most of the vampires they met, those who never declined any upgrades or red-carpet treatment. Usually, they demanded it.

A member of Ravyn's security detail filled in playing doorman for the day. After a quick phone call verifying her arrival, the shifter escorted Anya to the elevator and, as planned, entered it with her to bring her straight to Ravyn's temporary door. Someone had driven her, a tall, dark man who had lent her a proprietary arm getting out of the car and walking to the doorway. With a brief nod, he'd left her at the door but hadn't driven off until she'd entered the building.

From his phone, Bash watched the camera as Anya shuffled through the hallway toward the doorway. Ravyn's sister wasn't what he'd imagined. In fact, if anything her appearance and mannerisms shocked him.

Anya accepted the cursory pat down, as well as a metal detector wand that flashed over and around her without complaints. She only carried a small purse; it didn't even have an ID in it, just a few pictures that Bash hadn't seen due to the angle of the camera, but the guard had shuffled through them quickly and offered them back with a polite thank you. Anya rewarded him with a serene smile, so much like Ravyn's practiced smile it nearly bowled him over.

Too busy watching the exchange, not wanting to chance missing anything that constituted a threat, Bash didn't notify Ravyn that her guest was five minutes early. Already anxious, she'd paced her faux apartment, carefully choosing a blood infused wine to offer her guest, while adjusting furniture and flowers that didn't belong to her and closing blinds to filter the late afternoon sunlight. And, if he assumed correctly, counting, always counting.

"She's here." He spoke softly, knowing that Ravyn would hear, and at the same time, the "doorman" offered three sharp knocks on the door, another sign that everything looked above board. In a flash, Ravyn zipped from one room to another, before settling down on the settee and rising once again when Sebastian opened the door for her guest. Behind him he heard her lightly grumble, knowing that he blocked their view of one another, but best to put himself between the two just in case all wasn't as it appeared.

"Welcome, please come in. I'm Ravyn's friend, Sebastian Moldover," he offered as he took a subtle sniff of the lady before him. She smelled pleasant, with just an underlying scent of sickness; puzzling, but his wolf actually hummed a bit in satisfaction. Another test passed, but it still didn't explain everything.

Vampires didn't get sick, but perhaps her scent was just different and it registered in his mind as illness, and his wolf confirmed his suspicion. Her scent, however, was the least unusual thing about her.

Turning sideways, extending an arm in invitation, he said, "Ravyn, your guest has arrived." With no chance to warn her that Anya might not be the sister she remembered, Sebastion had to hope that Ravyn had truly braced herself for anything. Over and over, she had refused to see or hear anything about her sister's background check. It was either good to go or not. Cutting Bash off whenever he had tried to inform her that her sister might be different from what she remembered, had kept Ravyn fully in the dark.

"Sister…" The single word quietly escaped Ravyn's mouth, followed by a small gasp, eyes widened as she covered her mouth with her hand.

For a split second, Bash was pleased. He refrained from grinning, but seeing Ravyn shocked even momentarily was a sight to remember.

Clearly, the older woman who stood before them wasn't quite what any of them had expected. While Ravyn's age had stopped a breath past her bloom into womanhood, one might guess her as twenty, twenty-five, or thirty, but this woman's aging had surprisingly continued. Breathtaking beauties both of them, but a reflection of past and present. Ravyn's black hair had been brushed to the point where it shone and flickered deep blue even in the dim lighting.

Anya's hair, nearly the same length and just as shiny, was almost as white as the moonlight that drew the wolves out. A few darker strands contrasted with the shimmering white, but they were rare. Far from an expert in human aging, if Bash were to guess, the sister who stood before him was well into her eighties or even her nineties.

Ravyn's skin was olive-colored and smooth, the same as it had been the day she'd been turned, while Anya's spoke of a life well-lived, wrinkles and grooves lining a face that was a shade paler than Ravyn's. The laugh lines around her faded green eyes, which surely once had shone as brightly as Ravyn's own, spoke of laughter and life as she patiently waited for Ravyn's shocked perusal of her. Roughly the same height as her sister, sensible flat gray shoes encased her feet while Ravyn's heels added a few inches to her own. Despite the silver cane in her right hand her posture was still rigid, and the elegant pant suit and simple jewels she wore spoke well of her financially, although so had the background checks, so that much wasn't a surprise.

Anya spoke kindly, her voice slightly accented and familiar in tone. "Yes, dearest, I grew old."

With a cry, Ravyn clutched the woman in her arms. Slowly, Anya returned the gesture and for several moments, they just held each other in the comfort of a sisters' embrace.

"So beautiful," Ravyn murmured as she ran a hand

TOOTH AND CLAW

down Anya's hair and face, her eyes still frozen open in wonder. "So beautiful."

"As always, Little Bird, you are too generous." The older woman clutched Ravyn's arm, her wrinkled hand shaking a bit with the emotions of the moment.

Bash feared that she might fall over if Ravyn hadn't been holding her up.

Giving her an arm, carefully leading her to the sofa, Ravyn invited her to sit. She took her seat next to Anya, unable to stop herself touching her, as if afraid she would disappear if she so much as blinked.

Even as he sat across from them, Bash's eyes continued warily roaming over the two of them, trying to figure out this puzzle. Ravyn had claimed this woman as a sister, yet the woman who sat before them could much more easily pass as her grandmother or great-grandmother. Despite him keeping on edge for any potential danger, his wolf yawned, apparently still unconcerned. His mind told him vampires didn't age but at the same time, it argued that their very existence made anything possible.

"You have lived a life," Ravyn offered reverently, her initial shock at the impossible aging before her causing her voice to waver, or perhaps that was still the shock of having an actual sister before her.

"As have you, Sister; I just wear my years now. And I'll admit I've seen and heard a bit more of your life then you have mine, surely an advantage to living in the public eye these recent years." There wasn't even a hint of judgment from the different choices the two had clearly made.

Tilting her head at Ravyn, Anya examined her, as if it were Ravyn whom the years had changed. "The years have made you even more beautiful, if that were possible. It doesn't surprise me at all that you're an actress. Our little bird loved to act out stories, mimic those around us, dance and sing, although she never was a good singer."

"Still isn't," Bash admitted gruffly, sending Anya into peals of laughter even as Ravyn feigned dismay over the teasing, raising a haughty eyebrow at him while leveling a look that would fell mere mortals.

"And you, my sweet Ibis, you've…" Ravyn searched for the words. She'd refused to look at the reports Bash had pulled, saying that if he said Ibis was safe, then she would learn all about her on her own during their meeting.

"I've grown old, darling. I've grown old." Smiling with acceptance of this very human trait, Anya looked fondly at the younger version of herself.

Ravyn's hands twitched on her lap, and Bash wasn't the only one to notice. With a soft smile, Anya reached over to grasp each smooth hand in her own aged hands. Caressing the smoothness and softness, silently inviting Ravyn to do the same, she pulled Ravyn's hand to her lined face before kissing the back of it with a sudden ferociousness.

They sat in silence for a moment, each waiting for

the other to ask or explain and when neither did, Bash cleared his throat. "Anya, or do you prefer Ibis? I saw you have children? Three?"

"Either is fine. I suppose my days of being Ibis have passed and I will remain Anya until the end." She added wistfully, "Names have changed over the years, but all reflect a part of me." Patting next to her, Anya ensured that her small handbag remained by her side before continuing on in a proud tone, "Oh, yes, yes. Leo—that's my husband—and I adopted three children, two boys and a girl. They're all grown up now with families of their own. My oldest son lives here in California with his husband. I've been staying with them, while I've… um, I've been waiting. I usually visit them part of each year to escape the midwestern winters, but this year I needed to be here longer. Thank the goddess I did, since you finally received my letter. My other son and daughter each married, but they still live near me in Indiana where we raised them. I have eight grandchildren and even two great grandchildren. Can you imagine that?"

Bash knew that Ravyn could, in a different lifetime, imagine that of Ibis. Over the last few days, setting up the meeting, Ravyn had spoken nearly non-stop of her memories of Ibis. Back in the temple days, Ibis had talked of her dream to someday have a family. She fell naturally into mothering the little girls in the other groups and could always be counted on to have a cry with. Just as often, she could be found nursing baby birds that had fallen from nests and once for an entire week once, she'd carried a mouse in her pocket, feeding it bits of her every meal. While some girls had considered it an honor to be chosen to serve in the temple, Ibis had been devastated.

Most temples required strict vows and a commitment to a lifetime of serving them. For gentle Ibis, who wanted a simple life, a husband and children, it had been a yoke she bore silently. Temple life wasn't a life she would have chosen for herself, and certainly not eternal life. The woman before him in many ways hadn't changed from the young woman Ravyn had described.

Pulling out pictures from her otherwise empty clutch, she shared them with Ravyn and Bash. Leo was as tall as Anya was short. He was lanky, with large eyes and a smile that showed through in each picture; it was clear they shared a great love. With the pride of a mother, Anya pointed out who each of the children were, who they'd married, and how many children they had.

The final picture was a family picture, the entire family, taken just a year before Leo passed, Anya explained sadly with a shaky voice. Leo sat in a wheel chair in the front with a giggling toddler caught in mid wiggle on his lap. The family, a mixture of sizes and colors, looked happily straight toward the camera while Anya, with a hand on her husband's shoulder, looked at him as if she'd discovered the greatest gift of a lifetime. And truly she did.

"You have a beautiful family," Bash told her.

Ravyn seemed unable to speak, mesmerized by the picture and studying each of the faces as if one might hold a clue to the secrets of such a jubilant life.

"Thank you, it was a good day. The last before, well, before the days got worse for him." With a gentle kiss to the picture, Anya carefully placed it back in her handbag with the other three before offering Ravyn's hand an understanding squeeze. "I miss him every day, but I'm so thankful for the years we had.

"I suppose I should address the elephant in the room," she began, instantly putting Bash on edge. Had this sweet, gentle lady been behind the terrifying gifts and threats? His instincts screamed no, but often the most benign of creatures could be the deadliest.

"After that night when, well, when it happened," Anya began, "I ran. I mean, I suppose we all did. I could barely think straight; the pain and hunger were all consuming. Running was all I could do after..."

Ravyn nodded slightly in sad agreement.

Bash couldn't imagine the confusion and pain the young women had encountered after they were given to demons to re-form in a new image. His wolf snarled once again with the desire to rip the heads from the supposed priests.

"I ran and ran and ran. I didn't know where we were—none of us did—and I didn't know where I was going or where I would end up. It took days before the curse finally calmed enough for me to control it. But I suppose you know all this." The look that passed between the two women spoke of eons more pain than her few short words disclosed.

"Then I couldn't find anyone, any of you. It was like *poof*, gone. Some must have run farther or not as far or in different directions for who knows how long. I even tried for years to find the temple again, hoping that maybe others found their way back. But I couldn't find the little clearing no matter how hard I searched. During those years, the world was so big and later, the memories faded as surely as the temple eventually turned to dust. Time erased all proof of its existence, of our existence too, I suppose. Still, I made it my mission to search for you, any of you; anything not to be so alone."

Ravyn had previously told Bash that she herself had never looked for the temple, assuming that eventually the earth and river had reclaimed it. It was a place of nightmares, a place that had hopefully rotted away along with the secrets to eternal life. Ravyn had no desire to return to the place that had both destroyed and created her.

"I couldn't find it, but years later, I did find a few survivors. Survivors might not be the right word, maybe victims, but years passed us. Those evil men had several temples, not just ours, and more failures than successes, but they were so determined to beat death, to hold onto their feeble mortality no matter the cost or sacrifice of others. They soon learned that in defeating death, they only ensured theirs came much quicker. The others who had been forced to change—other originals, I suppose—hadn't met any of our sisters. After a while, I thought maybe you were just all gone and that I was truly alone."

They sat silently once more, and Bash sent a look toward Ravyn. Should he leave now? This wasn't his story to know. A tiny, discreet shake of her head kept him in his seat.

"I wandered for years and years," Anya went on. "Those years flipped by like the pages of a book, sometimes turning faster and faster and other times, slowly dragging on. During those years, I learned control but I also learned loss. Always loss. Everywhere I settled, those years would flip by along with the lives of those around me, those I cared about. I tried several times to find a piece of love in this world, a man with whom to settle, one willing to call me his wife, but as time went on and they began the slow descent to aging, their love grew to hate as I stayed the same, year after year. Love, hate, and loss, the circle of my life.

"I went into a deep sleep for years at a time, hoping that when I awoke, perhaps things would be different for me. They never were—different, that is. The world changed, but the cycle didn't. It couldn't. Even turning someone for companionship wasn't a sure thing. The curse picks its survivors. Despite my efforts, not all survived the process, and those who did, didn't want to spend an eternity with me. So, I often slept just to pass the years away."

"The deepest of sleeps can be the most healing," Ravyn confirmed.

"I did meet one of our sisters. Once upon a time, I suppose. So, I do know what happened to one beautiful sister. The other little one just bigger than you, Jackal. I don't know what she called herself, if anything. Jackal didn't speak to me. She'd given up on life, you see. I found her sitting in a village in Europe, sometime in the height of the plague. Surrounded in death and decay. Every family, every single villager sickened and died until there was no one left to bury the rest and they just lay there, filling the air with the smell. Her clothes were in tatters, her beautiful hair matted with mud and sickness. She lay in the street of an empty village next to a small child, mute and unable to so much as cry. I don't even know how I recognized her.

"But daylight was coming, you see. At this point, the sunlight was already making us a bit weaker and burning our skin during its zenith. So, I pulled her into a nearby burnt-out house where she moaned and cried, beating her fists against me. And once the sun rose high, in a burst of impossible energy, she ran out into it, arms stretched, reaching out and begging for the sun to take her. It burned and sizzled her skin and she screamed in pain as I watched from the shadows of the shell of a house. But still she was too strong for even the sun."

Silently, Bash went and poured water into a glass and handed it to Anya, who with trembling hands took a long, slow, deep drink. "My thanks," she said before setting the glass down.

Clutching Ravyn's hand in hers as if to steady both women's hands, she took a few deep breaths. "When the clouds blew in, I covered myself and shot out of the house as quick as I could in my own weakened state and gathered her up like a tiny bundle of charred rags, dragging her back into the safety of the house as she silently fought against me."

"In the hours that followed, I tried to give her my blood to heal, and she clamped her lips so tightly closed that her teeth bit through them as her body battled the pull of the curse. She hated me in those moments, cursing me with her bloody eyes, begging me with strained vocal cords to end it for her. So, I did. Maybe if I hadn't, I could have convinced her to keep going. Maybe if I had tried harder, I could have saved her. Maybe I could have walked away. But in the end, I helped her along her journey. I stopped her pain. And after that, I simply quit looking for the rest of you." With a shrug of one shoulder, Anya added, "Maybe if I were stronger, but I couldn't face doing that ever again."

"Those first years were so difficult," Ravyn agreed softly, understanding as memories filled her eyes. "The rage, the guilt. We had to learn to reconcile the two or there was no survival."

"Your man there knows about reconciling two sides. It's a fine line we must all walk. And we must change with the world or be left behind," Anya added solemnly, holding her water up as if to toast the memories. "But for me, being left behind was the hardest, the most difficult part. Love and loss. Then repeat the cycle until I couldn't anymore. More than once I wanted to find a way to end myself as well, but I suppose I was too much of a coward. The alternative was to sleep. Sleep for years and let the pain fade, I suppose."

"I understand," Ravyn softly affirmed. "I've slept as much or more than I've lived. The earth asks for nothing."

Anya nodded in agreement. "And it gives nothing in return either, love. Surviving is not the same as living."

Bash pondered her words and Ravyn's admission. He knew vampires could hibernate within the earth for long periods of time, barely sustaining life in a deep trance state, until their body woke them to enter the land of the living again. However, he had no idea how long Ravyn had slumbered until that moment. Did others hide away from immortality the same as she did or was she an anomaly?

"I met my Leo seventy years ago. And I knew the rush of new love, the thrill of a first kiss and the honeymoon that follows; goddess knows I've done it enough times."

"Here, here." Ravyn raised her own glass in agreement, and the pang Sebastian felt in his stomach amplified when his wolf cried in its own sorrow. Whining, the wolf pulled back from the pain of Ravyn's confession.

With a glance of astuteness that seemed to lay his pain bare, Anya offered a slight nod at him in… understanding?

"And I was done. This love was so different than the others over the years. I wanted to experience new things with him. I wanted to raise children with him, children whom I wouldn't out live, children who would watch me grown old, not the other way around. I wanted to experience growing old with a man who could really see me. Pipe dreams they were; imagine one of our kind growing older and older until the light dims and then fades from our eyes."

"But you made it happen," Ravyn observed. "How did you make it happen? It shouldn't be possible."

Shuddering with the memories, the older woman admitted the horrors. "The process may have been just as bad, if not worse, than the original transition. There were rumors, folktales really, of witches who lived hidden in the swamps of the Czech Republic, near a castle they safeguarded called Houska Castle, built over a gateway to the underworld. Rumors floated around that in this generation it was being guarded by powerful twins from one of the oldest lines in Europe. A man and a woman, equal in power, sharing it, they claimed, like they shared their mother's womb."

Twins were a rarity in the witching world, and seldom was a male born who could harness the same power his female counterparts did. There was power in being a single female from a powerful line, but twins were an anomaly and historically, they weren't generally permitted to happen, no matter the cost.

Bash stumbled over the words, a mixture of shock and awe, but not disbelief despite his words. "You… you crossed through the Gateway to Hell? You went into a hell gate?"

Of course he'd heard of Houska Castle; one of Oliver's side projects was the safeguarding and occasional monitoring of mystical sites around the world. This was something their third partner Malthazar specialized in, spending most of his time off the grid, investigating. According to Malthazar, it was the real deal—and nothing to mess around with.

The mystical castle in the middle of nowhere, a hot spot for paranormal activity, stood atop a seemingly bottomless pit or what some claimed was an entrance to hell, designed to keep the evil bound there. Others had been sent to determine its origins, but he himself had never laid eyes on it, just read the reports to fill time and listened to Malth's stories.

It was one of several places that claimed to be a gateway to hell and, in truth, one of only three that could legitimately claim such a title. The false gateways were a good distraction for the tourists who wanted to visit magical, dangerous sites. A visit to a pretender kept them safe from the true gateways and gave them something to brag about to their friends.

So many legends surrounded Houska Castle: demonic beasts were seen trying to escape the pit under the castle; screeching, flying winged creatures and legless crawling monsters that could still cover a hundred feet in seconds were a few drawn out in old text books. At one time, prisoners who were sentenced to death were offered pardons if they agreed to be lowered by rope into the hole and share whatever they saw. Results varied. Most died screaming within minutes of being lowered, before they could be pulled to safety. One survivor who was winched to safety within seconds of screaming had aged what looked to be thirty years, complete with wrinkles and pure white hair. And the few others who survived were out of their minds, unable to utter a coherent word about what they'd seen, babbling and shrieking nonsense until they left this world. Going to Houska Castle and hoping for help and mercy was a gamble for anyone, especially considering that much more was unknown than known about the nefarious structure.

"It was horrifying, but at the same time beautiful." Anya explained being ripped apart by shadows before being reknit back together, again and again.

"It felt like I was down in the pit for hours, maybe

even days. The screams ruptured my raw throat and I tore at my face, trying to escape. Endless, relentless, but when the twins pulled me back out, it had apparently only been a few seconds. Seconds. Imagine that? Days to recover, to heal wounds that at one time would have healed nearly instantly, but then I was human. Whatever happened to me down there returned my humanity and stripped away the demon inside me. The endless days and nights were over, but my, how different the days were! Sometimes I might find a new wrinkle overnight; that's how quickly humans change, you know. It's remarkable. My skin started to sag, my bones ached, and my eyesight faded. But it was wonderful, a miracle to do it with my Leo. When I looked at him, I could see myself and the love… the love grew and grew. His wrinkles became my wrinkles."

Sebastian felt a pit growing larger and larger in his stomach. The pressure nearly bowled him over. Was Anya here because she wanted Ravyn to turn her back into a vampire? Had she really not been able to find her sisters or had she just waited until she needed them again?

Her love was gone. Her children grown.

Now that death stared her in the face, had she come to regret her choices? His claws lengthened slightly and he curled them into his palms, where they bit into the skin as he held himself in check. *Let Ravyn draw her own conclusions*, he chanted to himself as he

TOOTH AND CLAW

eyed the visitor with new distrust.

"Hold now, wolf, steady on," warned the old woman, seeming to read him well enough despite being human. Anya's soft gaze turned back and forth between Sebastian and Ravyn, examining them both intently.

She smiled gently once again. "I'm glad to know that you know love. Sister. It's a gift to both receive and give love. When I die, my heart will be happy because if you and I both know how to love, then surely our surviving sisters can be granted no less."

When the short introductions had been made, Bash's reason for being there hadn't been laid out to Anya. The ache in his stomach subsided just a bit, imagining what the woman must see to decide that they were lovers. Of course, Bash simply being present for this exchange did suggest an intimacy between them that just wasn't possible.

"We're dear friends," Ravyn serenely told her older sister, while Bash struggled to explain himself, and his damn wolf preened under the older woman's insight.

"Of course you are." Anya patted Ravyn's knee while giving Bash a sympathetic but knowing glance. "Just like myself and my Leo."

"What a life you've led." Bash wasn't imagining the wishful tone in Ravyn's voice. "To have a love like that, and your family... How precious and beautiful."

"I have been a very lucky woman, and I can rest

easy knowing I've laid eyes on you." A troubled sigh left her before her smile returned a moment later. "I have been writing you for a few years now. Ever since I recognized you, I have sent letters to your agency, knowing the chances of you getting them and believing in who I was could be impossible. But here we are at the final hour. I know your wolf already sees it, but I'm dying."

Holding up a hand as Ravyn opened her mouth, Anya continued. "No, *this* is what I want. It's my next big adventure and the final chapter of my human life. It's everything I have wanted and more."

Anya spoke of her inevitable death as if she looked forward to the event. Surely, Bash prayed to Fenrir, when Anya faced the scales, it would lean heavily on the love her heart held for her family and not what the priests had forced her to become.

Chapter Eight

Death upon her eyes would carry her away

Anya stayed for hours, until her pain medicine wore off, laughing, crying, and sharing special moments with Ravyn. The goodbyes were quick and for the two of them, they were final. The cancer-stricken Anya insisted quietly and firmly that there wouldn't be another meeting, at least this side of the veil.

Anya even gave Bash firm kisses on each side of his face, as well as whispering to him to always follow his heart. Clearly Ravyn heard this, although she feigned that the words were a secret between the two.

Waving off the other members of the security team, Bash carefully walked Anya out to the safety of her car, handing her off to her son, who gently arranged her in the front seat of his modest car, nodding firmly to him before driving off with her. Had Anya's husband known the truth about her? Did her children know? Were they able to love her without knowing her darkness? How could one hide centuries of living from those closest to them? The thought gave Ravyn pause.

Could she give and receive that kind of love? Could she sacrifice that much of herself to love someone? Could anyone? If anyone could, it would be Ibis and her gentle soul. Tears filled Ravyn's eyes as she watched them through the security feed. Despite thinking her sisters lost so many years ago, this reunion of sorts unfurled a plethora of unexpected emotions and possibilities.

Back securely in her own apartment, or at least as secure as one could feel when some sort of creature was attempting to scry one's every movement, Ravyn attempted to relax over the glass of wine Sebastian had silently passed to her when he returned. She refused to set it aside even as she imagined the long, slow wink of a solemn eye staring out at her. Dammit, she would *not* cower, and she refused to check the crack in the window. Damn it all, none of that mattered at this moment.

Although she'd wiped her face clean of the tears before Bash returned, the ache of loneliness intensified after her sister left. Admittedly, she could be just as lonely in an empty room as well as a roomful of people, but this was the bone-aching loneliness of knowing yet another sister was lost. Anya, the little Jackal, and another. Another.

Three sisters gone, or would be gone when Anya left this world. At least. Ravyn would like to hope that the other three were out there carving out a happiness of sorts and that if they were gone, someone other than

Tooth and Claw

her would mourn them.

"Stay." Short and not a question or a request he might possibly deny. She knew she was being rude, demanding that Bash stay with her longer. He'd already spent days making this meeting happen and then stayed by her side throughout it, allowing his quarters to be their meeting ground. Immediately after she demanded he stay, regret settled in.

"I'm sorry. I should be thanking you and here I am just taking more and more from you." Her hands grasped the wine glass tightly, more out of habit then any desire to drink from it. "You've been at my beck and call, and I continue to demand you cater to my selfish whims. You have your nephew to check on, and you need to rest."

"Tobias is fine. He's happily been playing video games uninterrupted while I work."

Work.

Yes, his words were a good reminder that he worked for her. A knot formed in her throat, and her heart sputtered a slow beat or two as the sadness in the pit of her stomach enlarged. Bash wasn't there for her all day because they were friends. He simply was good at his job, good enough that she could forget that he was paid to be there with her day in and day out. Her suddenly dry mouth opened to demand he take his leave. After all, he'd earned it.

"I think I'll have that drink you're always offering." His dark eyes watched and waited. He never drank with her, always claiming he was on duty and of course, he was. Always.

Still, Ravyn moved toward her bar, floating a hand over the liquors before pausing over one. Pulling it out and up, she tilted the label toward him with her brows raised in question. His smile and nod of acceptance gave her a tiny thrill, and she found herself once again smiling as well, as she generously poured the brown liquid into a tumbler.

Handing it to him, she realized as he practically reverently took the drink that this was the first time she'd served him something. On the other hand, she couldn't remember the last time she'd needed to pour or fix herself sustenance. Bash seemed to anticipate her needs and have a drink at the ready before she knew she needed something. Ignoring the thrill that idea brought her, she tapped it down with her mind.

Don't read too much into it.

This time, they settled down on the sofa, Ravyn watching Bash out of the corner of her eye as he took a long drink from the glass.

"What a day," he began just as she blurted out in a jumble, "I… lied… lied to my sister… my sister Ibis… Anya."

Once she said the words, others began to bubble out of her mouth, despite her need to relax. The need to reveal her truth overruled all. "I lied. I did find one of our sisters. But even after Ibis told me her story, I couldn't tell her about this. I couldn't take away the hope that the rest of us have loved and been loved like she hopes. The hope that bits of her will still remain in the world long after she's gone."

Bash looked at her over the top of the whiskey glass as he drank deeply from it, raising an eyebrow, asking her to continue. With a deep breath, she quickly stood to top off his glass. After another thought, she dumped a generous serving in her nearly empty wine glass before placing the bottle within arm's reach instead of returning it to its space.

The words started hesitantly, slowly and then building up speed as she poured out the words that had weighed heavily on her since telling her sister—no, lying to her sister—that she hadn't seen as much as a glimpse of the other four over the years.

"My sister died on a battlefield. Not a battlefield filled with machinery, mechanisms and tech, no, but a battlefield with warriors—loud, ruthless, bloodied warriors. The oldest of us, I believe, or at least she acted as such."

Ravyn paused as her mind filled with the memories, trying to piece things together, to understand. So many wars over so many years. Death and war, war and death. No wonder she'd slept for so long. The violence proved over and over again that she couldn't escape it.

"I think we've been living—or un-living, as the case may be—the legends of old. For a while, I played goddess in various temples until that grew boring. I played the righteous Ma'at at a small temple for years, dealing out justice, maintaining the harmony of the land and seasons while I lived among them. Surprisingly enough, the real goddess never struck me dead for my blasphemy. The stories of Valkyries, Sirens, even the Four Horseman make me wonder where we've landed in history, the things we've all touched. Clearly, we weren't the only vampires made. The ability to beat death made us vain and bored. Why not have humans worship us? Fear us? Truly, these legends could involve any one of us. Surely, I wasn't the only one to live as a goddess to take and live on what the followers would happily give me.

"Like Ibis over the years, I would slumber for long periods just to escape the endless of it all. I'd been awake a few years after a long sleep, before I began hearing stories of a Morrigan enticing men to war on an island. I couldn't help but hope one of my sisters had found a life there.

"I arrived in Ireland, wet and cold, frozen to the bone, on an old merchant ship with tattered, patched sails and a leaky hold. I'd lived on rats during the short voyage from England. Rats. Can you imagine?"

Ravyn found herself being swept back into the memories: the biting taste of the salty water as it splashed and sloshed in the hold where she hid among the barrels and rotting food. The tainted, unsatisfying taste of rats' blood, the gnawing hunger.

The initial blood lust after her turning had her

determined to never drink from a human again. She eventually amended that to include those worthy of death, an easy enough option to find when traveling as a woman alone. After learning she could control the thirst, she amended her rules again to only those who gave willingly, even if she wiped their memory of the event afterward. The brutality of war ensured all bets were off. The only thing the dead and dying had to offer was their blood.

"The stories spoke of three Morrigans, but when I tracked the stories to the battlefield, I only found one. Either they used the story of three to explain how quickly she moved, how she could be in two or three places seemingly at one time, or she latched onto the stories and simply claimed she was a Morrigan. Or maybe there had been three, once."

Shrugging one shoulder, Ravyn snuggled deeper under the soft blanket, instinctively shifting to snuggle against Bash's hard body, finding comfort in the closeness. "It's so difficult to know when the legends began. Did the stories come first or did the demons? Did we create them or were we created? I found her on a battlefield. Pakhet, our fierce lioness. Like a whirlwind she swept through them in a barely noticeable blur, killing indiscriminately, friend and enemy alike. Beautiful—a deadly, beautiful, raven-haired goddess of war. Spinning on the shadows, she appeared here, then there, cackling on the wind as she shred them with tooth and nail, then casually shifting away to the next. Their shocked cries were drowned out by the battle around them. Was she on a side? Did sides even matter? She whispered her taunts and challenges into the wind, causing strife, fighting against and alongside all and none.

"I screamed her name. Over and over, I screamed her name. Laughing, she whispered in the wind, 'No, not today.' 'Stop,' I begged. 'Never,' the wind replied. She was so beautiful, even while standing in death; perhaps that made her more so. With tears on my face, sorrow filling my black heart, and with my own blade, I stepped within her swirling, dancing path with my knife extended slightly, and then I simply cut her down as she appeared. With a shocked gasp, her movements slowed and then ended, frozen. Her hands replaced mine on the knife shaft that extended into her chest. Frozen in the wind now she was, as the battle raged on around us."

Stumbling back from the shocked look on Ravyn's face, the Morrigan had smiled. Pakhet, the fierce lioness, smiled at her. A soft, gentle look entered her eyes. The harpy smiled, a happy, bloody smile, her white teeth barely visible against the mud, soot, and blood. Then with a grunt, she gently pushed the knife deeper as she whispered, "My thanks, little sister," and suddenly dusted away, disappearing among the swirl of smoke and bloody mud of the battlefield.

"I loved her, but I loved humans more. Those weak, weak humans. Already they were so fragile. A dry summer could kill a village, a single disease wipe out a city. War destroyed entire nations. They constantly teetered on the balance and there she was killing for pleasure with not a sense of remorse. Once upon a time, those shadow demons had shredded her humanity along with her body. But she'd embraced the shadows and become the fearsome legend. I couldn't allow that, and so I didn't. One small step and I could end it. And so I did. I loved her, but sometimes that isn't enough."

After all the years, Ravyn could still remember the details of those moments: the way the air rippled with the hate and anger of men encouraged by the Morrigan's dark, magical whispers. The way the mud, wet with the blood of the fallen, had sucked at her feet, trying to keep her in place while it bogged down the men in battle. The stench of sweat, fear, and rage mixed with the putrid odor of sliced intestines. Her sister reveled in it. She hadn't battled with shame or remorse; she embraced the change. And despite the horrors of those days, even now Ravyn could admit how beautiful the girl had looked with her black braids dripping in blood. Her battle-worn tunic swirled and danced among the fallen, gracefully bending and weaving amid the battle axes and swords aimed at her head while blood clung to her hands and forearms. Her face was painted with the mud and blood of anyone and anything near her. Horrifying, yet beautiful at the same time. So damn beautiful.

"I couldn't bear to tell Anya. I couldn't destroy her hope that the rest of us were well. She can go to her grave and rest knowing that we're all good. Or if she is granted this knowledge on the other side, at least maybe she'll be granted the wisdom of understanding why I did it and why I needed to lie to her. May the gods allow her to rest easy."

A part of Ravyn knew with absolute certainty that her sister, the fierce lioness, had wanted to die but just lacked the ability to take that final step. Unable to control the curse, death might have been the option to choose and Ravyn simply the instrument that allowed this blessing for her. Perhaps this final sacrifice would allow Pakhet, the goddess of war, to rest well on the other side. Perhaps even to see her sisters once again.

"I want you to stay tonight," Ravyn admitted softly, watching Bash slowly set down his now empty glass of whiskey. "I'm asking, not telling. And only if you want to," she anxiously amended, already seeing the hesitation in the wolf shifter's clenched jawline. She fought the urge to refill her own empty glass and sling it down but also didn't dare to look away from the man before her.

"Ravyn, if you knew how badly I want to. But this day... this day has been well charged from beginning to end. I don't want to take advantage of that, of you."

He placed his hands on his thighs, and she watched the hair on his arms rise as the wolf clearly had something to say about it.

"Even if that were true, it's not a reason to say no." Flippantly, Ravyn added, "I mean, I could tell you I've had sex with men under worse scenarios and that's not necessarily a bad way to remind yourself that you still have some humanity in you. Bash, I want to remind myself... I need to remind myself with you."

Silence sat between them as they each watched the other warily, nearly afraid to lay themselves bare. "That kiss," Rayvn began, "made me..." Another long pause as she tried to explain herself. "But even if it didn't, we could just ease the tension a bit between us. Scratch the itch, if you prefer; it doesn't have to mean anything."

"But what if it does?" Bash asked in a low voice, watching her with his deep predator gaze. "What if it does mean something?"

"Right now, I can only promise tonight. This moment right here." Rayvn considered her next words carefully. "You don't need to promise anything either. You can leave whenever you want."

Already feeling the sting of rejection, she stood, ready to make another graceful exit.

With a growl, Sebastian pulled her down on his lap, spreading her legs so she straddled him. His mouth met hers and although surprised, she found herself matching his passion.

Sucking his lower lip between hers before slowly

pulling away and meeting his dark brown eyes with her own, she informed him, "I need to hear you say yes, that you want me and this as much as I do." She could feel the heat of his body against hers and the blood pumping faster and faster with each breath. Even as she asked, she nestled her hips closer to him in an attempt to hit that once perfect spot against his hardness.

"Yes," Sebastian growled out as he reached up with both hands to cradle her face. "Yes." He pulled her against him and devoured her mouth, holding her in place behind the neck. As his other hand worked its way down her hip, he pulled her closer. Reaching down, he brushed the heat of her core, and she thrust her hips closer to him. Anything to get closer. "Not yet, my princess," he teased, brushing the spot once again, teasing her as he took her mouth in his and leaving his hand to roam over her hips and down the back of her thighs.

The kiss took over, growing wild, promising things to come as she tugged at his waistband, determined to remove the clothes that separated them.

"No hurries, Princess. We have all night. I want to worship your body."

"Then do it," she murmured, pushing herself closer, not even sure where she wanted him to touch next.

"Fucking hell, you make me so hard."

"Show me," she demanded, panting as that

hardness rubbed her sensitive core. "I want you inside of me. Fucking show me how bad you want me."

"I could take you right here and do unimaginable things to your body. Gods, you're so beautiful." Scooping her up, he added, "But it will be in a bed. Not out here."

"You're like the sunlight and the moonlight wrapped together as one to create perfection," Bash whispered to Ravyn, pulling her closer into his embrace. "You're the culmination of the best parts of both."

"Tell me about the moon," murmured Ravyn, looking up at him contently while tracing the lines of his chest and stomach, following the ups and downs lightly with two of her fingers.

"The moon speaks to us, and we don't always need to listen, but it's there always in the backs of our minds. But for three days, the pull is irresistible, so strong it's nearly indescribable. For you I'll try to find the words." Bash pulled her closer, rubbing his scent along her, and for a second, Ravyn imagined she could hear his wolf echo her purr of contentment.

"The full moon tugs at your soul. The day before and the day after are nearly as strong. You can feel your wolf thrumming under your skin, begging to be let out to be closer, I guess, to the moon. Before I shift, the air crackles with the magic of each shifter and the moon, as if they're reaching out to each other. I suppose they are. It's mind-blowing that wolves all over the world simultaneously feel the pull of the moon so strongly for twenty-four hours. During those hours, we're all drawn by the inexplicable siren call of the moon, connected every single month through our creator, Fenrir."

Pausing a moment as if considering and collecting his thoughts, he went on, "But the pinnacle point, the absolute point of perfection is the apex of the full moon, the moment it's truly full. You see, really it peaks only for a brief moment, a single perfect moment of perfection. But also, this moment of time is different wherever a wolf might be in the world. By man's perspective and even scientific definition, the full moon is an entire rotation. It's not, though. Everything before or after it is simply just a little less. For that single moment, moonlight runs through our veins absolute and powerful. A perfect, beautiful moment in which we neither control nor are controlled, but have perfect balance, harmony, so to speak. It's when our wolves feel most free and sing strongest to the moon."

Pausing, seeming to consider his next words, Bash added, "I may have been too quick to settle on the sun and moon. You're the peak of the moon, its zenith. That is perfection."

"I don't deserve that," she whispered as he tightened his arms around her.

The silence settled back over them as Ravyn considered his words about having a perfect moment of time every single month. It was amazing and almost incredibly cruel of the gods to allow that, only to take away that balance the rest of the time. "You sound almost romantic, Moldover."

Pulling her up on his chest, he added as he ran his hands down her thighs, guiding her to straddle him, "They say that Fenrir was chained because he wanted to burn the world, plunge it into total darkness, but that's not true. Not entirely anyway. He wanted the world to burn because they kept him from his chosen mate. The gods hoped to prevent him from finding happiness; by chaining him, they forced the prophecy. He was an instrument they used and a mate interfered with that. He never agreed to being chained, and Fenrir bit Tyr's hand off because it was the hand that had been raised against his mate. On his own, he could bear being the brunt of their anger and hatred, but when they raised a hand against his fated mate, the gods themselves couldn't prevent what was to come. They made him the villain in his own love story."

Settling his hands on her hips, a slight laugh rumbled through Bash—
one that a listener knew was meant to fill an awkward or uncomfortable silence. "Silly, right?"

Ravyn rocked her hips gently against him. There was more to Bash's words than what he said, and she feared what he was leaving unsaid. A chosen mate meant a forever mate. It meant that neither gods nor the Fates could keep them apart. A part of her could imagine how Fenrir felt when he wanted to burn the word to get to his mate. Bash was wrong, however, if he thought the world was worth burning over her.

It wasn't.

"Absolutely. Not. It sounds perfect." Lifting her hips as she held onto his hands, guiding herself onto him, she let out a soft gasp. "But..."

He sat up with a groan, pulling her core closer to him. Leaning against him as he moved inside her, she forgot that she needed to tell him that she couldn't be the perfection he was looking for.

But together right now with him deep inside her, she felt the world burn.

Chapter Nine

Moonlight on a raven's wing

The full moon was upon them. All the shifters took the day off the day before and the day after to answer the call of the moon. They could change at will or not change any day or night of the month, but during the full moon it was impossible for a wolf to ignore the moon's beckoning.

On the one hand, Ravyn didn't have to face an awkward day after, trying to figure out how, if at all, last night affected her relationship with Sebastian. Bash had left during an unexpected bout of blissful sleep during the sun's zenith. His side of the bed was still warm but no longer held the intense heat of the wolf. For a moment, Ravyn allowed herself to imagine a spot of warmth on her lips where he'd kissed her a final time before he left to follow the moon.

On the other hand? Ravyn didn't like to think that he'd crept out after she'd fallen asleep. She could even admit to herself that if he had, doing so was a bit childish and a lot hurtful.

So, she simply imagined that when he saw the

time, he hadn't wanted to disturb her sunlight slumber. Surely, he needed to prepare and leave immediately with the rest of the shifters to chase the moon for the next few days. Besides, he had a teenager to get moving too. Bash had taken the time to scrawl a quick note, simply saying "Full moon," but he signed off "X Thor," so that had to mean something good, didn't it? Ravyn was a bit embarrassed to admit she'd held the note much longer than necessary to read it, before smoothing it flat and placing it in her side table, closing it regretfully in the drawer.

Her ever silent and oh-so-efficient housekeeper had stripped her bed and had her sheets in the wash before Ravyn had even returned from her shower in a bathroom with the mirror still tightly covered to keep out prying eyes. This time, she tried to shove down the feelings of loss and hint of annoyance. There went her plans for the day. Clean sheets ensured she wouldn't languish in bed, reliving the night they'd just shared. Or smelling the pillow he'd lain on while imagining he hadn't left her.

She was wrong. One night wasn't enough. Every time she touched him, she wanted to touch him more. Each time he touched her sex, she wanted him back inside of her deeper and deeper.

Before the sun dragged her under to sleep, Bash had held her and whispered to her all the things he still wanted to do. Promised her that she wouldn't be able to see a cock without thinking of him. Promises.

Tooth and Claw

The vampires currently on duty wouldn't be likely to engage her in idle chit-chat like the wolves did, and they certainly wouldn't hang out drinking coffee with their feet on her furniture like young Toby liked to do. The best she could hope for was that they would fix themselves a cup of black coffee and station themselves outside whatever room she was in. Both species took their job seriously, but sometimes the vamps just seemed a hair too serious about it all, although the entire group of them would take insult to that particular observation for different reasons.

The wolves knew she was considered important, and despite the fact that Sebastian liked to jokingly call her "Princess," it was a bit too close to the truth. She was important to the vampires. Important, intimidating, untouchable royalty due to her creation and even if they didn't understand the process, they revered it deeply. They were each several generations removed from whichever original vampire had sired their line, so for them, Ravyn was possibly the only vampire they knew who had been created without a master. Despite the fact that there were few vampires in the world, there was little to no record, keeping many ignorant of their direct sire. It made sense in theory that they idealized any potential esteemed sire they came across. Hand in hand with that reverence came the inability to engage in casual conversation with her, let alone—gasp—joke around.

No matter how often she requested that they relax

or call her by her first name, they would simply smile politely, nod in agreement, and still address her formally. "Yes, Ms. Ravyn Sinclair; no, Ms. Ravyn Sinclair." Their idea of relaxing the formality toward her was addressing her as Ms. Sinclair and, unfortunately, even that made them very uncomfortable. Ravyn hoped they didn't have a title for her outside of their interactions with her. If Bash found out she had a title, he would most likely use it every chance he got. Imagining him bowing deeply to her, kissing the back of her hand, and calling her "Your Highness" in his low, mocking tone made her stomach flutter. Although the idea had merits under certain circumstances, Ravyn blushed faintly at the thought.

Toby, on the other hand, had no cares for formalities or hierarchies. Just the other morning, he'd come in with both food and coffee and tossed her a casual, "What's up, Sis?" It earned him an eye roll as well as a cuff on the back of his head by his uncle, but she carried the pleasure his simple, three-word question gave her all day long.

Last night, she'd been Ravyn to Bash, and many other terms of endearment that made her blush a bit from the pleasure of the memories. Her favorite might have been when he called her "mine" while deep inside her as she screamed in agreement.

Love sick? Love struck? She was definitely feeling more struck than sick. Reluctantly, Ravyn admitted that today might be a day to work uninterrupted, since the shifters would be gone. Because no matter what, this threat would be gone soon. If it wasn't it didn't matter; she would still be returning to work. No longer would she put her life on hold for some maniac who may or may not still be fixated on her. A small part of her hated to admit that if she didn't keep her mind busy focusing on other things, she might become that girl sitting by the phone wondering when he would call. And worse was feeling that way while knowing that Bash's shifter form clearly didn't have the appendages needed for using a cell phone.

Still, when her phone rang, she jumped in an excitement that nearly embarrassed her. Clicking Accept on the video call, Ravyn forced herself to hide the disappoint that it wasn't Bash somehow figuring out a way to call her without opposable thumbs.

"Hey, girl." Pulling from her acting ability, she pasted a full smile on as Eva's face filled the screen. "Aren't you supposed to be enjoying a honeymoon of sorts?"

Eva flushed. *So cute*, Ravyn thought with a hint of jealousy, not for the first time, at what Oliver had found.

"Taking a break from all the sight-seeing and stuff," Eva replied pertly. "And something just compelled me to give you a call." Eyeing her strangely, Eva continued, "Although I don't know why I felt worried. You're the one glowing this time. Is house arrest over or at least looking better?"

"Ugh, no, definitely not over. Just quiet," Ravyn quickly amended, knowing that anything she said to Eva was as good as telling Oliver. She definitely didn't want to be responsible for ending their trip early. "It feels like all we do is wait for their next move."

"They'll make another mistake." Eva's words were serious. "And when they do…"

As Eva drew a finger across her throat to emphasize the plan to destroy Ravyn's stalker, a couple of tiny marks on her neck caught Ravyn's notice.

"What is that?" she screeched, feeling like a teenager's mother. "Why is Ollie marking you like that? He can heal those marks."

Wide-eyed, Eva covered the aforementioned dots with the slap of her hand to her neck. "It was a game"—her voice went up a strange, high notch—"it was a game, we were playing a game!"

Ravyn snorted and attempted to cover it with a choked cough before settling a serene look back over her face. "I can imagine," she finally responded dryly, dragging out each word while Eva squirmed. And she could—imagine, that was. Imagine that Bash might agree to play such a game with her. He would, but would he be the prey or the predator? Both were intriguing options.

"But in all seriousness…" Eva's voice took a solemn note. "Are there any updates at all?"

Shaking her head, Ravyn couldn't keep the note of annoyance out of her voice. "Nothing, nothing at all is different. I almost wish something would happen so we had a clue if he's given up and moved on or if he's just waiting." Only a tiny white lie; nothing had been proven about the growing crack in the window. It could simply be as it appeared, and a poorly constructed frame placed pressure on the wrong side in the wrong conditions. And nothing had been proven either way that anyone was watching them through reflective surfaces. A trick of the light, a reflection of one's own eye; frustrating, yes, but still nothing concrete. And nothing to worry Eva or Oliver about during their time away.

Promises were made to get together after Eva and Oliver's extended vacation. And empty assurances that Ravyn would let the two know if anything changed in California.

The call ended too quickly, leaving a hollow feeling in her chest. The connection to her unusual prodigy, although previously unknown, now seemed to vibrate as a reminder of what once was. How could you miss what you never knew you had? It was silly.

The quietness of the apartments settled in quickly as well as the boredom. Fixing her eyes on the crack in the window, Ravyn tried to determine if it had grown larger in the last hour. She squinted, tilting her head up at it before closing the drapes once again. The witches had specifically shorn up the area with their wards but couldn't give a valid reason for the crack.

Ravyn refused to accept scripts from her agency via email. Give her hard copy of five hundred pages, if necessary, but skip the digital version. She enjoyed flipping through the pages, reading at leisure, marking it up, adding sticky notes, and making it her own. Call her old-fashioned, but she simply hadn't gotten the hang of reading through works on her laptop or Kindle. Eva devoured books that way, but she still liked the feel of paper. Three scripts awaited her attention; her manager weeded out the ones that wouldn't make the cut, saving them both time in the long run. Ravyn trusted her manager to only bring her the stories that she might be compelled to be a part of.

One had a couple of highlighted sticky notes attached to the outside of the envelope:

"Sort of different choice for you to consider."

"Producer insists it's written for you. Calls daily."

"Insists" and "daily" had both been underlined multiple times; so many that it looked like there was a danger of it ripping through the paper. Clearly someone had been overly persistent but at the same time, also important enough to not immediately put off her manager.

The cover sheet listed the production company, and Ravyn immediately understood why her people hadn't just ignored an overzealous, hopeful producer. If they didn't at least have Ravyn look over the work and consider it, this man could and would black ball

TOOTH AND CLAW

all their clients—future and present—due to the insult. The mere ego of the man made her want to trash the entire script without even considering it.

He was a bully. But he *was* brilliant. Ravyn could never work again and still be fine, but she enjoyed her work and didn't want to close any doors because of her own pride. Besides, it was a tough market out there, and she didn't like the idea of being responsible for others losing opportunities due to her choices.

She did, however, decide with a self-satisfied smirk that it could wait for last. The small act of rebellion gave her a tiny bit of satisfaction as she began reading through the other scripts. And for the next day and a half she read… and read… and read. She made notes of things to check on, considered potential casting choices and each director's production vision.

Her housekeeper kept her fed, discreetly setting glasses of warmed liquid near her; no matter if she sprawled across the sofa or lay on the bed, they appeared and disappeared when she finished. It felt so good to be normal again. Considering work and the excitement that accompanied filming left her vibrating in happiness. In the end, Ravyn wasn't sold on the idea of either works yet and penned a few questions to ask. Ultimately, at this point, she decided that one had enough possibilities that if she could fit it into her wide-open schedule she would take it, but better works could easily replace it.

Finally pulling out the script that she'd originally set aside, she attempted to look past the pushy yet widely successful producer who'd sent it to her. A bird immediately hit the window when she pulled it out, but this time she no longer jumped from the impact.

Bertrando Roland. Mr. Roland of Land and Sea Cinema, founder, producer, and apparently, a force to be reckoned with if you hoped to stay in Hollywood's good graces. An industry powerhouse, and for him to be sending out a script with her specifically in mind was actually damn exciting and almost guaranteed to be another box office hit. Still, it irritated her that he'd been aggressive with her manager, even if his works were amazing.

Holding the binder, Ravyn contemplated what sort of script it could contain. Tapping it against her chin, she allowed herself to briefly consider what a movie deal with Land and Sea could do for her career. Admittedly, she was already popular and wealthy beyond imagination, but a movie of Roland's caliber could catapult her to the next level of fame. Beautiful actresses were replaceable; interchangeable, really. Every season a new young scarlet waited in the wings, ready to claw her way in to replace those who stumbled even slightly. And the fickle public didn't even blink, eagerly embracing whichever beauty they were told was the next big thing. They followed, imitated, and secretly wanted to be whomever they were told to watch. But the right movie, the right script, the right role, could make one a legend. A role that years from now, even when Ravyn retired and hid from the public eye, they would talk about and reminisce about how stars these days weren't the same as the old days. She could be *that* star. If she could deal with him, of course.

A single short, handwritten note lay on the front, loose from the binder: *R. Thanks for considering. B.R.*

B.R. was clearly Bertrando Roland, but they were also the initials on two separate floral arrangements she'd received on set several months ago, as well as another, enormous arrangement that had arrived at her apartment before her last movie premiere with congratulations as well as the initials. She simply hadn't realized or even considered that Mr. Roland was the sender. Had he been considering her for a role for a long time? Ravyn had no doubt that her agency would have notified her directly if he'd expressed interest. Certainly, she received flowers and gift baskets regularly and quite often didn't know the sender, but Ravyn was certain her agency sent thank you letters to every sender when possible. Had the flowers been an attempt to reach out to her and gauge interest early on? Thankfully, he didn't seem to hold that possible oversight against her and was still willing to chance her interest in working with the man.

Setting his note carefully aside, she wrapped up in a soft blanket that still lingered with Bash's soothing scent before making herself comfortable once again on the sofa. Then began the story of legendary Giulia Tofana, a skilled seventeenth-century poisoner who invented a colorless liquid called Aqua Tofana to help subjugated women gain their freedom from oppression.

The Catholic Church had painted her as an evil, villainous woman, a witch who murdered for money, killing good, decent men and ripping families apart. While Ravyn herself had never met the woman, she knew through the hushed whispers during those years that Giulia only helped those who were helpless and punished only those who were evil and preyed on the helplessness. A heroine lost in history by the men who wrote it.

Amazing. Sitting back on the couch, she wiped away the tears, still clutching the script in her hands, unable to let it go quite yet. This would be amazing.

Ding.

Her phone interrupted her revelry. It was her agency with a text and contact info.

"Mr. Roland asks for you to reach out at your leisure to discuss."

It was almost as if he knew she'd just eagerly finished reading the project script.

Quickly, Ravyn typed off a message, caught up in the moment. This was the project she'd dreamed of since starting this life in Hollywood. Nothing superficial, but something worth doing and sharing. A mark on the world; a legacy of sorts, to live long after she left the glitz and glamor. A mark of herself and a legendary woman who deserved to be showcased and remembered for her deeds as well.

An equally quick response dinged back at her with a pinned location. Sighing, she stretched, moving her neck side to side as it popped gently, easing the tension.

If only Bash was back to talk this over with. He was the one she wanted to share this with and not just because she entrusted her security to him, but because the news, the possibilities, were exciting.

What to do? What to do?

A flash of guilt rippled through her, knowing that Bash would want her to wait. Want her to wait for the background checks, the security detail prep, the location checks. He would definitely hate the idea of her meeting at a location that someone else had chosen. He would hate everything about the situation. But this was Bertrando Roland, giving her the chance to tell Giulia Tofana's story.

One, two, three, four, five, six. Six lines on the last page. Six lines. Ravyn considered. Dipping a finger in the dredges of her wine, she began flipping and counting through the pages despite the fact that they were numbered. Reaching page seventy-five, she stopped. Her decision was made.

Standing up with a stretch, she pushed open the drapes on the window. Hesitantly, she stood directly in front of the window. No eye—imaginary or not—twinkled at her. Surely that was a positive sign.

Feeling a tinge of guilt as she once again examined the window, she noticed that the crack had grown. At nearly twelve inches long, it was well past time to call in a window expert. Magical examination had proven futile and it had to be assumed the integrity of the glass had been compromised and a replacement needed. Unfortunately, no one had called for a repair.

After this meeting, she promised herself. If no one else remembered, she could do it herself.

Chapter Ten

Fly free little bird

The vamps agreed with her evening plans.

Of course they did. Ravyn made a mental note to talk once again to Bash about their unprofessional deference to her. The point of security was to make the hard decisions and to tell her "No" when needed. They either didn't have it in them or were so sure of their vampire abilities to keep her safe, they were willing to ignore all other security protocols.

Sloppy and irresponsible. Clearly it worked in her favor today, and despite the guilty feeling she had at taking advantage of the situation, Ravyn eagerly squished it down to finally prepare for an evening out.

Dressed in a simple black sheath dress that hit just at her knees, Ravyn twisted her dark hair into an elegant bun, securing it with a blue lotus clip with silver claws before touching up her lipstick. A small, intimate gathering was what Bertrando Roland had suggested, a chance to get together, relax, chat, and see how well they might work together. Three guards would accompany her, one as her driver and two following in a separate vehicle. Roland's secluded mountainside home, as well as it being an intimate gathering place, wouldn't permit two or more random men to wander about undercover. It was better to be straightforward with her need for heightened security. And if the wolves returned from their time away before she and the others returned home, they could patrol the outside of the grounds.

Final pieces in place, Ravyn stepped into her lounge area just as Toby wandered in, freshly showered with wet hair combed back, eating from a party-size bag of chips. His low, wolfish whistle of appreciate pleased her, and she ignored the dark, glowering look her driver gave him as the vampire stood stoically by the door awaiting her.

Giving a slow twirl, with a pleased smile, she asked, "You like? I'm not always in grubby sweat pants and lounge wear, you know."

Toby nodded, brushing a few chips off his tee-shirt before swallowing the ones in his mouth. "You look great. Got plans for tonight?"

"I do." Not intentionally vague, but a bit cautious about his earlier-than-expected appearance. Admittedly, she'd lost track of time while reading the scripts. "You're back early? Is everyone here?" she inquired, although honestly, she only cared about one person.

That person's name went unspoken, along with a flash of both guilt and excitement. Part of her jumped at seeing her... her... whatever Bash might be defined as, but the other part immediately considered that he would squash her plans to venture out tonight to an unseen location. Her paramour? "Paramour" sounded more involved than "lover" and not as committed as "mate." Since when did labels matter so much to her? Were they anything?

"Nah, I came back earlier with one of the guys who wanted to get back and spend some time with his girl. Bash and some of them always hang back and decompress for a few extra hours, but I like to get back and do my own decompressing."

It took a second for Ravyn to recognize the unfamiliar feeling settling into place. Hurt. She was hurt. Bash could have been back already, but he chose to stay away from her for a few extra hours. He hadn't chosen to immediately return to her side. Apparently, no matter how old she got or how many lovers she took, she still found herself susceptible to hurt and jealousy. Ridiculous. And wildly embarrassing. Bash wasn't really to blame. She'd told him one night; insisted upon it, in fact. But then it just felt different. She'd changed the rules and it wasn't fair to expect him to know that.

"I'm going out to a small, informal gathering." Glancing at the frozen-faced vamp by the door, she made a decision. "Want to be my date? Or do you still need time to decompress?"

"What... really?" Toby spit a few chips out in his

haste to answer. "I mean sure, if you want me on your detail." His chest puffed up a bit, before deflating as he looked at her outfit as well as her well-dressed driver. "I'll need to change, and I don't have anything too fancy." He waved a chip-laden hand in her direction in explanation.

"Pfft, you're young. You can wear a band tee-shirt, hoodie, or jeans and easily pull off edgy, as long as it's clean," Ravyn said, noticing that his current tee not only bore chip crumbs, but a few other stains.

"Yeah, I can do that," Toby reassured her eagerly. "Can you give me, like, five minutes?"

"Take ten," Ravyn offered with a wave of her hand as he scuttled toward the door.

The black wrought-iron gates loomed high over the car and disappeared on either side into a densely forested area. Ravyn wondered if they enclosed the entire estate or if they were simply for show and ended a few feet into the tree line. If Mr. Roland valued his privacy and security, they would continue on, guaranteeing to keep possibly anyone or anything out. Of course, even at that height, they were no match for a vampire or wolf shifter. Before her driver could push the call button, the gates smoothly opened, as if the guards inside were watching and waiting for guests' arrival. They closed smoothly
and quickly as soon as the car's rear bumper cleared the gate.

Tooth and Claw

"Fancy," Toby murmured in appreciation, his wide eyes, so similar to his uncle's, flickering back and forth, taking in the tall fencing that did seem to expand well past the drive into the underbrush, as well as the guards' shack with its darkened windows.

Ravyn found herself nodding in agreement. Bertrando Roland took his security seriously, nearly as seriously as Bash did and that, of course, was only what they could see. The unseen security could be equally as impressive or completely non-existent.

"I still don't understand why you're so eager to work with this guy. He probably needs you more then you need him. I mean, everyone knows who you are. Him, I've never heard of."

Ravyn considered his words as well as her answer. "Yes, while I'm popular enough here and now, Land and Sea Cinema makes timeless, classic works. The work I'm doing now is similar to fast fashion: here today, gone tomorrow. Maybe it will stick around longer, maybe it won't. But Mr. Roland's work could be considered similar to a timeless suit. It has a much higher likelihood of being held onto and viewed long-term."

The young wolf's blank stare had Ravyn reconsidering the fashion metaphor. "Or just trust me, it's a good career move. And I would be part of telling the story of Giulia Tofana."

That was at least met with a grunt of acknowledgment, if not understanding. He didn't understand. Long after the actress Ravyn Sinclair was gone, the story would stand. This might be her chance to make a mark that would outlive her current lifetime, a mark that she herself might see decades in the future.

Her driver opened the window and gruffly informed the approaching guards that another car with Ms. Sinclair's private security followed about sixty seconds behind and would require entry.

"Of course," the tall, thin, angular guard agreed, without actually making a move back toward the gatehouse. "We will need you to park your car down here in the side lot. Ms. Sinclair will be taken by cart toward the main house. Mr. Roland doesn't allow vehicles too close to the house; it scares the wildlife."

The vamp shifted in his seat, prepared to argue, but the guard smoothly added, "Of course, you and your men will be immediately taken up after we've secured your vehicles. No point in making either Mr. Roland or Ms. Sinclair wait on the help."

Ravyn cringed at the "help" comment. However, she recognized that the man had a strange way of pronouncing certain words and sounds, as if his tongue didn't quite want to cooperate—or maybe it was an unrecognizable accent. Perhaps something didn't translate well between languages.

"That's perfectly fine. My date will accompany me now, though; no need for both of them to park a car. It certainly doesn't take two to do that." Ravyn added just a touch of coercion to her voice, willing to push more into it, but the guard seemed to willingly accept her option.

"Certainly." He smoothly opened the door for Ravyn before gesturing toward a golf cart hidden beside the gate. Glancing at the gate where the second car had pulled up and idled, he added, "It seems the gate isn't opening correctly. We have reset it, and if that doesn't work, we can manually open it to allow your remaining security through. I apologize for the inconvenience."

His monotone didn't actually sound very apologetic, but maybe this was a regular occurrence that merely annoyed the man. Two other lanky men stepped out of the guard house, their torsos and arms incredibly long, similar to the guard who had greeted them. One went to slide into the driver's seat of the golf cart, while Ravyn was escorted to the passenger seat and a strangely quiet Toby slid into the seat directly behind her.

The ride uphill took several moments and, after attempting unsuccessfully to engage either the driver or Toby in conversation, Ravyn simply enjoyed the scenery, watching as they passed a few more guards standing stiffly alongside the driveway. Tall trees grew into a natural tunnel over the paved single-lane roadway, and the twists and turns along the route hid the house from view. After several quiet moments, they finally stopped in front of a house with tall, tinted windows and natural stucco siding; a beautiful house that fit perfectly in the still wooded area. No yard to speak of, just the paved drive and pathways under the dense trees which filtered out most of the sunlight, leaving the forest floor bare around the home.

Still not speaking, the guard remained motionless as the two passengers exited the vehicle with a thanks that he appeared not to notice. He spun the vehicle around and headed, presumably, back to the front gate, driving at a quicker pace.

"Shall we?" Ravyn asked a still quiet Toby, who hesitantly followed her.

"I don't like this," he whispered. "Something just seems off, odd. Both of us agree, something is terribly off here." Toby glanced warily around, looking for any apparent danger.

"Both of us" clearly referred to his wolf, and while Ravyn could agree the place seemed a bit odd, she couldn't say that anything screamed "danger" or "stay away." In fact, it was very inviting to her. She didn't want to embarrass Toby, but perhaps he and his wolf were a bit uncertain about entering a Hollywood party. It could be overwhelming, especially if you weren't used to such things. Coming off the full moon could be very emotionally charged as well. The combination of the two events was bound to cause some confusion.

Pulling his arm into her, she leaned into the lanky wolf shifter. "It's really just a small gathering where we're going to get to know a few people and see if a new project is a good fit for me and vice versa. Very

TOOTH AND CLAW

low key, I promise." She gave his arm what she hoped was a reassuring squeeze.

Toby was nearly as tall as his uncle and, most likely, his father had been tall as well. In a few years, he would stop growing, start filling out more, and he would certainly rival his uncle in looks. With a maternal feeling, she smoothed a wayward curl down on his head as he still rather reluctantly kept pace with her.

The door opened before they had a chance to knock. Ravyn stepped slightly in front of the young wolf as he attempted to do the same to her. Ravyn deferred to his movement, knowing his wolf's protective instinct might take offense if she placed herself first.

"Welcome, Ms. Sinclair. Welcome to my home," the jovial voice boomed from the man who opened the door. Similar to the guards, he stood tall and lanky, his limbs seemingly awkward and long, but his toothy smile was a sharp contrast to the impassive guards' dour expressions. His silver-and-dark peppered hair, parted severely on one side, looked freshly cut around his ears and neckline. As with many in Hollywood, few wrinkles marred his face, the skin pulled unnaturally tight and unmoving, despite the open and eager smile that filled it ear to ear.

"Please, Mr. Roland, call me Ravyn. It's so delightful to meet you. I've been traveling and unaware that you've been trying to meet with me," she lied, covering that fact that she'd been in hiding.

"The pleasure is all mine, and you must call me Bertrando, or even Bert, as many of my friends do." Again, a strange accent or perhaps a speech impediment marred his smooth, welcoming words.

Extending her hand in greeting, expecting him to grasp it and shake heartily as was so often the case when meeting new people, especially men, Rayvn was a bit surprised as he gently, almost reverently, grasped her hand between both of his. Holding it a bit longer than necessary for a greeting, his long fingers carefully rubbed her hand as if attempting to warm them up. Carefully, she began extracting her hand before Bertrando seemed willing to do so.

After a long second, he did—albeit reluctantly—release her hand, before turning his attention to Toby.

"And who is your handsome young escort?" he questioned, not sounding condescending like some might with an extra uninvited guest, but truly interested.

"This is Tobias Moldover; he was kind enough to escort me this evening." Ravyn smoothly made introductions, while feeling the uncomfortable waves rolling off the still silent Toby. Neither man attempted to shake hands, and Toby nodded curtly, while the other man welcomed him into his home as well.

"You have a beautiful home." It wasn't a lie; the place was amazing. Armor and weaponry from

TOOTH AND CLAW

different times and different places around the world decorated the space, as well as artwork depicting battles between monsters and heroes, devils and angels, and good and evil. High ceilings and dark woodwork emphasized its grandeur. Their footsteps echoed on the ceramic tiles as they walked. It was a little large for Ravyn's personal taste—she preferred cozier and homey—but an amazing design nonetheless.

"Thank you, it means a lot to me that you find it so." Bert settled them down in a lounge area before offering them drinks. A wisp of a woman in dark clothing seemingly appeared out of nowhere, settling a glass of red wine at Ravyn's elbow and passing what Ravyn assumed to be a soda to Toby, who examined it carefully before drinking deeply from the glass. After a transformation, the shifters were always thirsty and hungry, especially after the three-day moon requirement.

"I'm afraid I may have misunderstood your invitation," Ravyn admitted before taking a sip of the dark wine. By the goddess it was good; spicy with a warmth that exploded gently in her mouth. She nearly forgot she was speaking. At Bertrando's questioning look, she righted herself. "I thought there would be others involved in the work here tonight."

"Ah, Ravyn I did say intimate, but yes, I do have a few others who will be joining us later." Again that smile from ear to ear, a bit off-putting as it stretched the skin tightly, drawing it thin. "I feel like I already know you, but at the same time I wanted a chance for us to get to know each other a bit more outside of the work. What makes you tick and all that. To see the real you and how you can make Giulia Tofana come to life, or even more than that—how you will be able to embody her.

"So, darling, tell me: has Ravyn Sinclair ever killed a man?"

Ravyn nearly choked on her wine. What was he asking?

At her shocked look, he offered, "I jest, I jest. Surely, you won't need to kill a man to get inside Giulia's mind. But you're a beautiful woman who must have seen what men can do to those they find powerless."

Nodding her understanding, Ravyn sipped more wine, allowing it to warm her through. This she could understand; gatherings, no matter how intimate they claimed to be, were also a time to don a mask of sorts. Everyone did it no matter how hard they tried not to.

Clearing her throat, she forced herself to say the words that might get her removed from the project. "I'm not sure if you know or have been told, but I suffer from a severe sun allergy."

"Pfft, I heard you suffered from an infliction. Causes a rash or something?" With a wave of his hand, Bertrando brushed aside her concerns. "Most scenes are in the shadows; poor form to be setting up poisoning and murder in full daylight, although my conniving Giulia will be a beacon of light, a vessel of hope for these poor trapped souls. It will be her—or hopefully, you—who is the shining light on the set." He grew more animated as he spoke, punctuating each word with a jab of his hand and, in some cases, both hands.

"Tell me, Ms. Sinclair: does Giulia read like a cold-blooded murderess or a heroine taking up a fight for the fairer sex?"

"I would like to imagine a heroine," Ravyn admitted, "but I can also question if a serial poisoner must have some murderous qualities about her."

Bertrando Roland frowned as if the answer irritated him. "But how can one be both? To murder is a sin, is it not, no matter the reason? I mean, I could hardly imagine you murdering someone. Because we don't want beautiful people to be evil. It almost makes it worse that these women came to her for help and were drawn in by her beauty. Did they ask themselves if they were committing a sin? Was it a crime? They say Giulia's beauty made her trustworthy. Did they trust that it couldn't be a sin because of her beauty?"

Ravyn shifted in her seat before smoothly meeting the man's eyes. "Those are important questions. It has been claimed that before Lucifer fell, he was the most beautiful of the angels. So, the reverse could be true, that her beauty alone was already a crime. A sin against nature. Perhaps knowing that she was already deemed by the Church to be a sinner just for existing, how could she not help women the Church and kingdom sided against?"

"How was your drive up? Any difficulty finding the place?"

The abrupt change of subject gave Ravyn pause. Apparently, they were finished talking business, at least for now. Rich men in the movie industry could be odd, as odd as they wanted and the rest of the industry just pivoted with them. Talking points and jumping around kept their audience on their toes.

Ravyn finished her glass of wine, surprised to notice it was all gone. Before the evening wrapped up, she absolutely needed to find out what this vintage was. The wisp of a woman quickly swiped the empty glass away and replaced it with another full one before disappearing into the background once more with a short nod to Bertrando and her. There, but not there, the woman managed to stay just in Ravyn's peripheral vision. Her long, free hair hung in front of her face, hiding her features even when Ravyn attempted to subtly track her. Long, bell sleeves covered her hands even when she was quickly refreshing their drinks. Her dark navy shift hid her body but, in turn, apparently allowed her to move quickly and quietly about the room, mostly keeping her back to the group.

Still chatting and sipping her second glass, Ravyn briefly realized that the remaining of her security detail hadn't joined them yet. In fact, none of them had, not even her driver who had accompanied them inside the grounds. Concern for the men disappeared as quickly as it had popped into her mind. All was well; of course, it was.

A side glance at Toby showed the boy about to fall asleep. Clearly, the last few days of chasing the moon had taken a toll on him, but the producer didn't seem to be concerned about what could be considered rudeness on the young man's part. Ravyn blinked slowly as Toby came in and out of focus for a moment. Shaking her head cleared the fog that seemed to settle over her. Odd.

"I have to admit, I'm surprised you reached out to me," Ravyn admitted, "and honored that you know my work and would consider me for Giulia. And that script... Seriously, that script is amazing."

"I knew we had something special when I was approached with it." Leaning back, he spread apart his lanky legs while gesturing toward her with his long hands. "But truly, it was written for you. I think you embody the spirit of Giulia. I think everything you have done up until now has prepared you for this role. Don't you agree?" he questioned, his intense look never leaving her face. Apparently, he needed an immediate answer.

"Certainly. I certainly hope so," Ravyn demurely agreed, setting down her glass once again.

A quick, sharp nod from the producer had the wispy woman gliding over once again, this time topping the glass off before pressing it back into Ravyn's hands. For a moment, his intense gaze left Ravyn as he glanced toward the woman's retreating back.

"Do you like the wine? When I tried it, I felt like it would be perfect for you." Again, the intensity of the question seemed a bit out of place, but perhaps he was just as eager to see her in the role as she was about working with him, and it came off a bit forced and awkward.

"Absolutely. In fact, I was wondering—" For a second, the room shifted in and out of focus, tilting sharply on its side. "Oh." She raised her empty hand to her head to settle the unusual feeling, before gently shaking it off. Taking another long sip of wine, she decided maybe this particular vintage wasn't sitting well with her. Odd, but not impossible.

Once again reaching to place the glass down on the table, determined that she'd sipped her last drop, her head suddenly began to swim. She immediately froze in place, trying to find her equilibrium and, when unable to do that, Ravyn attempted to at least get the red wine out of her hand before she splashed it on Bertrando's pale furniture. "I'm sorry, I'm..." Her dry mouth swallowed the words that her swollen lips refused to form.

Blurry-eyed, blinking, she struggled to hold her head steady as she slowly lowered the glass toward the table.

Tooth and Claw

Bertrando swooped in to take the glass. "Ah, darling Ravyn, did this go straight to your head? Tsk tsk. Let me take this from you."

Her now distended tongue filled her mouth, refusing to cooperate as she struggled to form words, as if her mouth were filled with dry cotton. Her limbs suddenly were foreign to her, hanging heavily from her body. Her head swum against the darkness pulling her down as both panic and realization filled her. Nearly paralyzed, she blinked slowly, heavily, at the still grinning man directly in front of her. His extended smile seemed to deepen and expand farther in front of her, covering the entirety of his now blurred face despite being just inches from her own face.

Poison... Her mouth attempted to form the word, even as her brain refused to comprehend the possibility. Impossible. Unable to move or even hold up her heavy head, her eyes tipped toward Toby's now still form. His head hung loosely onto his chest, with long, slow deep breaths entering and exiting his body. A fuzzy form appeared beyond him.

In the distance Bertrando clapped his hands, "Our other guest has arrived."

Two women? The wispy woman covered from head to toe and another? A woman with straight black hair and red lips who appeared and disappeared with each slow blink of Ravyn's eyes. Familiar, yet Ravyn couldn't quite grasp why as she attempted unsuccessfully to bring this new woman into focus, struggling against the heavy water that pulled her down.

Oh, Bash, I've f'ed up. And then nothing as she simply floated away.

Chapter Eleven

My sweet love returns to me

With a grin that wouldn't stop, Bash eagerly entered Ravyn's apartment without even stopping by his own place first. He was exhausted, but ready to be back by her side where he belonged. For the first time since he began shifting, he'd been in a hurry for the three days and nights to be done. He'd spent three days fighting his wolf to stay in the wild and not run miles to be at her side. Now they were both eager to lay eyes on her. Maybe next month, they could find a way to make it work, and he wouldn't need to reluctantly drag himself away from her bed while she slept.

Immediately upon entering, he could feel the emptiness of the apartment. Surely, she hadn't been gone long? He could still smell her scent in the air, the sweet floral with a trace of spice, and even a hint of his nephew, who had been sent back earlier while Bash and the other men lingered over a beer or two, relaxing over the shared camaraderie. Despite the fact that he'd immediately wanted to leave with his nephew, he fought the urge to change the monthly habit and draw suspicion from the other wolves. They needed this time together with him not just as a leader with his soldiers, but the comradery of the shift. Although the wolves would joke and elbow him, they would also understand, but Bash wasn't ready to share or explain this new twist in his life.

Sebastian's heart dipped a little when he realized Ravyn wasn't eagerly waiting for him in the apartment. Then it completely sank in his now tight chest at the realization that she might have left the building completely during his absence.

Damn it all! Anger and a bit of annoyance caused his face to flame as he thought about her sneaking out without proper scrutiny the moment his back was turned. Had she planned this all along? Damn it all to hell. Rubbing his jawline before pulling his hair back into a pony tail, he cursed himself and then her. He'd thought... Well, it didn't matter what he'd thought. The job was what came first, always the job.

His nephew had been here. Here and gone maybe back to their shared apartment downstairs. So eager to see Ravyn, he hadn't even stopped in to check on his teen or shower the stench of the last few days off his body. What a fool he'd been.

Despite the fact that it had been running to exhaustion for the past few days, Sebastian's wolf whined anxiously, pushing against the edges of his mind. His mate hadn't abandoned them, it insisted. Bash argued back sharply that you couldn't be abandoned by what you didn't have. Sulking, the wolf remained quietly watching but no longer pushing forward.

Where the hell was she, then? Thankfully, the wolf didn't answer the rhetorical question; now wasn't the time to get in an argument with his animal.

Then he saw the note. After reading it, his hands tightened in fear and frustration, crushing the flower he held within it without even realizing it. The delicate flower he'd called nearly a dozen flower shops in the region for crumbled into fragrant blue and yellow pieces on the pristine floor.

He chastised himself for his momentary weakness. There was no place for it in this line of work! Dammit! He knew better. He knew better than to care too much, to make it personal. That was where the real danger lay; allowing yourself to get close to someone left room for them to leave or disappoint you. His heart tightened, as he momentarily flashed back to his brother. He should have been there for James too. The real danger was in not being there for someone you cared about. Bash turned quickly, immediately preparing for the what-ifs, the heel of his boot making streaks of the blue petals on the floor.

Chapter Twelve

Hunted, the raven flies to the heavens

Ravyn's mind woke up first, her limbs and even her eyelids too heavy to react as they typically would. The synapses crackled to life, firing up as she began hearing groans, light clangs, and even soft shuffling noises around her. Testing and feeling the heaviness, the aching of her limbs, and the smell of rotten meat, her brain slowly and dully considered the possibilities. Eyes heavy and closed, she floated, hearing and feeling but not comprehending or reacting to any of it as it wormed its way through her brain.

Then an internal shot fired in her brain, screaming, *"Danger, wake up!"* And so, her subconscious alerted her that it was time to reconnect to whatever occurred outside of itself. Not quickly, though. Despite the insistence that something bad was going down, her mind remained dull and not connecting the things that it was hearing and smelling to the sensation of danger.

With a moan of her own, her eyes began fluttering heavily, begging to simply stay closed. That moan made another part of her brain realize that some of the sounds were coming from her. But the lights were too harsh to even open her eyes. His nose wrinkled as it was assaulted with the scents of old blood, decay, and overpowering fresh bleach.

A cruel hand twisted into her hair, pulling her head back before whispering crassly in her ear, "Wakey, wakey, darling Ravyn." The hot breath assaulted the skin on her cheek as he made his demand, which he followed up with a wet nip to her ear, hard enough that it would draw blood if she were merely human. Again, Ravyn couldn't stop the cry that escaped her and she found herself cringing away when her tormentor laughed harshly before holding onto her chin and whispering at her, "My beloved, we will have so much fun together."

Awareness pooled throughout her body as her limbs stretched and prickled, as if they too were waking from a deep sleep. How long had her limbs been stretched out like this? The back of her neck ached where it hung forward with her chin near her chest, while her arms stretched out to the sides, pulled so taunt they held her straight up from the ground, holding the weight of her body, her now bare feet barely touching the floor. Her wrists burned where shackles held them snuggly in place.

A rough hand firmly, painfully, lifted her chin up once again, holding her head upright and drawing her up on her tip toes.

Ravyn stood quietly, aware that her captor stood in front of her, most likely face to face, waiting for her to acknowledge him, the situation, or anything at all, but her mind couldn't stop rolling, attempting to make sense of the position she was in. Attempting to capture the fleeting thoughts that rolled around, hinting, taunting at some sort of idea or observation that seemed to remain just out of reach.

The jarring, harsh voice taunted, "You've been a greedy, greedy little girl, Ravyn. Tsk tsk. All that wine. You just couldn't stop yourself stuffing yourself. Gluttonous. Unlike that pup you had with you. He drank so little that we barely had time before he woke up."

Mewing softly, Ravyn's scrambled brain attempted to latch onto his words. The wine? The pup? Toby? Toby!

"I truly thought that thisss would have been more of a challenge," the voice continued, hissing a bit as the words bit through his teeth. "Ah, but dangle a script in front of you and you forget all about, well, anything. Everything. I spent so much money on mages and witches, tracking and spells, taunting and watching. Waiting, but in the end, I just offer you another glimpse at immortality and you come running and nearly truss yourself up like a Christmas goose for me. At least your friends took care of the old mage problem for me. He clipped your little tag-along for me and then got himself killed before I needed to make the final payment to him."

Tag-along? Eva?

The words sank through the mist and waves in Ravyn's head as the pieces began clicking together in her mind, like a puzzle. The stalker, click. The gifts, click. The invitation, click. The wine, click. Tobias, oh goddess, click.

Slowly she forced her eyes to open. Only moonlight filled the room, unusually bright moonlight reflecting off the walls of her prison. Wide, nearly rabid eyes met her own sensitive eyes. This fool literally shook with glee as he held her face up to meet his.

Dead. He was a dead man; he just hadn't realized it yet. Hissing, her eyes boiling red, she met his look with a glare and a snap of her fangs toward the hand that simply gripped her chin even harder, then gave it a firm shake.

"Ravyn, you still don't seem to be grasping this situation fully or correctly." Holding onto her chin, he forced her to look down first at her right arm, then her left. "Silver chains for my lady."

Silver. That explained the burning in her wrists. Each wrist had been wrapped several times with a small chain of silver links. Those chains were then pulled through to the opposite walls and could be tightened or loosened depending on how much slack the captor gave or took.

Savagely pulling her chin over toward his right

shoulder, he stepped a bit to the side.

Toby kneeled on the other side of the narrow room in an alcove she assumed reflected hers. He, too, had silver chains holding him to his spot, but he had enough slack that he could kneel. Matching links lay on the ground behind him, attaching to the wall, which Ravyn fearfully assumed also attached to his ankles. His angry bright eyes met hers, and he gave a small, tight nod that made him grimace. Then she realized that a thick silver collar had been snuggly placed around his neck. Holding his head high helped alleviate a small point at which the deadly silver touched exposed skin. The pain would be excruciating, especially to a young, untried wolf.

Ravyn's eyes twitched frantically as she tried to convey that everything would be okay. Of course it would.

Bopping her nose almost playfully, Bertrando Roland emitted an eerie, high-pitched giggle that echoed from the walls, so unlike his gently congenial voice from earlier. "Is it starting to clear up yet, my lovely?"

He let loose her chin, and she struggled weakly to hold her leaden head up on her own, refusing to allow him to see anything but anger and death in her glare. "You, my queen, my greedy queen, downed a bottle of spiked wine. An entire bottle!" Another shrieking giggle rolled through him and a hiccup escaped as he attempted to calm himself. "Spiked with… vervain and wolfsbane." The dramatic pause had Ravyn wondering if the fool actually expected them to applaud him.

"Young master back there had the same, but in a bit of cola, or do you say soda? Or pop? I love all these American colloquialisms. What a time we live in. Make up your own slang, call it your vernacular, and see who follows you."

What in all the levels of hell is he talking about?

About every other sentence made any sense, and Ravyn suspected that it wasn't due to her being drugged at all. This brand of crazy was all him.

Bertrando's back was to her as he examined Toby, tilting his head from side to side as the young wolf shifter silently glared up at him. Ravyn tested pointing her toes, trying to reach the ground completely to ease the strain. Thankfully they weren't burning as if they, too, were wrapped in silver. Not great news, but it could be worse. After all, they were still alive.

For now.

"Mr. Roland—Bert—so you've wanted to meet me. My, what a lot of trouble you've gone through." Ravyn desperately wanted his attention off the teen as her gut screamed at her that his attention on Toby was a bad, bad thing. Nothing made sense. How had Roland trapped her?

Well, sadly, the wine made perfect sense. And she begrudgingly admitted it was brilliant. The bold, spicy wine had covered the taste of both the wolfsbane and the vervain, but how had he known to use it?

She'd never seen him before in her life. Everything about the man screamed human. Rich human. But money didn't necessarily mean that a human would have the means and ability to carry off such long-term stalking and kidnapping. Repeated kidnapping, in fact, considering the orchestrated kidnapping and subsequent torture he apparently had ordered on sweet Eva. Who was this man? Insane, sure, but what could lead a person to basically take on one of the most ruthless predators ever created?

"Ravyn, Ravyn. I'm honestly surprised at you. I courted you with gifts and visits, and you denied me at every turn. When that didn't turn your head my way, I decided you needed to be rid of that albatross around your neck. That filthy half-demon who tied herself to you, blocking my attempts. Yes, those were my attempts to get closer to you. She didn't even know what she had, being a part of you, inside your mind. One can only dream of that sort of... intimacy. But with such filth."

Bertrando's disgust dripped from his every word. Clearly, if he could have killed Eva outright to break the bond, he would have. Obviously, his witches had given him the same lecture about magic backlash that Delta had given Oliver and her. The magic slap from recklessly breaking a bond could kill even a vampire if they were on the receiving end. So, while his minions hadn't taken any care in cutting the magical bond, it could have been much worse.

Eva had protected her without even knowing, but Ravyn had no intention of trying to explain anything to this madman. Despite his obviously thorough research, Bertie Boy was wrong in saying that Eva had tied herself to Ravyn. In fact, the opposite was true, and it was beginning to sound like both of them had benefited from the now broken bond. The bond had allowed Eva to see Ravyn's past and present through dreams. Although the stories were often incomplete or random, she'd managed to weave them into some fairly impressive bestselling novels. And despite the fact that Ravyn had been magically assaulted several times, the bond had allowed Eva's magical protections to settle over Ravyn as well.

"Truly, Bert," Ravyn lied smoothly, dropping her voice a treble and adding a mild testing of coercion, "why me? I'm flattered, but…" Setting her eyes upon him, she dropped her lids for a long second before looking back up at him, mentally screaming, *"Look at my eyes!"*

"Ah, you little wicked minx." Surprisingly, Bert easily met her eyes, his own flashing with excitement and his tone hinting at amusement at her. Before she could blink, he drew a fist back and struck her flat in the face, surprisingly strong for such a soft-looking man. Stunned, her head violently shot back several inches before stopping sharply and bouncing forward again, as the chains holding her arms quivered and shook from the impact.

Gritting her teeth tight, barely feeling her fangs tingling in anticipating, Ravyn braced herself, forcing her head to hold still despite the ringing in her ears. She would kill him. He was a dead man. An animalistic roar shot out from Toby and his chains clanged as he fought against the bindings.

"No," Ravyn whispered to him, knowing that his sensitive hearing would pick up her voice, begging him to stop, commanding him if she could.

Bertrando shook a long, bony finger back and forth in front of Ravyn's face while his head followed slowly. "Oh no, no, no, no. None of that mind voodoo. It doesn't work on me, and if you try again, well, you will make me angry—and you most certainly don't want that, my pretty Little Bird." His eyes twitched maniacally back and forth, as if judging whether she understood his threat. Perspiration beaded on his forehead as he watched her. "I will clip your wings, and you won't like that. You won't like at all."

Had his fingers been so long before? Her muddled brain attempted to remember how they'd looked wrapped around his wine glass, the one he'd simply held while he peered over it at her. The excitement in his beady eyes hadn't been from the thought of working with her; it had been in anticipation of something much more sinister.

Little Bird. Ravyn wanted to spit in his face and tell him to never call her that name again. It was the name her sisters had once bestowed upon her, and this madman had no right to use it. Even more than before, she wanted to rip his face off and stomp upon it.

Another strong shake of his head, then the maniac reiterated his promise with his sharp nail just inches from her eye. "You do not want to make me angry. If you try to use those eyes on me again, I will pluck them out and feed them to you. Oh, yes, this I promise, my Little Bird." The strange tone of affection mixed with the amusement in his voice hit Ravyn harder than the punch she'd just taken. Spit flew with the enunciation of each word, as if his tongue had suddenly grown too large for his mouth.

Swallowing the blood pooling in her mouth from his hit, Ravyn promised herself she would do much more than spit on him when she got the chance.

"I've been searching a long, long time for you, my queen. You are all I could have hoped for. Magnificent!" The lanky figure stood tall, examining her under the moonlight that filled the room, allowing the same finger that had threatened her eyes to run down her cheek, then her neck and lower.

Ravyn stared forward, remembering the exact route his finger took down her body and promising herself that he would feel her own claws mapping down his body all the way to the bone—after she broke his wrists, of course.

Twitching, his entire body spasmed before he seemed to regain control of it, shaking off the tremors before gripping his hands together.

The cement slabs that lined the floors, wall, and tall ceilings felt like a basement, but the wide windows that lined the top of the room let in moonlight from all sides. The tail end of the full moon shone in all her glory tonight high in the sky. It had been light still when they arrived at the mansion, and many hours must have passed for the moon to reach its zenith. Bash would be back. Surely, he would be back by now. He just needed to get the update from the remaining security and track them to this location. Anytime now, reinforcements would be arriving. She and Tory just needed to hold out until then.

"Why?" Ravyn asked, genuinely curious. She could feel the dripping of blood from the edge of her mouth. Noticing him watching, she slowly drew her tongue out and lapped up the wayward drops while staring at him.

His breath hitched while he watched, mesmerized by her every move, enthralled by the sight of her nearly black blood. War was a game, and she wasn't out of moves yet. He would be ripped apart by her hands, Ravyn promised as she suggestively shifted her hips toward him, sucking in her swollen bottom lip, which still burned from his hit.

Bertrando gulped, looking rapidly from her eyes to her mouth before drawing himself up taller, stretching deeply, once again seeming to shake off tremors from his body. Was he growing? Under the moonlight and shadows, his body seemed to gradually grow longer and thinner, lankier as his torso expanded and his limbs lengthened.

Blinking, Ravyn wondered if it were a trick of the light or the poisonous herbs still floating around in her system. Disorienting, but it still didn't change what she planned to do to him.

"Because, Ravyn, you are the living flesh, the flesh of the dead. Neither and both. And to reach eternal life, I must partake of such a flesh. You are the origin of the undead flesh that offers eternal life." His words peppered out quickly, as if he needed to get them completely out before his tongue stopped them. More perspiration dotted his upper lip as he bounced before her on his toes, seemingly excited to share the news with her.

This creature was certifiably insane. And he apparently knew exactly what she was. Seduction suddenly seemed like a useless weapon in this battle against insanity.

"My body has an affliction," he offered as he bounced on his toes, swaying back and forth as if not quite comfortable with his body. "This affliction has haunted me for over a hundred and fifty years, well over. It's the hunger, you see. I just get so hungry." Bertrando's eyes turned woefully upon Ravyn. "So hungry," he pleaded, his voice growing shriller, higher with every word. "That hunger just grows and grows and when I eat it feels so good, but then I'm just so hungry again."

Chapter Thirteen

Alongside the wolf, feasting on the carcass of the fallen

Horror and realization filled Ravyn, yet she couldn't stop herself from asking, "What do you eat? What fills you?"

"I didn't want to eat it in the beginning, you know? It's just that I was so hungry. We all were, surely, but not all of us were strong enough to eat. But I was. I was, but I'm still so hungry." He beseeched her to understand his apparently endless hunger, even as her mind flipped through possibilities.

Hunger? His body remained in one place, but his muscles spasmed and twitched, bouncing from one place to another as he waited for her to understand. The perspiration on his forehead began pooling its way down his face. He rolled his shoulders, as if his body had suddenly become too uncomfortable to be in.

"What did you eat?" Despite trying to remain calm, Ravyn's voice instinctively rose an octave. *Goddess, please.*

"They said it was a shortcut. It would save us so much time, they said. Easily done, they said. The expedition was cursed," he spat in his eerie, high-pitched voice, sounding as if his vocal cords were stretching along with his body. "Hastings's riders told us it would be better, that we were making history traveling through the pass. We made history, all right, but not how we wanted to." Another maniacal giggle escaped before he could swallow up the noise.

"But they convinced Donner that leading this expedition would give him infamy. They were wrong. That smooth bastard convinced us that he could handle anything thrown his way, and so we followed him. We followed him to the gates of hell, if hell were a desolate, frozen wasteland."

Gulping, the man took a deep breath as if struggling to control himself, holding his chin up proudly to stare down at Ravyn. "Which was worse: the cold or the hunger? Both grind away at you, little by little. The cold and snow went on endlessly, reaching deep into your bones to twist them until they shattered. The hunger grew and grew, starting in the pit of your stomach, so little at first you barely noticed it. But it grew, reaching deeper, moving out more until it was so vast, so endless that it was all you could think about. Just how hungry you were. The cold made you numb, though, but that hunger, that hunger just grew and grew, twisting and twisting."

The Donner Party... This man claimed to be a

member of the Donner Party, the ill-fated group of migrants and pioneers who had trusted the wrong people, followed the wrong path, and ended up stuck in the treacherous, snow-covered mountains during the winter of 1846. Eighty-seven souls entered the mountains full of hopes and dreams; only forty-eight survived.

"Wendigo..." The word escaped Toby softly, almost reverently, or more than likely fearfully, as similar feelings flooded through Ravyn. A legend? Impossible.

A wendigo? This man claimed to be a creature from a nightmare and Toby believed it, if his tone was any indication. Her eyes flickered to him, taking in his whispered word. A subtle but quick movement of his hand flashed the fig sign to ward off the evil, not appearing to notice the pain as even the slight movement moved the silver chains, which once again drew blood as they tore at the already raw skin of his wrist.

Despite her own bondage, Ravyn found herself following his movement, cupping her own fist and sticking her thumb between two fingers to ward off this mythical daemon. *Damn, he should fear her.*

"They're not real." Even to her own ears her false bravado fell flat, but she pushed forward as if disbelief alone could destroy such an evil incarnate. "Bedtime stories told to children and pups to keep them in line. Fireside stories to entertain away the long, dark nights."

Bertrando's long face looked plaintively at her once again. "How could you, of all creatures, say that?" Waving his elongated hands, he took a few steps away from her before turning back to implore with large, round eyes, "You, the destroyer of death, the defeater of the grave? Yes, and I suppose all vampires are fanciful stories and shifters are just imaginative ramblings of drunken encounters? But a real monster must be a story? A fairytale, I suppose? And you, you of all people, deny my existence?"

A now knobby accusatory finger pointed across at her, and Ravyn wondered if she'd made a grave mistake in questioning him as he once again began pacing and huffing around Toby.

"So, you choose this, this immortality?" *Keep him distracted, keep him talking*, she chanted to herself, wondering how much wolfsbane and vervain she'd ingested. He wasn't joking when he pointed out her greediness; unfortunately, often a downfall of vampires. She could still barely hold her head up and the only reason she stood mostly upright was due to the chains holding her arms outward and supporting her weight.

"A choice? I suppose you could call it that," he scoffed. "Cold and hunger do strange things to a person. The wind whispers things, cold and dark ideas. And after enough days, you would do anything to quiet the whispers and the hunger, that deep, bone-rotting hunger. The wind whispered that I could end the hunger. Why let all of that... all of that go to waste when we were starving? But when I listened to the whispers, all I did was prolong the hunger. And so, I eat and I eat and I eat, but all is not lost."

If legends were true, the whispers that rode the wind belonged to a lost spirit—he spirit of a demon that could only be allowed to enter a body if the person agreed and then consecrated that agreement with human flesh. The shared body committed to an eternal shared life with a creature that needed to continue consuming human flesh to live, to stave off the endless hunger pangs.

"At first, I was weak and scavenged for food to keep the hunger at bay. My life was a cycle of hunting and eating. Then I learned the true art of the hunt, and I embraced the gift I had been given. Let them come to me. Some lifetimes they would come for a job, or a meal. You see, I learned that the more I offered, the more they came to me. In California everyone comes searching for something: riches, fame, love. If I dangle that they come right to me. So many desperate meals came straight to my doorstep. My favorite has been midwestern dreams that land them straight here, desperate and trusting, and then gone. The bonus is when you make enough money, no one looks twice at you."

He mocked in a lilting voice, "Who, me? Why would I allow some girl from Kansas to stop by my house, when I make Hollywood stars? Fools, fools, fools," the creature chanted mindlessly, mockingly the girls who had come before. The innocents who had thought they were coming for answered dreams, Hollywood fame, but had ended up a meal for the monster before her.

They were being held by a manic, one who either was truly a wendigo or someone who thought he was, but either way, he was clearly out of his mind and that made him even more dangerous—especially to Toby. Ravyn hadn't survived thousands of years by being weak or stupid, but today's stupidity might get the young wolf killed.

"Ahhh," the creature before her groaned as his body elongated once more, surely making him twice the height as when they first met him. "The moon calls to me." Turning his hungry attention once again to the young wolf who eyed him with both fear and anger, he said, "Surely you know what's that like, when the moon controls you? There is no fighting its dark call, is there?"

He shuddered as spasms moved through him.

Ravyn wasn't sure if it was pain or something else.

She knew Toby bit his tongue to avoid angering or arguing with the man. The wolves revered the moon; it brought forth their true selves. They lived in harmony with the moon, and its siren call wasn't a curse but a blessing bestowed by their ancestor Fenrir, the gray wolf. Whatever this man felt was a foul blasphemy compared to the beauty the wolves found in their relationship with the moon.

Hunched over, gasping in pain or ecstasy as bones snapped and crackled, the man's features twisted and turned as his body arched this way and that. Fascination and horror forced Ravyn to watch, unable to look away, as a transformation overtook the creature. This wasn't the smooth transformation of the wolf shifters, but a painful, unnatural transformation. Once it began it went quickly, though, and with a shudder, the wendigo shook off the last remaining remnants of its human shell, rising to an upright position, nearly doubling again its original height.

This time, Ravyn's fist instinctively curled in with panic to ward off the evil in front of her. Bertrando Roland—or whoever he really was—wasn't trapped in a delusion. Her heart sank in the fear and realization that what stood before her was like nothing she'd ever seen in her long lifetime.

She realized that her warding was a feeble and futile attempt as she stared in the face of true evil, feeling the power emanating from its grotesque body. Tight, ash-gray skin pulled tautly across its transformed features. Having doubled in size, its blood-stained bone antlers nearly brushed the ceiling of the room; the humped neck prevented it from quite reaching it. Its head had stretched out in a parody of the deer skull its antlers represented, stretching longer than a normal deer's head might. Double rows of sharp carnivore's teeth ran along its jaw, firmly ending any likeness to a deer, real or imaginary.

Gray skin so thin that Ravyn could count the row of ribs along its torso, long arms dangling close to the ground. A mixture of skin and sinew ended with elongated fingers that formed into claws appeared to be stained with the blood of previous victims. Lean, muscular thighs supported the mismatched body, with tufts of fur hiding most of the thin skin on its waist and thighs. The legs looked more likely to support a creature on all fours, but this one somehow defied logic and stood upright on feet encased with two cloven hooves, as well as a third clawed toe that seemingly appeared out of the side of its foot. And a stench, the smell of decay and death, floated off the creature, unpleasantly tickling Ravyn's nose.

In short, it was terrifying—a nightmare brought to life.

She and Toby might truly be screwed if backup didn't arrive soon. Ravyn simply wasn't regaining her strength quickly enough to ensure her own safety, let alone the safety of the young wolf whom she'd foolishly brought into this den of death.

The wendigo lifted its bony snout, sniffing the air, testing it, before its snake-like tongue darted from its mouth, tasting the air with what looked like an expression of pleasure.

"Ah, yesss," it hissed, stretching once again, shaking its shoulders to remove the last dregs of humanity, "to remove the shackles of that body is, well... is relieving." Focusing its large, glassy eyes on Ravyn, it gave a mocking half bow, its body bending at the waist a hair, with one long, distended arm crossed across its waist and the other tossed back dramatically. "My queen is here; my savior, surely." With a casual look over its shoulder toward the frozen wolf, it added, "And dinner."

Toby let out a small whimper before curling back away on himself as far as his chains would allow on the cold stone floor.

Ravyn tilted her chin up, determined to hide the fear that assailed her, looking the creature directly in its dead eyes. Clenching her jaw, she swore to herself, *This wendigo is dead. A dead man walking.*

"You, my beloved, will be my everlasting meal, the one that will conquer the hunger... the hunger." Another plaintive howl escaped the creature as it clutched at its stomach. "You have conquered death, and so will I as I partake of your undead but ever living flesh. Night after night," it promised, once again running a long-clawed finger along Ravyn's body, this time not quite touching it, but the cold that followed along its path chilled her deep in her bones.

Realization struck Ravyn. Toby's death might be quick, but hers wouldn't be. If this creature had its way, her pain and suffering would be endless. The regenerative properties of her body would ensure that, a never-ending cycle of flesh torn from her body, to grow anew, then repeat until this creature grew bored or tired of the situation and tore her to dust.

"Your body has conquered all, and now you have the honor of sharing that with me. It has taken me years to track you down, but to see the results in front of me." It shook its head in disbelief, and Ravyn could almost believe it was touched by the situation. It actually believed that her body had powers beyond what it had. "Finally, you are mine, and no one will stand between us again."

"Vampires can't offer eternal life beyond their own." Ravyn took a stab at arguing with the creature, tentatively adding a pleading, "Bertrando," to the end of statement.

Throwing its head up, the creature howled with laughter. "Oh, you are funny, my dear. Bertrando is gone now." Titling its head as if to listen, it amended, "Ah, he is in here somewhere, but he doesn't want to play anymore. I have tried numerous vampires over the years. What an experience that has been. Kill them and they dust. So, carving them up while they scream is a rewarding experience all of its own. But their immortal flesh doesn't satiate this hunger. So, I continued studying and observing. I think you are like me. I think the hell spawn that created you have inadvertently created a buffet for me."

It tilted its oversized head as it heard something outside the room before what might pass as a macabre smile crossed its face. "Ah, my queen, I have a visitor for you."

The soft click of a well-oiled door sounded to her right, and Ravyn struggled to turn her head toward the sound, as nearly silent footsteps tapped gently into the room. A blurry figure entered her peripheral vision as she struggled to focus. Shrugging off a cloak that covered her from head to foot, she stepped into Ravyn's line of sight.

With a shrieking giggle, the deranged creature awkwardly clapped its hands together. "I love a goooood family reunion," it hissed, followed by an awkward half bow. "My queen, let me introduce you, or ssshall I say reintroduce you, to your sissster. My witch."

And Ibis stepped fully into her vision. Not the version that Ravyn had met just days before, not a grandmotherly Anya. And not a young Ibis from years ago. A version, but just slightly different. If Ravyn was the youth and Anya the elder, then this version was slightly middle-aged. Where Anya's smile lines had creased with love and happiness, this version's age lines bespoke anger and hate. Her sharp eyes cut through Ravyn as if she could barely stand to look at her without cutting her to pieces.

"Impossible," Ravyn whispered as she took in the aging beauty before her. And she was beautiful; the evil that emanated from her didn't change that.

"Well met, Little Sister." This version of Ibis spat in her face.

Chapter Fourteen

And the unkindness of ravens tore the flesh from its bones

*H*orror passed through Ravyn, and she fought to control her emotions. If she let the fear overtake her, she might not ever regain control. Right now, her only chance of survival was to remain in control of her thoughts and actions.

Sister? Another sister? Or the same? How was it possible? Clearly, this doppelganger in front of her wasn't her sweet, motherly sister Ibis. Unable to look at this woman any longer, Ravyn dropped her chin to her chest, before a smack immediately reverberated across her face and through her.

"Look at me!" the almost familiar face demanded of her, pinching her chin between fingers that dug deeply into Ravyn's skin, forcing her face back upward to its own. "Look at what your 'sister' did to me."

Ravyn did as the woman demanded, examining the creature in front of her—familiar, yet not. "How is it possible?" The words tumbled out, tripping over themselves. It was surely Ibis, just the same as Anya had been her.

The same features were etched upon this woman's face, but like Anya, she was changed. Where Anya's face had aged with soft, gentle laugh lines, this woman's face had harsh, angry lines drawn across it. Her scent was unfamiliar but closely resembled burnt, blackened ash, not the sickly sweet scent that had surrounded Anya.

"That bitch sent us into the Houska Gate..." The woman spat the words at Ravyn. "And yes, it chewed us up and re-molded us into a new image. But it has left us connected in ways you cannot imagine."

Us? This made no sense. Anya had claimed she'd gone into the Hellgate alone. Nothing about her story had seemed to be a lie, and usually Ravyn could tell truth from lie, although she begrudgingly admitted that the present situation might prove that she wasn't on top of her game lately. "You're not Ibis," she stated flatly to the enraged woman.

"But I am, you stupid whore." The rage emanating from the woman was palatable in the air. "Your stupid sister wanted to give up her immortality for love, of all things. But the Hellgate didn't absorb what she gave up. It separated it. What the twins pulled from the hold was the useless creature that visited you. But me... I had to crawl my way out inch by inch, like the demons that used it as an escape route." This Ibis sounded almost proud of herself. "It took me days to do so; all the while, other demons tried to pull me back in, crawling over me or latching on as their ticket to freedom. I am what that selfish bitch Anya left behind: the magic, the immortality, the greed, and the insatiable appetite."

This explanation settled over Ravyn as she tried to understand what sort of thing stood before her. "But you're aging," were the only words that she could think to utter.

Examining her fingernails coolly, the woman hissed, "Of course I am. Those demons stole what they could from me while I clawed my way out. And my reward for reaching the top? Those twins kept me as a 'welcomed guest' for decades." She sneered over the irony of it all. "They experimented on me for decades just for surviving. Called my magic an abomination, as if they were any better. What should have been eternal youth and life was distorted. I am aging—slower, of course, than a mortal—but still that which was rightfully mine was taken from me and I want it back. What I'm left with now is a shell. The magic that remained molded me, but I can't even yield the magic. I am the magic and the magic is me. So much power and others have to harness it."

The woman angrily spat once again in Ravyn's face, and Ravyn willed herself not to flinch as the spittle ran down her face. "I was one of the most powerful creatures in existence and now, I'm relegated to boosting others' magic and using them to channel my own power. I'm nothing. That mage you killed off thought he was powerful until I allowed him to channel his magic through me. Nearly unstoppable, that one was. The scryer? Barely a blip on the power scale. But channeling through me, we could see you wherever you hid, whatever you did. I am magic, but without magic users I'm nothing.

"You waste your power, your immortality, trying to fit into a life with humans. You—we—are above that. We were created as death-bringers to crush life. We should rule, not hide in the shadows like rats scurrying around for scraps. We were remade in the image of a goddess and you, you as well as Anya waste that gift. You deserve what you have wrought."

The remnants of Ibis paced the room, anger seeping from her every pore; anger and hatred at what had been done to her and what sort of creature she'd become. If she wasn't a psychopath and working with a psychopath, Ravyn could almost feel sorry for her.

"For seventy years, I've lived with the knowledge that I was the left behind parts of Ibis, the parts that Anya wanted to forget. But she didn't really leave me behind, not like she thought. This connection will be broken soon enough when she dies and leaves that retched existence, but I've also been able to influence her a bit here and there. Anya never thought of you and the other sisters, not really. She wanted to leave it all behind for her family."

The woman sneered the words. "No, I gave her nudges in dreams, in the moments she relaxed and let her guard down. 'Find Ravyn. Find our sister.' I knew I couldn't get close enough to you, but she could if she tried hard enough. I'd nearly given up on her, but finally, she found her way to you and left behind a token in the couch. A single spelled picture, one she didn't even realize she'd delivered. One that left yet another barely discernible crack in those wards and those determined little minds of yours. And she delivered you here to us. After all the work we'd done, you walked straight to us."

"Sister," Ravyn rasped out, her throat barren but pleading, questioning. Her sister's convoluted dark magic explained so much. Suddenly, it was clear why none of the wards could keep the wendigo's spirit from dropping off gifts, as well as the spying eyes. This unfamiliar magic had been free to assault her simply because it was unrecognizable by her security team. This magic didn't exist and shouldn't exist.

"Don't bother." Ibis turned her back on Ravyn as the young wolf curled around himself drew her attention. She examined him intently while Ravyn mentally begged for Toby to remain quiet. "And I thank you for bringing us leverage against you. All wrapped up in a neat little bow, this pup will work quite nicely."

"Ibis, this can't work. Surely you know that, Sister," Ravyn cracked out, anything to get the witch's and wendigo's attention off Toby.

"I sssee the wheels turning, my little queen," the creature hissed, its raspy voice barely able to curl around its forked tongue, unable to remain ignored for long. "But there is no hope; there is only time. And the time isn't quite yet. You have a gift for the both of us." Gesturing a curved claw toward itself as well as the evil remnants of Ibis, it went on, "You shall give your sister back her immortality, and be done, but you and I will be together a much longer time."

Ravyn struggled to comprehend the words as Ibis once again twisted her face to look her in the eyes, her beauty so much like her beloved sister it hurt. "I'll spell it out simply enough that even you can understand. You'll be re-gifting me eternal life soon, very soon, and as for him… Well, you'll be gifting him plenty for all of your remaining eternal life. And if you think for even a moment that you won't do these things, then realize that my magic will simply make you and it won't be nearly as pleasant or as easy as it could be." Pausing to let her words sink in, she added, "Not that I would mind either way, Sister. And anything I do to you will be done to the pup as well."

At least for a short time, Toby's life was ensured, even if was meant to be used as a way to control Ravyn.

With a swirl, Ibis stood just a breath away from Ravyn. Leaning in with a soft whisper that a mortal would never hear, she admitted, "He's a tool for me to yield. He delivered you to me, but once you change me, you are his. He believes you can satisfy the hunger, but nothing and no one can. You will turn to dust beneath his teeth and then you will be no more. Remember this, Little Sister: after you're dust, you'll be no more remembered than I was. Gone, forgotten, and still unloved."

Flipping around so quickly that she was nearly a blur, Ibis once again took in the room before settling her gaze on the wendigo, which whined under its breath long and low while its lanky legs rocked back and forth under her scrutiny. "I will retire for now and began my preparations for my purification. And under no circumstances are you to begin anything without me or before my own change is underway," she reminded the wendigo before leaving the cold room with a flurry of movements. Not as fast as the vampire she once was, but certainly faster than a normal human, Ravyn noted from under nearly closed eyes.

"That damn witch told me that the ritual must be done under a new moon. The wolves have power under the full moon, but my power lies within the new moon. So, until then we must wait." With a coy look toward the cowering pup in the corner, it lisped, "Although sssome of us have more time than others."

Ravyn bit back the threat she wanted to spit at the creature. If she angered it, she realized it wouldn't be her who paid the price, at least not this night. She caught a glimpse of a quiet Toby over its shoulder, silently observing the exchanges from his spot of the floor, trying to not draw any attention to himself. It would be too much to hope that he would be forgotten, especially not when he was recognized as a weapon to control her.

"But you and I can play before the new moon." Dropping its shrill, hissing tone, suddenly the deep, comforting voice of Bash came out of it. "Do you like this voice better, my love? If you close your eyes, I can be whomever you want." It ended its offer with another shrill giggle, amused by its own abilities. "Or I can play both parts," it offered suggestively in Ravyn's own voice before dropping back to its own. "Ah, yesss, I can do that if I decide to cut out your vile tongue for a night." It thrusted its hips toward her in a threat as well as a gross parody of its plans for the inevitable future. "You might even grow to like it. After all, you are but a whore who lies down with dogs."

Her stomach twisted as the wine she drank earlier seemed to curdle inside her before she emptied its contents down her front and onto the floor, gagging and retching as it spilled out of her. The smell of blood, vomit, and poison filled the air, nearly overpowering the creature's own stench.

It drew back from her in a look of disgust.

"You are better than thisss filth, my queen." Its own lispy voice was filled with revulsion. "I expected more from you."

Toby cringed back deeper into the shadows as the creature eyed him.

"Ah, my young pup." Pacing toward him, it veered off to the bracket in the wall where it harshly pulled up on the chain, forcing Toby to stand as one arm was pulled upward by the unforgiving silver chains.

Toby attempted to shrink back but the chain forced him to half stand, facing the wendigo. As it reached him, he curled up his hands to fend off the evil, but to no avail. Its oversized, clawed hands curled around his chained wrist, prying the fingers open.

"Foolish superstitions," it muttered. Once it held the thumb, index finger and middle finger open in its paw, it studied them intently as Toby quietly struggled to close them back up.

The wendigo opened its mouth as Ravyn gasped, knowing that Toby stood face to face with its rows of tiny, sharp canines.

"Wait, wait, wait!" Ravyn shrieked, not recognizing her own voice. "She said not to hurt him." Straining against the bonds that kept her in place even as they ripped into the skin around her wrists, she fought to get closer to the two.

It didn't matter. Swiftly and without preamble, the wendigo chomped down with a loud crunching sound that snapped across the room. For a brief second there was silence, then a shocked Toby let out a scream of pain that surely could be heard for miles.

Turning half toward her, the creature crunched the

Tooth and Claw

fingers loudly in its half open mouth as it hummed in apparent pleasure, watching her while it savored the moment. Still it held the wolf's shackled hand as the boy continued to scream. The blood shot into the air before spewing from the two missing appendages down the monster's clawed hand. It observed the flow intently, fascinated and completely oblivious, uncaring, to the wolf's horror and pain.

Toby's screams nearly broke Ravyn. She hadn't been able to stop this.

"Kill… She didn't want him killed, but I can cccertainly ensure that doesn't happen. For yearsss I have perrrfected that art."

The creature loosened its grasp on Toby's bleeding hand before cupping its palm to hold the warm liquid in it, turning slowly and shuffling almost reverently toward Ravyn, bringing to her its grotesque offering.

"For you, my queen." It held the cupped hand dripping with the strongly scented blood.

Ravyn's nostrils flared as she scented the horror and fear the blood offered and she wanted to cry when her fangs dropped down, cutting into her clenched lips. Closing her eyes against the tainted offering, she shook her head no, not daring to open her mouth to say a word.

"Drink," it ordered in Sebastian's dulcet tones, then repeated the word in Toby's youthful voice. "Please, please," it pleaded before grasping her cheeks between two sharp claws, forcing her lips open, and rubbing a rough, blood-coated finger along her gums and teeth.

Rayvn's mind begged her to stop even as she instinctively swallowed the boy's unwilling life force before suckling the offered bloodied finger. After the first tumultuous years, she'd never taken from an unwilling victim and certainly never a child, but her body betrayed her. When it weakened briefly against the onslaught, the wendigo forced more blood into her unwilling mouth.

With a low laugh of satisfaction, it smeared yet even more blood around her mouth, as if daring her to lick off the offering.

This time when it released its grip, Ravyn's head fell forward in defeat. She hadn't even the strength to hold it up after this brutal violation of both herself and young Toby.

"Sssee, I can take care of you, and you will take care of me. My queen, you will keep up your strength until the new moon." The wendigo wiped its bloody fingers across her face before finding a clean spot on her dress to continue wiping them clean, ignoring her tears and the tears from a sobbing Toby. Disgust entered its tone once again as it tsked. "You are a messs. I will send in my Lilith to clean you up. I expect more from you."

Ravyn remained silent, raising her dark eyes to watch the wendigo stalk from the room. Closing the door tightly behind itself, it left the two alone in their pain.

Rage replaced the disgust she felt in herself. He would die. Perhaps not tonight, but soon. "Toby," she whispered softly to the crying pup, "I'm so sorry. Can you shift?"

The sobs quieted for a moment as he struggled through both pain and shock. If he could shift soon enough, the magic of the shift could heal his missing fingers. If not... well, she refused to consider that right now.

"I-I can't," he hiccupped after a brief pause. "The chains won't allow it, and if I fight through it, if he told me the truth, the collar will rip my head off." A gasping sob escaped the wolf as he fought to control the pain and staunch the blood while applying a tourniquet of sorts with his uninjured hand.

"Just breathe deeply. I know it hurts, but breathe through the pain, in and out, in and out. Let your wolf shoulder some of the pain," Rayvn encouraged him as her brain frantically ran through the options, any options available to them. She might have time, but Toby didn't. If they stayed here, his time was limited to days or even hours with the unpredictable, ravenous wendigo.

So many mistakes. Her ego would be her downfall and worse, Toby's young life hung in the balance. At least one of her men had made it inside the gates with them, but she began having doubts about the chances of his survival. She'd seen roughly half a dozen men at and around the gate. If human, the vampire would easily be able to cut them down, but if they were imbued with magic or other supernatural forces, the chances that her driver was gone grew exponentially.

The other car had been left outside the gates. Regrettably, this creature seemed to have planned for every situation, so it was doubtful they'd made it inside; if she was lucky enough, they were at least alive. But help hadn't arrived yet, and it might not come. She had to plan for the fact that no one would come. Like the old days, she was on her own to save herself; however, Toby's life was also held in the balance.

Despite the mess of vomit down her chin and dress, hurling had been useful in clearing out more of the poison from her system. And despite the regret of ingesting even a tiny bit of Toby's blood, it had, in fact, helped to clear her head as well. Her extremities moved a bit easier now, and her previously immobile feet tingled as new blood circulated through them. If she had her way, forcing her to take the boy's blood might prove to be a fatal mistake. Hope rose through her as she tested wiggling her toes; the feeling was returning to them. Hissing as her wrists shifted against the silver chain holding them in place, she continued testing the restraints to no avail.

"Uncle Bash will come," the boy whispered, his words more of a prayer than a promise. The room began to darken a bit as the moon continued its path across the sky, marking the slow passage of the night.

Chapter Fifteen

On the eve of your death the wolf will come

Sebastian fought the urge to rip the heads off every single vampire in his employ. The fools. The damn fools. Three nights and days, actually less than seventy-two hours, they needed to keep Ravyn's safety above their need to defer to her every request. If they'd even remotely put their foot down, Ravyn would see reason, but they seemed unable to even say, "Hey, let's wait a few hours." No, they let Ravyn sneak off as soon as her slumber ended.

An itinerary had been left behind for him, written out on a single sheet of paper. It wasn't emailed or texted for approval, as if the foolish woman had known. Surely, she'd known he would deny or at the least delay the evening's plans. But no, he'd found out late. Much too late. And no one answered their phones. Not her, not the security detail that accompanied her, and not even his nephew, who kept his phone glued to his side, deemed his angry, frantic calls worth answering.

Tooth and Claw

His wolf's panic-stricken anger howled inside his own, carelessly reflecting back and tripling his emotions, driving them both to the edge of sanity. Curling his fists tightly in an attempt to allay his emotions, his claws driving into the balled-up palms, he took one deep breath, letting it out slowly before repeating the process. Losing his mind wouldn't help the situation; the rational part of his brain knew this and tried to convey it to the animal fighting to be set free.

Smoothing out the now crumpled message, he focused his eyes, still blurry from anger, at it. She'd left an address for this man, this producer whom she planned to see, the names of those driving and accompanying her, as well as the tentative times of arrival and departure in neat block handwriting. A quick note scrawled at the end, still clear but not as neatly written stated that Toby would accompany her as well.

His every instinct screamed that this entire evening was a dangerous mistake. Had no one considered that the invitation had arrived after all the wolves had left for their three days away, leaving her vulnerable under the magic of the full moon? He knew the vamps had a weakness for her, but he'd never considered that she herself would drive them all straight into danger. There just weren't any stronger options against the moon than the vamps, but even they couldn't take on a revered original vampire.

Ravyn was more than a golden princess or regal queen who walked the earth with them; for the vampires, she was the embodiment of a goddess even if they didn't come from her line. The fools should have been prepared to lay down their lives for her, not follow her every god-awful foolish command.

The next full moon, I'm locking her in a vault, Bash swore to himself. *Inside a damn padlocked coffin, inside a locked vault with me carrying the only keys*, he amended, pushing his hair back away from his face. A shudder ran through him, the pinpricks moving over his body as fur threatened to sprout. His worried wolf insisted on coming out. *No, wait!* He demanded of the beast as he struggled to contain it.

His curled fists barely relaxed enough to punch out a single message, but he managed to fire off a brusque text to the remaining exhausted security team to prepare them for an immediate extraction effort. This Bertrando Roland could be just as he appeared, but his team needed to be prepared for any scenario. Yet anyone with even a hint of common sense could see the red flags in this scenario and that was even before everyone on the team quit responding to their phones.

Right now, anger was a better motivator than the fear and panic creeping up from behind. Hitting a few other buttons, he tracked both Ravyn's and his nephew's phones, confirming that their last known location as of many hours ago matched the address left in the note.

"I need you people to hurry, and has that witch arrived yet?" Bash barked out to the team who were already moving quickly and efficiently to assemble for a departure in less than twenty minutes. The panic was beginning to creep up and overtake the initial anger. Even his wolf paced anxiously in the back of his mind, lowly whining in anticipation for whatever was to come.

"Sir," several of the shifters sounded off in response as they continued gearing up. This on-the-cuff mission meant they needed to be prepared for anything. They could be facing a hostage situation, magical, monster, or if all was well, simply nothing except a dead zone in the countryside.

After several minutes of waving her hands around, the witch nervously admitted to him, "It's solid, sir." Stepping back, she dipped her head as she angled herself half behind one of his men. "And not all the magic is recognizable; it's strange and convoluted. I'm proceeding with caution and it's going to take time."

Bash wanted to lash out at the witch to check the wards again but this time, he managed to hold his tongue. Losing control was for fools, and fools didn't complete rescue missions. Of course the wards were solid. On arriving at the gate, they'd tested and retested them. Two teams of three had been sent out to circle the compound and see how far around the wards went. The tall fence that framed that gate on either side wasn't the real protection; it was an illusion of security that ended a few yards into the dense forest. The real protection was the impenetrable wards surrounding the acreage.

"Get another witch," he barked to his men, ignoring the woman whose stench of fear had begun to penetrate his senses and for a moment, he felt a flash of guilt. None of this was her fault and all he'd done since she'd arrived at the apartments was to snarl and growl at a now shaking, timid witch.

"Moldover?" one of his team members began, clearly preparing to call him out if his judgment became questionable. "Never mind," he immediately amended, running a frustrated hand through his hair, loosening it from his pony tail.

"I'm sorry," Sebastian bit off to the witch, who refused to meet his eye. If there was one better, Oliver would have already had them on retainer. His partner didn't accept second best, and burning bridges with this one would cost them all in the long run.

When—not if—he got Ravyn back, he would kiss her senseless, but not before spanking her for putting herself and his nephew in danger.

"How far out is Delta?" Bash had requested that particular witch's presence as soon as he recognized that Ravyn and Toby were gone. Something in his gut told him she would be needed, and even it was a false call, he would rather be safe than sorry. However, it was looking more and more like the situation was as dire as he feared.

Unfortunately, Oliver's helicopter was still here on the west coast, remaining at Ravyn's disposal. Dispatching one local to Delta took time; money could smooth the path, but it still took time. Time that wasn't on their side, Bash feared.

"En route. About three hours out. We've secured landing about twenty minutes from our current location." The same guard once again spoke up while the others remained silent, looking out into the perimeter they'd established.

Breathing slowly in and out, he released his hair before smoothing it back into place, replacing the band holding it up, as his mind clicked through what they knew and didn't know. Two of the team members who had accompanied Ravyn had been trapped outside, held into place by a spell that the witch had easily broken. That spell was just meant to trap and slow down entry, nothing permanent like the wards. Their minds were muddled and after questioning them extensively, Bash couldn't even confirm from them that Ravyn had gone inside.

The entire setup could be a false trail designed to occupy them while the producer or whoever he was took Ravyn to a different location. Occasionally, the landscape past the magical barrier would flicker in and out of focus, leading the group to acknowledge that whatever they were seeing wasn't real time or could be a complete facade. They'd lost contact with the driver as well, but with the magical illusion he could be standing on the other side of the gate and they might not see him.

And Toby. Toby surely was still with her; Bash couldn't bring himself to think about the alternative. If something happened to the boy, Sebastian didn't know if his sister-in-law would recover. Only Tobias and his siblings had given her the strength to continue when her mate, his brother, was killed. The time Bash hadn't been there, his mind filled in.

Focus. He needed to focus on the next step: bringing them home.

A background check had been run on this Bertrando Roland and what had come back so far was absolutely nothing of interest or unexpected. Not even a parking ticket, which actually sent up major red flags to the group. No one had no history, or at least such a shiny history, especially in the movie industry. Only child, parents dead, inherited money, and major success in the movie industry, as in doubling or tripling the money his parents left him. Every film was a success; everyone who worked for him said the same thing. Genius, high standards, a joy to work with. Again, this level of perfection was impossible. Someone had to hate the man or at least dislike him a little bit.

Oliver's side of the business had people continuing to work on it. Bash had demanded they look into Roland's primary school records, discover where his parents had made their money. Everything. He wanted to know everything about this man.

"Incoming!" one of his shifters shot off, and half the team turned their focus toward the edge of the forest while the other half began scanning for other potential unknowns. Two still in wolf form trotted to the front of their group, ears perked and hair rising on the back of their necks, while the others in black-and-gray fatigues raised unnecessary weapons to their shoulders. If a human approached, they would see a group of mercenaries in training with large dogs, and if the threat were supernatural, the team could be fighting tooth and claw in a matter of seconds.

A man, a youth really, perhaps a bit older than Toby upon closer examination, stepped cautiously out of the shadows, hands raised slightly above his head, a walking stick in one, green and black paint blended over his face as well as spots on his hands. His shoulder-length black hair was held down by a leather strap tied around his head; his eyes, nearly as black as his hair, peered out from the face paint.

"Easy there," the stranger intoned lowly at the group. As he stepped into the roadway, the group could see he was dressed similarly to them except his clothes lacked the crispness of the team's. His black cargo pants were streaked with clay and mud, speaking of hours or even days in the woods. While his long-sleeved black tee fit snuggly against his chest and arms, hinting at an unseen strength, it was covered with the same dirt and debris. Brown leather straps wrapped around his shoulders, but the pack wasn't large enough to be seen from the front. The small bag, together with his appearance, made the man seem to be simply a lost day hiker.

Sebastian subtly sniffed the air, trying to catch the man's scent. Strangely, there was no hint of sweat, fear, or body odor clinging to him despite his disheveled appearance. The man looked expectantly at Bash, despite the fact that one of his team members had already begun his spiel.

"Sir, we must ask you to leave this area. Our team is conducting training exercises that the State of California have approved and we have the necessary paperwork on file in the case of..."

The tawny man ignored the cover story, studying Bash as if making a decision. Slowly lowering his hands, he held the walking stick loosely at his side with a wide stance that had Bash deciding his instincts were right: this man wasn't simply a tourist or even a local out for a hike. Despite his casual stance and the fact that he looked barely older than Toby, he held himself at the ready, his eyes frozen on Bash's but still appearing to take in the entire group at the same time.

"Sir, are you lost? Do you need assistance, sir? If not, we ask that you leave this training area immediately."

Gripping the walking staff lightly between his

forefinger and thumb, the youth opened the remainder of his palm in an outwardly friendly greeting followed up with a slow, almost respectful nod. "Greetings, Sebastian Moldover and shifters." Pausing, he waited for that revelation to sink in, keeping his stance loose and open while glancing among all the men before settling back on Bash. "I am Kai. I do believe we have an enemy in common."

The men holding weapons shifted uneasily, casting quick glances to each other before Sebastian told them, "Stand down."

His instincts were screaming that this unassuming man was friendly and his wolf bounced around, downright giddy to see him. Strange. "Kai…" He nodded in a not quite formal greeting, but still holding to the old ways, he asked, "Might I ask how you know my name?"

The man shifted from foot to foot, which was when Sebastian noticed he was actually barefoot as well. Odd. Not for a wolf, of course, but for a human, definitely. He held himself with the confidence of an older man although with the face camouflage it was difficult to ascertain for sure if he was as young as he'd first appeared. With a small grin, his white teeth flashed as he spoke. "You all aren't quite as quiet as you think." He pointed to and correctly rattled off the names of each of the team members, who looked at each other uneasily once again. This youth was clearly more then he appeared.

"Hold," Bash ordered, reminding the group that despite how it appeared, they weren't amateurs.

Leaning a bit to the side, the stranger pointed toward the witch, who now stood fully behind one of his men. "Apologies, ma'am. I didn't catch yours, but I'm assuming 'Witch' is a title, not a name."

A cocky grin with yet another short nod had Bash ready to jump on top of the man to thrash him in frustration, but his wolf's giddy excitement held him short. The wolf appeared to recognize the man or at the very least was ready to make his acquaintance far more exuberantly than human manners dictated.

"So, Kai," he drawled out, hoping he sounded much more relaxed than he felt, "might I ask what you're doing way out here?"

Kai shrugged and then pointed out, "Well, Sebastian…" He hesitated and appeared to consider before a slow nod. "Or do you prefer Wolf? And I could ask you the same."

Bash mentally snapped at his wolf as it preened under the boy's acknowledgment. "It seems you would like to appear as if you just know everything."

"I'm getting the feeling I know more than you," Kai admitted without preamble. "And as for what I'm doing here"—he spread his arms out wide in guiltlessness—"I was here long before you. Your men stumbling about and shouting orders is what woke me from my nap. Right over there." He pointed over his shoulder into the foliage, raising an eyebrow when one of the wolves trotted into the forest to check on the story.

Silence settled upon them until the wolf, now a man, walked back out of the forest naked, carrying a sheathed knife in his hand. "Bash, he's got a site right off the path, hidden, but a nice hidey hold. We've been walking right past him for hours. Had this in there." Handing the still sheathed blade to Bash, he effortlessly transformed back into a large gray wolf, sitting back on his haunches, awaiting his next order.

Bash examined the outside of the old leather sheath, turning it back and forth in his hands. Unassuming, battered and beat up, the leather nearly black in its creases, it spoke of years of use. The handle, perhaps bone, matched its sheath in age and use. The groves worn into it fit perfectly in the flat of his hand and his fingers wrapped around it as if it had been made for his palm. A tremor ran through him, as if the knife spoke to him, calling out to him to release it. Refraining from pulling the knife from its holder, he grudgingly loosened his grip. He'd been around witches and their athames just enough to know that despite how a blade called to you, it was never safe to pull someone else's. The magic kickback alone could kill you and that was before even knowing anything else about it.

Reluctantly, he flipped the sheathed long blade, offering it to Kai to handle first. Placing his walking stick on his back, Kai took the few steps toward him and accepted the handle with yet another nod. "I thank you for not releasing it."

"A piece like that deserves respect," Bash answered gruffly, feeling an odd sense of loss. Despite the fact that he'd held the knife for less than two minutes it had felt right in his hand; comfortable, like it was home.

"Did it speak to you?" Once again the head tilt as he watched Bash, awaiting his answer.

"I felt... I felt... something,"

This time, the nod wasn't questioning, but pleased. "It's the athame of my people. Forged together by my ancestors... and yours, the sons of Fenrir." Continuing as if he hadn't insinuated an impossible connection between them, Kai explained, "It's used in the hunt and the protection of mankind. It calls for blood when it leaves its sheath." Carefully, he unwrapped the leather strap holding the blade in place, then smoothly slid the knife from its holder. The other wolves trembled as a small shockwave moved them. Bash found it almost impossible to stay upright in the split second the magic hit. He was unable to take his eyes off the bone blade that twinkled for a moment before smoothing out and reshaping into a sleek silver blade.

Silver. A death sentence to any of his kind, yet it had an unimaginable siren call to it that whistled through the air.

"It won't harm you," Kai assured him. He looked around the rest of the group, who stood frozen, watching the beautiful, shimmering blade settle back into aged white bone once again. Unlike the sheath and handle, the blade had writing etched along its entirety from top to bottom, the tiny drawings meticulous and unreadable by Bash.

Kai turned it over in his hand. "Vanadium steel and silver. It's been spelled by the ancestors to only harm evil and can be wielded by my people as well as yours. It was meant to be used in battle by one such as yourself, but the years haven't been kind to its legacy."

"Wait, hold up. Kai, was it? I've never heard of a silver knife that a wolf could hold." The disappointment that Bash felt battled with the simple beauty of the knife that called to him. Glancing around, he continued, "I don't mean to be rude, but are you here alone or is your dad or someone around? If this blade is what you say it is, it seems a bit odd that you're out here hanging around waiting for a wolf to show up so you can pull it on them."

Dismay crossed Kai's stoic face as he slid the knife back into its sheath, carefully rewrapping the leather holding it in place. "I haven't exactly been waiting around for you and I wouldn't expect you to understand this, but your people and my people have had an understanding for years. Only… well, only they've died off. Died off or been killed," he amended.

"What does that even mean? You work with other shifters? Other wolves? Where are they?"

Impatiently, Kai pushed back. "I just told you.

Dead." Looking toward the heavens, he took a deep breath, re-centering himself before looking back at Bash. "I'm making a mess of this and we don't have time for that."

"Well, we can agree on that," Bash huffed out, crossing his arms across his chest. Ravyn needed him and they were wasting time with this interloper. "Although it appears to me you have all the time in the world, camping out here and all."

"A long time ago—think ancient times—my people and yours teamed up to fight an unspeakable evil that haunted the land. We hadn't always gotten along and some say that the gods unleashed this evil to force us to work together. Not that it really matters when or why, but we did. For years and years, my tribe and the wolves in the area had an agreement. The strongest wolf of the pack would wield the knife and the strongest of my tribe would wield the magic."

Bash snorted. "Your gods played a joke on you, then. I'm no Alpha and if you're the strongest of your tribe, then, well…"

Kai interrupted and for the first time, he sounded angry. "First, I'm the strongest of my tribe, because I'm the only one left. The last one. The rest are gone. And second, you big idiot, I didn't say the Alpha, I said the strongest. The two don't necessarily go hand in hand as much as you all try to convince yourselves of that. And I assure you if the gods had said the smartest, then it wouldn't be you. Besides, have you noticed a lot of options around these parts? There isn't a wolf pack for miles and miles. Their natural population was pretty much decimated within the state. The knife calls to you, you've already said that much. And if the knife says it's you, then it's you." He begrudgingly added the last bit, as if it pained him to admit it and would have preferred a better choice. "Excuse my impatience, but we're running out of time."

Bash opened and closed his mouth. His father had once said if a wolf kept quiet, folks might assume him a fool, but if he opened his mouth, he might prove to be one. This seemed just like one of those moments. He gestured to continue with his hands, keeping his mouth closed.

Kai closed his eyes briefly, as if once again centering himself. "The evil that we fight has been here for centuries, picking off my people. I've only heard tales of the time when we worked together with the wolves. Whenever that alliance was broken or killed off was well before my time. My father never met a wolf. My grandfather spoke of the last wolf when he was a boy. If it weren't for him, I wouldn't even have believed. I've been hiding and watching that thing in there but without a wolf, I'm as good as useless against it, but still I..." Unable to articulate the words, the young man's voice drifted off.

But Bash understood that their numbers dwindled among the supernatural. Still duty called. Duty above all else. And the boy's duty was to watch, but watch what? *Fenrir!* Panic filled Bash. Was this boy a vampire hunter? If he expected Bash to blindly pick up a blade against Ravyn or any vampire, for that matter, he was sorely mistaken. Was he willing to kill a boy brave enough to stand against wolf shifters?

"What do *you* fight against?" he asked the boy, emphasizing the "you," refusing to put himself in a category with him.

"Wendigo. We battle for humanity against the demon wendigo spirit. I've been taught the magic to subdue and trap the spirit, but I need another to wield the knife."

His words settled over the wolves, and they broke rank as they murmured among themselves. Instinctively making the sign against evil, Bash surmised by their tone that he wasn't the only one. Wendigo! An unstoppable, insatiable killing machine. Humans feared the boogie man or the slender man, but pups were raised knowing that they wouldn't even hear the deadly wendigo going bump in the night. Deadly hunters and tricksters without a weakness, they could lure one out by sounding like a loved one and they would be dead at the same moment they discovered the trick.

Looking at Bash expectantly before he continued, Kai said, "And I feel like you might have a more personal reason if the vampires and young wolf who entered the compound a few hours ago are any indicator."

Sebastian perked up at his words. "You saw them enter? Why didn't you stop them? Are they still here?" His words shot out, peppering the youth before he could respond. If he had the ability to do something, why hadn't he?

Nodding his dark head, Kai waited a breath before holding up a hand. "Once they get this close to the gate, it's too late to stop them. The magic protecting this place has grown and evolved over the last few years. It's strong and I'm alone. I stop those I can, but my greatest weapon these last few years has been that the beast doesn't know I exist. As far as it's concerned, my line has died out, and along with that any threat to it."

"Whose skin does it wear?" All signs pointed to this Roland fellow, but he could just be a pawn to the demon.

"It goes by the name Bertrando Roland these days." Kai spat after the words left him. "He likes to pretend he's from Europe or something. Since Dad died, all I can do is try to head off those he brings here before they get here, and I watch. It feels so secure here—invincible, in fact—it has settled here for years."

Chapter Sixteen

And death sought the raven

Ravyn once again wearily raised her head a degree. Ibis hadn't been wrong in knowing that Ravyn, weakened with loss of blood, would still only need to slumber a few hours when the sun hit its zenith. Her body had known the moment the sun stood high, and her world went black.

Immediately, she knew outside of Toby that she wasn't alone. A *drip*, *drip*, *drip* echoed around the chamber, and she found herself counting the drips in her head without realizing. She reached 224 before her mind once again caught up with her situation, and she prayed to the goddess that Toby's bleeding had stopped. The hours were too long for the pup to be bleeding so freely. Before she even opened her eyes, she checked on the soft, often rattling, slow breaths he took in. Thankfully, he slept as well. The dripping continued echoing in the chamber, but her fuzzy eyesight couldn't determine the direction it came from.

Tooth and Claw

Slowly one, two, three, four drops echoed as Ravyn waited for the sleep to pass and forced herself to stop counting the sounds.

Taking a deep breath, she could taste the evil of Ibis's magic tainting the air. Why was she back? Waiting to taunt Ravyn with more threats?

"Wakey, wakey time." Ibis's voice cracked through the air, and Ravyn couldn't help but compare the grating sound to Anya's soft tones. A small chuckle escaped the magical being. Ibis spoke with both glee and wonderment. "I knew you were stronger than the sun. It's been centuries since I could take such a short nap."

Lifting her head slightly higher, Ravyn took in the figure of Ibis sitting primly in a chair, her legs crossed at her ankles as if she were sitting at a garden party and not participating in kidnapping and torture. How could one so beautiful be so evil?

"You, my dear Little Bird, are the one I hoped for. Even with continual draining, you still managed to wake up faster than vampires half you age."

With horror, Ravyn realized the dripping—*seven, eight, nine, ten, eleven*—came from her. The sound of her blood pinging on the floor echoed through her head. This bitch had spent all afternoon draining her slowly and as the cuts healed, she would begin again. With a bit of focus, Ravyn could feel the blood pooling from her wrists even as her body fought to heal her wounds.

Ibis's wide, maniacal eyes met Ravyn and without looking away, she brought up the knife that had been used for hours to maintain the blood flow. Dried as well as fresh blood still appeared on it, as if just minutes ago Ibis had used the knife. Slowly, without breaking eye contact, she brought the knife to her lips and licked off the edge of the blood, expelling a deep breath of satisfaction as she did so.

"Even now I can taste your power." Ibis shuddered and closed her eyes as the bit of blood rolled around in her mouth before she swallowed it. "It's so difficult to not drain you now. But for the highest chance of success, we'll wait for the new moon just as those priests did millennia ago. With one shot at this, we want the most chance for success. Right, my Little Bird?" Ibis asked, as if Ravyn were a willing participant in this plan.

Standing up, with a wave of the knife Ibis added, "Don't worry about Bertrando; he wore himself out last night. The fool likes to eat and then chase after the moonlight—as if he could catch it. Thankfully for me, he's now sleeping the day away, so it's just you and me." Pausing, she glanced toward the end of the room where a sleeping Toby still half stood, chained in place. "Except, of course, for your little friend. Tsk tsk, Ravyn. I didn't realize you'd taken up feeding from children."

Ravyn seethed silently, waiting for the point—whatever it was—that Ibis was trying to make.

Tooth and Claw

There was no point in arguing or begging. She refused to give Ibis the satisfaction.

Ibis just stood with her head tilted, bouncing the flat side of the knife in her hand as she examined Ravyn for several long moments.

"Do you even comprehend how special you are? The gifts you, and maybe you alone, received? Seventy years ago, before my immortality was ripped from me, I hid from the daylight twelve hours a day. Twelve hours," she reiterated, biting out the words sharply. "Half the time we're given in a day. And we slumbered like the dead for eight of those hours. I'll bet the only time you slept that long was when you chose to go to ground for a few decades."

Ibis flipped the knife lightly in the air, the steel shining and catching tiny bits of light as it flew. "You feign weakness, but I see you. You hide away for barely eight hours and I'm not certain you need to do that. And your slumber? Your slumber is nearly a choice. Even drained, your body fought to waken. I was busy, busy for several hours, but if those damn Houska twins taught me anything, it was patience. Yes, patience and more importantly, perseverance with experimentation."

"I had nothing…" Ravyn began weakly, her vocal cords swollen from hanging so long with the coils around her neck.

A curl of Ibis's lip and a shake of her head cut off her words. "Little Bird, don't. There is no one else. I want you. I want your blood to pump through my veins. The power of your blood was enough to awaken the little succubus half-breed." Ibis shuddered in anticipation. "Never before has that been recorded. With your blood, I will transform into more. You. Will. Not. Deny. Me. This. You will not deny me my immortality."

Ravyn couldn't find the will to argue with her. She was insane. Not only magic held her together, but insanity weaved the cords as well. The twins had been right in locking this creature away. How did she know so much, though? Ravyn knew her aversion to the daylight hours, while weak by human standards, wasn't so much by old vampire standards. Already so many of them revered her due to being an original, but knowing that she stood better against sunlight than any other ancient put a target on her.

She did, in truth, need to sleep four or maybe five hours, but if she was well fed—and Ravyn tended to stay well fed—she could cut that in half. She did need to avoid the sunlight for around eight hours and as long as she stayed out of the sunlight, it didn't weaken her like other vampires, especially elder vamps.

She was an anomaly and clearly, her attempts to stay under the radar hadn't gone completely unnoticed. And if Ibis knew, then who else might?

Ibis wasn't finished yet. Having a captive audience, one who might understand her, certainly made her chatty. "For years—decades—I was kept in a

TOOTH AND CLAW

cage. Treated as less than. Worse than one might treat an animal. But I could see glimpses of Anya's life," Ibis sneered, "like sunshine in the darkness, one might imagine, but it wasn't. It was simply more torture. Living out her life, the grand, disgusting life she thought she wanted. It gave me a dream as well. I dreamed of ripping apart the man she loved while she watched before doing the same to her. But it turned out so much better than I imagined. She still had to watch her beloved die and now she's slowly being eaten away until death takes her as well. Fitting."

Ravyn knew she couldn't explain to the sneering, angry creature before her that that was exactly the life and death Anya had wanted. This wasn't about living an eternal life, but a life filled with love and loving. Ibis, with her anger and hatred, would never understand that. The creature who stood before her, the leftover magic that had formed Ibis, didn't have the capacity to understand that.

"She couldn't turn him, you know," Ibis added abruptly. This bit of news caused Ravyn to look quickly at her sister despite the fact that she didn't want to give her the satisfaction. "She couldn't be sure that he had any demon blood in him. Are you shocked, Little Sister? All those years ago, when they tasted and tested our blood, they were searching for the taint of demon blood. It didn't matter how little; they still took us from our families, even those they knew without a doubt didn't have enough to transform."

Despite's Ravyn's attempt to ignore Ibis, she couldn't. That was why they'd been picked, of course. But she'd known that already. Their tainted blood was why they'd been torn away from their families and sacrificed.

"How little you know despite your years, Sister," Ibis spat out. "Haven't you ever wondered why some can receive the gift of eternal life and others cannot? It's simply a matter of whether Grandma or Great-grandma or beyond hooked up with a demon lover. And of course, against all odds, the child survived on this plane and managed to procreate. So many things have to line up perfectly for us to receive our gift. Anya just couldn't be certain her human could survive the gift, so she killed herself to be with him instead."

Astonished, Ravyn considered those whom she'd attempted to turn over the years. Not many, but at the same time, even fewer survived. She'd assumed it was because they truly didn't want the gift of immortality, or they were simply too close to death to complete the transformation. This explained so much.

"Of course, you would never wonder why so few can complete the transformation. You're all about poor Ravyn. You dumb skank! The humans need to have enough demon DNA to accept the transition. Years ago, those bastard priests knew well before that night who would have the best chance of beating death. The rest were just bodies to distract us. Unless, of course, by chance they did turn; then they were a bonus prize. You, you with all your power would have been a boon to them. Your dear father? Most likely you were sired by a demon. They were probably thrilled to suckle your demon laced blood."

Slow, deep breaths in and out and with a cock of her head, Ravyn once again checked that Toby still breathed and his heart slowly pumped. She found herself wanting to cry like the little girl from long ago who'd played along the river's edge. Despite Ibis's taunts, the man who had raised her was still her father. Nothing she could say, would change that.

Would she see Sebastian again? Her heart squeezed tightly at the thought of never seeing him again. And she hadn't even got to meet his wolf. Would he mourn her or hate her for getting herself in this situation? And Toby too. Dammit and Toby.

"Pay attention, bitch. Although that might not be the insult it once was, now that you sully yourself.

"Those twins knew, though. They claim to be descendants of the vampire creators, the bloody priests who thought they could conquer death. They claim they're different, but still they trap, they control, they study. Anya feared her love couldn't transition. So, she gave all of it up for her shell of a life and a short, bitter end. I suspect as the hangman's noose tightens around her neck, she'll choke on curses of him."

But Ibis wasn't done. Goddess, couldn't she just take herself and leave in peace? But it was almost like she never got to speak to anyone and now, Ravyn was her chosen confidant—or confessor.

"Meeting the wendigo was a stroke of good luck. If the gods before had abandoned me, that day they smiled upon me. It's a clever creature in some respects. One must be to live this long, of course. Years spent gathering money and power, all as a means to feed itself. Otherwise, it's meaningless. Hunger is its driving force. Its only desire is to fill its hunger and early on, it found a way to do so. The coven your people killed off in minutes during your little half-demon rescue? It had spent years building it. They desired power and immortality. They worshiped the wendigo like a god, but only its need for them kept them from being food. Its guards are lesser demons, demons that crawled out of Houska and other hell gates over the years. They wear the skin of humans held together by black magic."

Ibis stopped pacing, holding her knife loosely in her hand as she examined Ravyn curiously. "Aligning myself with that creature, feeding it bits of information, hints of satisfying its hunger… it was all so simple. Now, the scryer, she was a surprise. It just saw her as a meal and didn't even realize what it had. A little wisp of a thing, barely any power at all. She didn't even realize what she could do until I saw the smallest of flames in her. Even with me channeling her magic, it was too weak to see the future or the past, but enough to see the present, to see you at least on occasion, once all of our other doorways closed. Thank the gods she didn't need all her fingers to scry and that the wendigo left her one eye." With a roll of her own eyes, Ibis admitted, "Its hunger will be its downfall, but I will be long gone by then."

Ravyn closed her eyes; the wendigo's threats weren't empty. Opening them again, she looked straight at Ibis and pleaded, but not for herself, "Help him, please." She looked toward Toby. "He's not a part of this and hasn't done anything to any of you. Just let him go so he can get help."

Ibis chuckled, slowly shaking her head. "Oh, sweet Little Bird, I don't think you understand. I. Don't. Care." With a wave of her hand, she explained, "I don't care what happens to the mutt. I don't care what happens to you. The whole world can burn and I still won't care. I want my life back. And you'll give it to me. You woke the succubus in your half-breed parasite, and you will do the same for me. Then I'll walk away and not look back."

After Ibis left, the silence sat thick and heavy in the cell. Even Ravyn's blood had dried up, no longer hitting the floor with timely pings.

Ravyn's mind raced as she considered her next move, any move at all.

A small, exhausted voice from across the room whispered, "We're going to die here, aren't we?"

Heart dropping, Ravyn couldn't bring herself to answer. Toby didn't deserve a lie, but unless Sebastian came through soon in a big way, they just might. As weakened as she was, she couldn't fight her way out.

Chapter Seventeen

Nevermore

Early morning sunlight began softly filtering through the high windows, offering long shadows instead of darkness. Another night had passed with no visit from their captors, but also no hint of rescue. With a soft click, the door cracked open, drawing their attention, and Ravyn could immediately smell the terror emanating from the young wolf. Toby had slept for hours and hours, barely waking to mumble delirious words, pleading for help from a mouth so dry it would surely crack. Ravyn had listened to his slow breathing for hours, counting the seconds between each breath, while praying to any gods that listened to keep his strength up.

The door slowly swung open, the first sound they'd heard in hours. Their heads shot toward the doorway in panic, but instead of a monster it was the tiny wisp of a woman, the same one who had served them their tainted drinks that evening. Although the wendigo had said it would send his Lilith to tend them, it had been ages since it uttered the words. It didn't appear the creature recognized the passage of time clearly, or perhaps it simply got derailed with chasing the darkness, if Ibis could be believed. Either it had awoken after its long nap or Ibis had sent her in herself.

The wisp floating in was once again covered from head to toe in navy linen that reached down past her fingertips, as well as a hood that wrapped along the bottom side of her face like a shawl.

Ladened with a bucket that emitted a strong bleach smell and a low, sloshing sound, the woman appeared to not even see them as she scurried around the room gathering supplies into a pile on the floor.

Ravyn eyed her suspiciously as she moved toward a spigot on the wall, filling the bucket to the brim with water before struggling to carry the full bucket closer to Ravyn, liquid sloshing over its edges onto the floor. Something about the woman made Ravyn want to avert her eyes, most likely a spell placed on her to avoid visitors examining her too closely. But Ravyn fought against the compulsion to look away, instead keeping her eyes focused solely on the approaching woman.

"Help us. Help him!" Ravyn frantically whispered toward the woman, praying to both her goddess and Fenrir that she had the compassion her master and mistress lacked.

Tooth and Claw

Setting the bucket down, the woman held up a single thin, knobby finger to her own gray lips, miming quietness. Ravyn realized that this woman was missing several fingers; her struggles with the bucket weren't necessarily due to its weight but her own handicap, more than likely imposed on her by the wendigo. The longer Ravyn looked at the bedraggled woman, the easier it was to remain focused on her. The magic that had been laid on her was light enough that if one chose to, they could push through it, but Ravyn suspected that by the time a visitor pushed through the magic it was much too late for them.

Using the same hand, the little woman pushed her long, gray hair back out of her face, tucking it consciously behind one ear. With horror, Ravyn realized that the missing fingers were only one injury that had been inflicted on the woman. This one-eyed woman was the scryer Ibis had discovered and used, the one the wendigo had called his Lilith and Ibis had claimed had a gift for divination.

The wendigo's threat of popping an eye from her head hadn't been made in vain, and even with Ibis's description, Ravyn wasn't prepared for the sight of the bedraggled creature before her. This poor woman's eyelid had been stitched together crudely and healed roughly, poorly. Another scar followed along the side of her face, and Ravyn suspected with horror that she'd been forced to care for her own injuries. Her scarred face was impassive as she began sponging the dried vomit from Ravyn's dress. She scrubbed and scrubbed, spending a bit of extra time running her fingers through Ravyn's soft, black hair once the mess had been cleaned away. Each time Ravyn opened her mouth to speak, the woman would place a finger against her own lips, silently shushing her even as her single fearful eye darted toward the door. Finally, she opened her own lips, showing her missing tongue before shamefully hanging her head, tightening her lips once again before continuing on with her slow, methodical cleaning.

Refilling the bucket with fresh water and more bleach, the woman called Lilith lowered Ravyn's chains slightly to loosen her arms. Gesturing toward the ground, she pantomimed lowering herself. Ravyn hesitated. Could she grab the woman and demand freedom? Even if she killed her, it didn't leave her any closer to freedom. Once again, Lilith urged her downward, followed with a desperate, one-eyed glance toward the door. Ravyn complied for now but regretted her decision when the woman dumped the entire contents of the bucket over her head. The bleach burned her skin and eyes as it trickled down her, the fumes heavy in her nose as she gasped to breathe around the toxins.

"Please," she gasped as the woman made to gather the items and leave the room. "Help him," she pleaded, looking toward the half hanging wolf.

Hesitantly, the woman considered, her broken face

Tooth and Claw

furrowed, pondering in a mixture of fear and uncertainty as she looked at him sadly. With a fervent glance around the room, her mind made up, she complied, lowering the chain that pulled his bloody, maimed hand up and away from him. Once the tension was released, with a pained, animalistic growl, he clutched his mutilated hand against himself, pressing away from her as far as the chains allowed.

With another apprehensive perusal of the room, Lilith impatiently slapped his good hand down, quickly pulling his injured hand free. With unwieldy movements, she roughly held up his bleeding hand to examine it for a moment with her one good eye. Tutting gutturally with her broken tongue, she patted his hand roughly. With efficient and somewhat awkward movements, she wrapped the same towel around the appendage that she'd used moments before to clean Ravyn.

With rough movements, she once again put water in the bucket—this time without adding bleach—and placed it before the trapped wolf. Cupping a gnarled hand, she dipped it into the water before placing it next to the youth's mouth. She repeated the process several times as Toby frantically gulped the drops of water down his parched throat. Lilith glanced fearfully between the door and the wolf before she pulled away to examine her makeshift bandage.

"Thank you," Ravyn whispered as the broken woman applied pressure to staunch the bleeding a bit more, before settling her own fragmented hand ever so gently and briefly on the wolf's tear-stained face before snatching it back.

Soundlessly, Lilith scurried across the room toward the door as if running from the good she'd just done. Once at the doorway, she paused as if considering her next move. Ravyn watched as the woman drew her slight shoulders back, bringing her hunched body up just a hair, as if a decision had been made. Turning quickly as if not wishing to second guess herself, she scuttled as quickly as she could back toward Ravyn until she stood directly in front of her. Her one eye stared at Ravyn with a defiance that had Ravyn shrink back a bit. Maintaining eye contact, she brought her wrist up to her own mouth, viciously tearing into her thin skin with her teeth and drawing blood. Gasping as the scent hit her starving, drained body, Ravyn's fangs burst painfully through her gums. Lilith shoved her thin wrist toward Ravyn's mouth and Ravyn drank deeply from her.

Ravyn felt the woman pushing on her head as she drank. It took several long seconds for her to battle the beast inside her who wanted to drain the woman dry. Panting, she reluctantly released her hold on the woman, who stood before her even paler than before.

Gripping her wrist to staunch the bleeding, Lilith ran from the room, leaving behind her meager cleaning supplies.

And just like that hope returned, flaring up in the

knowledge that not all was lost. Licking the last dredges of blood off her lips, Ravyn could feel the woman's gift strengthen her body as it rolled through her veins.

The wendigo faced the same fatal flaw as her: its ego overwhelmed all. Even its most broken lackey offered kindness to her fellow prisoners.

Slowly, Ravyn twisted her hands in the cuffs that bound her to the beams, cutting into them. As the blood began to flow, she meticulously began working one wrist through the narrow cuff, ignoring the pain.

Toby was silent. Perhaps he slept again; perhaps he simply watched her working herself free in the silence.

As she twisted and turned her hand, Ravyn began speaking as if he could hear her.

"My entire lifetime I've been a bird. Some have known me as Little Bird. I've had variations of Crow and Raven both throughout my life." Twisting and turning, slowly bending tendons and smashing bone, she continued working her way free.

"I even had someone write a poem about me. I mean, I'm certain I've had many poems and stories written about me over the years, but this one might be my favorite. A little-known writer at the time wrote about me. Poe. You've heard of him, right?" Ravyn glanced in the direction Toby lay.

He'd been forced upright for so long that he quite possibility collapsed with exhaustion when his chains had been loosened and the water coursed through his body.

"I think they teach about him in school nowadays.

"I used to visit him in the night and sit in a corner talking with him. Edgar intrigued me; such a quandary of emotions. First, he was afraid of me. Certainly, as one should be when a strange woman all dressed in black comes in through your bedroom window to watch you. But that fear passed and we chatted to pass the time. He thought me an angel or a demon and asked questions about the afterlife, questions I couldn't answer, but together we could guess and wonder. He'd lost a great love and wanted assurances he would see her in the afterlife. He would grow angry with me when I said I didn't know."

One hand free from the deviled silver bindings; not so bad. Ravyn found it easier to ignore the pain and tearing of her flesh while reminiscing. Her storytelling continued after a deep breath, stabilizing her mind and body. She twisted and turned the second hand as the first one knitted itself back together. "Some nights, he would call me Death. because only a beautiful woman could be Death, of course. Some nights, he would cry and beg me to tell him that his love was safe. He both hated and loved me. And he hated himself for loving me. I suppose he felt like he couldn't love more than one."

Ravyn could feel the sun making its path across the sky. Even with the blood given to her, she was still going to be subject to the weakness it caused. She needed to hurry. Time was of the essence and Toby's heart rate had slowed even more while she worked to free herself.

"Sometimes I was an angel, but he settled somewhere in the middle and decided I was his Raven. We talked about things other than life and death. We spoke of love, of war, of peacetime and if it existed or was even possible. As a man at war within himself, he understood conflict all too well. The push and pull between caring too little and caring too much. Poe understood the frailty of mankind or, I suppose, humankind. His work reflected his life, his fears, and his killing of those fears and shortcomings over and over again, attempting to bury them away. But that's not possible; our sins always come back to haunt us."

More wiggling as the wrist band slick with blood slid back and forth. "Almost there," she murmured without looking toward Toby. The best she could do for him right now was to free herself.

"Almost there, Toby."

Chapter Eighteen

Thy hallow beauty in death

Perspiration beaded on Ravyn's upper lip as well as her forehead, as she readjusted her grip on the dead weight of the young wolf. She couldn't remember the last time she'd broken a sweat like this. Most likely it was due to the remnants of the poison still leaving her system as her body fought against it. Perhaps this was what the flu was like? She'd run barefoot from the house of horrors. Her feet would recover from their trek across the coarse, uneven terrain, but despite what others believed the injuries still ached as the skin shredded and blistered. Her injuries from the silver still burned and bled. How many times had they given her poison in her unconscious state? Surely, she shouldn't be so weak and injured still.

With a comatose Toby tossed awkwardly over her shoulder, she questioned the wisdom of ordering him to sleep but knew her discomfort was nothing compared to what the young wolf's would be if he were awake. Carrying him, while ungainly and

Tooth and Claw

questionable, was better than him trying to control his pain and injuries. Despite his size and bolstering, he was still barely more than a pup and untrained, at that. It wasn't until Ravyn had run well away from the house that she dared to stop and consider her next step. Staying hidden in the underbrush, she watched and waited for any sign that they were being followed.

Ravyn slowed her breathing as she strained to hear. The bastard had burst one of her eardrums with his last punch and the whoosh of air in that ear distracted her from possibly hearing what could be around her. Her healing was slow, too slow, and time wasn't on their side. Ravyn suspected that Ibis's time with the twins had introduced her to the ways of subduing vampires for extended periods of time. That sort of thing seemed right along their range of interests. Tilting her head, she quieted her ragged breathing and strained to hear anything out of her good ear, anything at all.

Silence… No birds chirped, no animals rustled in the underbrush. Either they'd all fled or been hunted to extinction by the creature or its minions. No alarm had sounded, so perhaps their escape hadn't been noticed yet—although the estate's alarms could be silent, or the creature could communicate through unseen bonds with those who served it. An entire plethora of reasons could explain the silence, and it was much too soon to celebrate an escape.

A sip of Toby's potent shifter blood, no matter that

it had been given unwillingly, had helped bolster her strength and burn off some of the vervain and wolfsbane. Lilith's willing sacrifice helped even more, but still it wasn't enough to have her at full strength after the poisoning and repeated draining.

Freeing herself, although difficult, had proven to be only the first step. Breaking apart Toby's manacles had been even more difficult. Every time the silver chains moved, they burned deeper into his already tender wrists and neck. Combined with the shock and pain of his maimed hand, forcing him to sleep had been the kindest thing to do. Tearing the bottom of her already ruined dress apart, she'd attempted to wrap strips under the manacles to alleviate as much of the contact as possibly. She didn't dare unwrap his hand to reuse the cloth; she would rather escape completely naked than reopen the wounds on his poor hand.

Even with the protection of the mangled cloth, his body had burned and he'd cried out against the silver as she ripped the manacles apart as quickly as possible. Shame flooded through her as her fangs dropped at the sight and smell of the fresh blood that dripped from his wounds. She couldn't. She wouldn't unless there were no other options. Surely, she had the strength to free them without resorting to taking more from him.

"We've got this Toby, we've got this," she whispered to the unconscious pup as they waited in the underbrush for any sign that their escape was being monitored.

A low whine escaped Toby as his wolf responded to her nearly silent prayer. The creature within him had avoided her compulsion, leaving her feeling a bit less alone when its let its presence be known to her. Laying a clumsy hand on him, she attempted to soothe the beast inside the boy. Her eyes moved quickly over him, making certain that their run hadn't jostled any more injuries. Her knowledge of human health was limited, to be sure, but Toby seemed the same; at least no worse. A bit feverish, warm for even a wolf; the same perspiration that drenched her hadn't left him unaffected either.

The humidity felt so high in the vicinity that if someone told Ravyn they were trapped in a terrarium in full sunlight she would have believed them. The wounds on Toby's wrists and neck seemed to have dried, and the dirty rag wrapped around his injured hand had remained in place.

Keeping low, Ravyn moved through the bushes, keeping her body between the still form of the young wolf and the house. Moving in the direction of the gate seemed like the best option. The grounds of the estate could go on for miles in the other directions, but the gate stood less than a mile away. Still, anything could lie between her and the gate. Although she'd only seen half a dozen of the wendigo's demonic security guards, she couldn't be sure there weren't more. They also seemed short on witches, and Ravyn prayed to the goddess that Ibis and the wendigo hadn't replenished those numbers in the last few hours.

Zigzagging through the undergrowth, Ravyn paused on a particularly dense spot, once again catching her breath as she examined the terrain in front of her, mapping out her next moves and stopping points. *Focus.* Losing focus or panicking could mean the difference between life and death. Prey panicked, and she was too old to be prey; refused to be prey. Never again would she be the young girl led to slaughter. Breathing deeply in and out, Ravyn refused to suppress her rage, imagining it growing as each breath of oxygen fed the tiny spark until it flamed. Fear couldn't grow where rage burned, and it was rage that would keep Toby alive. Even if it killed her, she would get him out. How could she face Sebastian without his nephew? How could she face him when her own arrogance had led to him becoming maimed?

Ravyn held onto the hope that a transformation might still heal the young wolf. Given the chance, surely his fingers would regenerate as Fenrir's magic overtook him? She wouldn't allow herself to consider otherwise. She had to get Toby to Bash.

"Okay, Toby, hold on. We're going to move again," she whispered to the still wolf, once again hoisting him onto her shoulder, adjusting him to fit the best. Her waning strength wasn't the only problem; the youth's size definitely put her at a disadvantage. If the pup were even a few inches taller, he would be dragging on the ground. For the first time in her long life, she mentally cursed her height.

Ravyn had made it just a few steps when a sharp back hand across her face sent her flying back several feet through the undergrowth. Toby's inert body flew in a different direction as she fell despite desperately trying to keep her grip on him.

Without giving herself a moment to even catch her breath, she landed and rolled up lightly onto her feet, her fingers forming claws. She positioned herself so that she still remained between Toby and the wendigo in front of her. Looking at the creature, she opened up her stance, keeping her clawed hands upright as she shifted her weight to a defensive position, expecting the enraged wendigo to immediately launch an attack at her.

Instead, the depraved creature let out a low laugh, showing rows of tiny, viscous teeth, tossing its deer-shaped head back, even exposing its furry neck as it did so in a sure sign that it saw her as weak.

"Awww, my queen," it hissed between peals of gasping laughter. "You are all that I have been promisssed." Laying its beady black eyes back on her, without a care in the world, it brought one blood-stained claw to its rows of sharp teeth. It picked absently at one tooth as it watched her, before removing the claw and flicking a piece of something that Ravyn decided not to imagine onto the ground beside it. The disproportionately long fingers tapped briefly on one another as it watched, waited for her to make a decision.

Bending her knees, Ravyn shifted her weight briefly, as her mind clicked through the possibilities. Run or attack. Neither were a good option. Outside of the wendigo's arrogance, she knew next to nothing about its weaknesses, and more than likely it was as fast as her, if not faster, in her still weakened state. Perhaps she'd made a mistake in not having another sip of Toby's blood? Too late for regrets now.

Despite the fact that she wore the mantle of being one of the oldest original vampires in existence, the creature didn't appear to have even a smidgen of fear of her. Arrogance. A trait they both apparently shared.

"You did not disappoint me." It spoke as though it had expected her to run. Its heavy, antlered head tilted as if considering the possibilities.

Ravyn wondered if it had known what it was doing when it forced Toby's blood into her mouth. But did it know its ranks held a traitor? Or had that been a part of its plan? Every move continued to appear calculated and still she'd underestimated it.

"I wasn't sure if you would take the pup or not," it admitted. "You would have gotten farther without it. Dead weight, that one." It huffed at her with a glance past her to the still silent Toby.

"Is this a game to you?" Finding her tongue, Ravyn bit out the words harshly, barely recognizing her voice, before realizing her nose had been broken.

Tooth and Claw

That would be why her face hurt so badly, but already she could feel the bones ever so delicately reshaping as her innate healing instinctively moved to fix the damage.

Damn, I need more sustenance.

"The biggest," the creature admitted, watching her and apparently expecting some sort of reaction. With a wave of its lanky arm it added, "This is my hunting ground now. Roland, he hunts in the cities, but once he brings them here, it's my turn. This is where their hope turns to despair. This is where they truly find out how badly they want to live." After a pause it added, "They don't live, of course, but some want it much more than others. And some humans want it surprisingly little. Ironic, isn't it?"

Twisting its neck, it waited before Ravyn finally answered, "I suppose."

Yes, yes, it nodded, bobbing its head as if pleased with her reluctant agreement. "I knew you were perfect for me. You see me. Just as the mage claimed."

Was it referring to the decrepit old mage who had kidnapped and nearly killed Eva? Or to the magical remnants of her sister? Ravyn wondered but didn't want to give the creature the satisfaction of her asking. It had been patiently playing the long game, perhaps even before she knew there was a game afoot. Damn her arrogance. The long years had made her lazy and complacent. If—when—she corrected herself, they got out of this mess, she was going to begin training again.

Her muscles already ached from carrying the pup only the short distance. In her prime she wouldn't have broken a sweat, let alone had to feel screaming muscles over such a task.

"Yesss, I regret his losss, and I'll admit, I was so angry when he was gone. But in the end, he served his purpose. He broke those disssgusting bonds with that halfff-blood abomination, leaving you ready for me. I suppose a favor was done. I owe that witch nothing now." A strange chittering sound left its mouth, perhaps a giggle at how things were working out so well.

"Fool he was. Even your sssister's power boost wasn't enough to keep his head attached." It cackled at the idea.

Clicking its nails together as it spoke nearly drove Ravyn to lunge forward to rip the hands from its body. Fighting the urge to count the taps with a sharp shake of her head, she cursed the weakness. Tapping, tapping as it struck each nail against another, clearly in love with the sound of its own hideous, broken voice. But a weakness—it liked to hear itself speak—and Ravyn got information from the wendigo without asking a single question. *Arrogance and ego will be thy death*, she promised.

Spreading her hands to her sides, Ravyn offered, "You could let us leave now, and all is forgotten, forgiven." She mentally spat at the creature, knowing it wouldn't take this offer, but figuring it didn't hurt to ask. "Your mistress is just as likely lying to you, offering me up after I transition her? Sounds suspiciously like she doesn't expect me to break your curse. Using you to help her get what she wants and then in the end you get nothing. I would think eating pure magic might be a better option than my second-rate demon blood."

"Awww, my queen, if only you were as clever as you are beautiful," it cackled with a gurgle. Waggling its hips lewdly at her, it added with a sly hiss, "Thankfully, we don't have to wait till the new moon to completely explore this new relationship of ours." Adding a thrust in case she didn't understand, it watched her carefully. "Our relationship is ssso much more than that. It has been ordained."

Holding her face devoid of expression and steady, Ravyn promised herself that she would rip her own head off before she allowed that creature to touch her. "I would rather not," she declined diplomatically.

The creature began gasping and hissing as mirth overtook it. Bending at the waist as laughter coursed through it, shaking on its deer-like legs as it fought to speak, it gasped the words out, "As ifff you have a choicece."

With a blur so fast that she missed its movement, it appeared in front of her, laughter abruptly cut off. Ravyn gasped in shock at the speed it appeared. Before she could react, it slashed her face with a single claw, cutting her skin to the bone of her cheek and jaw.

Simultaneously, it grasped the front of her tattered dress in the other hand, ripping down to her waist as its talons grazed the skin of her torso. Dropping its voice low, it promised in a new, dark voice, "I could pluck your eyes out before you could react and be inside you before the blood hits the ground."

Unblinking, Ravyn refused to drop her eyes at the horror it suggested. Taking slow, deep breaths as the creature stared back at her in the same unblinking way, she took the time to settle her frantic mind. Insane. The demon within the man was insane. Either it had always been insane, or its time on earth had made it so. Hell, maybe even the vessel it inhabited was the reason for this insanity, but regardless of the reason, it was clear there was no talking her way out of this one. And holy hell, it was fast and quiet. The damned creature didn't make a sound if it didn't want to. Its oversized, ungainly body seemed patched together, but it moved with the finesse and quickness of a honed warrior.

For a moment, they both stood completely still watching each other, separated only by inches. The demon expected her to be cowed by its unexpected move as well as its words. But she'd faced demons much worse than the one standing before her. Her death and rebirth were proof of that.

They were running out of time. The previous soft rays from the sun were beginning to wear upon her as it followed its well-worn path across the sky. Age had gifted her many things, but it also made her weaker against the sun. In the early days, she'd hidden from it in fear. She'd soon learned that it held no power against her, but as the years clicked past that changed. She estimated by the time she was one hundred years old, she'd lost just a few minutes of daylight and at this age, several hours a day of sunlight made her as weak as a kitten or, at the very least, a human. Cloud cover helped considerably, but today's clear sky didn't promise any help against the unrelenting sunlight. Temporary weakness was the price she paid for living in California.

"I have an alternative," she offered, dropping her voice to a husky whisper.

The wendigo tilted its head as if eager to hear her offer, leaning in closer to hear her words. Interesting. Sharp hearing apparently wasn't one of its heightened abilities. What might be interest crossed its face.

Raising her right hand to the blood on her cheek, Ravyn leisurely swirled it around before drawing it down to her neck and running the finger along her throat, down between her breasts. Slowly, patiently. At first, the creature's eyes remained locked on hers but as her hand slid lower, it couldn't help but glance down to follow the bloody trail along the front of her nearly naked body.

Gotcha, Ravyn thought gleefully, casually breathing in and out, careful to keep her face blank as she watched the demon follow her finger. She brought the hand back to her face, swirling it around the blood that now began to congeal on her face, ignoring her throbbing cheek.

The wendigo watched her intently, waiting for her next movement. Haltingly, Ravyn brought her bloodied hand upward to the wendigo's face. She could only reach as far as its jawline. Steadying herself, she ran the finger along its jaw toward its now panting mouth, teasing the blood along its lips as its tongue darted out, trying to capture both the promise of her blood and her teasing touch.

Once again, Ravyn brought the finger to her own face to gather the tempting blood. This time she touched it just to its lower lip, sucking in her own as she gave her offering. From there, she ran the finger down the bottom of its long jaw, lazily, steadily. One of its clawed hands reached out, grabbing her by the hip and roughly pulling her against it; its touch once again nearly froze her to the core. As her hips settled against the creature, Ravyn forced herself to resist the urge to shudder or jerk way. Instead, she allowed a low moan to escape the back of her throat as she brought her hand down the long jawline and lower, where she could feel its throat swallow and pulsate against her touch.

Yes, right there, she thought as she let her claws extend.

With a vicious snarl, she wrapped her clawed hands around the creature's throat, fingers digging into

Tooth and Claw

its skin, breaking through as they grasped the tendons of its throat, tearing and ripping them away from the creature. With a hiss she released her fangs, pulling herself up while her talons held the wendigo in place.

Its eyes grew wide in shock as it frantically tried to push her away. Too late. Her fingers finished their journey through the flesh, grabbing the throat even as it attempted to pull away. With a wild screech, she dug her talons deeper as she simultaneously ripped away at its neck with her deadly fangs.

Deeper she squeezed her talons in and around its neck while ripping away with her teeth. Even as it finally desperately pushed her away, she kept her hold, biting down harder and digging deeper to hold her hands in the bits of sinew and flesh slick with its dark, sickening blood. The sudden spray of blood as its neck popped beneath her hands blinded her, burning her eyes, but she refused to let go, pulling its throat straight away and tossing it to the side even as she fell to the ground. Gleefully, she watched the wendigo's strange dance as it wrapped its oversized hands around the gaping wound that had once been its throat.

Ravyn was certain the look on its face was a combination of shock and panic as it realized what had happened. It was still attempting to hold its neck together as it fell to its knees. Her bloodthirst paused momentarily as she blinked her eyes rapidly to clear them of the creature's blood, unable to tear her gaze away from its downfall.

With fluid, rage-induced strength, she ripped a small sapling from the ground next to her and bounced lightly on her feet. Adrenaline filled her as she bounded back toward the wendigo even as it attempted to staunch the flow of blood from the fatal wound on its neck. Its mouth moved silently as if trying to form words—most likely threats against her. Nothing it said could possibly interest her and without a second thought, she drove the sapling up under its chin and through its head. With one slow blink, then a second, the creature's hands fell uselessly to its sides, head lolling in an impossible way, followed by the rest of its body hitting the ground.

Ravyn watched it briefly before adding a kick to its solid torso. Damn, that hurt her foot, but the creature didn't move again. Dead. It was dead. She and Toby were safe.

With a sigh she looked up at the sky. Closing her eyes, she allowed herself to briefly savor the moment. Wiping the blood away from her face the best she could before wiping her hands off on the remnants of her dress, she swiftly moved toward Toby. His heart still pumped slowly and softly, but he needed medical treatment. He needed the deadly collar off his neck and he needed to shift.

But there wasn't enough time. Already the bright rays of the sun reddened her skin and burned her eyes. Blinking rapidly against the painful glow, she frantically scanned the area for an overturned log or branches short enough to fashion a lean-to thick enough to block the ultraviolet light as well as hide them from the view of Ibis or any minions faithful to the dead wendigo.

Weakened, with an unladylike grunt, she pulled Toby's inert body deeper into the underbrush. The creature had kept the forest floor cleared, most likely to make it easier to tromp after his victims and allow them few places to hide.

Spying the trunk of an evergreen most likely torn from the ground by the wendigo and leaning against another, she hoped it was large enough to hide them both. Its wide roots draped with forest floor dirt and debris offered more protection against the rays than other options. With some effort, she pulled Toby under the macabre canopy, scooping piles of leaves over and around the two of them, knowing that an errant ray couldn't harm Toby but might be detrimental to her if it lingered long enough once the sleep took over.

Hunger gnawed at her stomach. She was beginning to fear that the vervain had put her under for at least an entire day and night instead of hours like she'd first thought. The hunger was too great for only missing a feeding or two.

Darkness overpowered the hunger, weakening her limbs as the sleep of the full sun overtook her.

It has to be enough, was her last thought as she curled herself protectively over the still sleeping pup. *Anything out here will have to get through me before reaching the boy*, she promised anyone who might be listening.

CHAPTER NINETEEN

When the wolf and raven come together darkness reigns

On the evening of the third day since their friends went missing, the team stood outside the impenetrable compound. Reinforcements had arrived, but even with Delta's help they were no closer to gaining entry against the magic. Yet in the end, they didn't need to break through the unrecognizable magic. Apparently going in was the problem, not leaving.

Ravyn burst through the thick undergrowth more beast than woman. *No, not a beast*, Sebastian amended, *a Valkyrie*. A blood-stained warrior of lore carrying a fallen hero to the hall. His wolf howled with relief at seeing her and then abruptly and solemnly cut off the sound. His heart nearly thumped from his chest with simultaneous relief and fear.

Alive. She was alive. Panic followed as he realized that the blood covered-woman carried the too still body of his nephew in her arms, a thick silver collar around his neck. Both bloodied, Ravyn barefoot with her dress barely hanging on her body, they emerged from the estate as if pursued by the hounds of hell themselves.

Seemingly impossible, she cradled Toby in her arms with half his body tossed over her shoulder. Even with her waning vampire strength, she'd brought the youth, twice her size, back from wherever they'd been. As she fell to her knees before the group, they burst into activity. Immediately, the team surrounded her. Armed with both tooth and gun, they protected her back from whatever might emerge from the growth after them.

Sebastian's heart dropped in his chest, fearing the worst for his nephew. So still, too damn still. How could he face his sister, his family, if...

Hanging onto her sanity by a thread, not a hint of white showed up around Ravyn's black eyes. Eyes that searched and found Sebastian's within seconds. Even as she wavered on legs with barely the strength to hold the teen in her arms, she was refusing to let him go.

"Bash," she hissed out with a lisp, her fangs extended as she fought to control her beast from within.

Sebastian realized with horror that her teeth had pierced her lips in her attempts to control her hunger. Instinct and training immediately replaced the combination of feelings that had surged through him when she stumbled out of the wooded overgrowth.

Tooth and Claw

"Help…"

"Medic!" Pushing his feelings down for Ravyn for a sharp, cold thought, Bash barked out orders as two trained medics—one vampire, one wolf—shot forward. The damn vampires had better be prepared to overpower her if needed; that was why they were on the job in the first place. As much as he loved this woman, what stood before him might not feel the same toward him.

Despite the speed of the medics, Bash reached the duo first. Gently he wrapped his arms around his nephew, whom Ravyn refused to immediately release from her tight grasp. Her fangs bit deeper into her lower lip, pinning her mouth closed while releasing fresh blood.

She was barely holding it together, yet she refused to bite the boy.

"Sir?" A voice hesitated, questioning the safety of approaching an almost feral vampire. Bash ignored the warning. Whoever said it didn't know Ravyn and couldn't see how she fought to keep herself under control even as her hunger drove her forward.

"Ravyn," he said gently, "you can let him go now. You brought him home." Relief flashed through him; he could feel the boy's wolf sitting silently watching and waiting, not wanting to antagonize his savior who stood on the edge of a precipice. He was alive. Thank Fenrir, he was alive. "Just let him go and let me take care of both of you."

The vampire medic tore open a bag of blood, and Ravyn's eyes lit up as the smell hit her. She twitched as she sought to find the source of the smell but still refused to let go of her charge. The vamp stepped closer but she snarled at him, lashing out with her teeth as she protectively pulled Toby closer to her breast.

Reaching back, Bash took the bag from the medic and pressed it closer to Ravyn's face. Caught in the lust for blood, her face twitched violently as the bag pressed closer. With a snarl, she released one hand from Toby and snatched the bag from his hand, bringing it greedily to her mouth, suckling the bag even while her eyes darted around the group and she growled at any bit of movement other than Bash's.

"Let me take him," Bash encouraged gently. "We can take care of him." Promises passed his lips even as he gently took Toby from her arms. The boy was so cold, and one of his hands was wrapped in a rag soaked with both old and fresh blood.

Once in his arms, he could feel the slow, steady beat of Toby's heart under his hands. Slow, too slow, but thank Fenrir the boy still lived. Where there was a heartbeat there was hope.

A snarl sounded from behind him as he turned away with his nephew in his arms.

"I'll be right back, Ravyn." This time he walked backward, maintaining eye contact with Ravyn even as she dropped the first blood bag and without looking at

TOOTH AND CLAW

it, greedily pulled another from the hands of the awaiting vampire.

The wolf medic followed, already evaluating Toby, but also being careful to not get between Ravyn and the two. One of his men kindly offered to take Toby from his arms.

"We got it from here, Boss." The emotion was heavy in the man's tone. Tobias had been with the crew for months and there was no way they could remain distant from the outgoing, precocious teen. "Take care of her. If she berserks, I don't think even they can hold her down." He kept his voice low, but still the vamps heard it and the air seemed to shift uncomfortably around them.

Bash realized it was true. In fact, Ravyn's agitation could potentially even set them off. Instead of one berserk original vampire, they could have several others incited by her powerful aura as well.

"Get him to shift as soon as possible, and if you can't get him to, come get me immediately," Bash ordered as he reluctantly handed his young charge over. Emotions had no place on this type of job and right now, he had plenty of them. The witch, Summer, followed the boy closely, already evaluating his injuries and taking action even as she scurried to keep up with the much taller wolf carrying the youth.

Delta remained behind, finally silent for the first time since she'd arrived. She observed the nearly feral Ravyn with hands on her hips, knowing better than to approach the vampire too soon.

Sharply, Bash reminded the vampires among his team, "If you can't control yourself, remove yourself."

The vamp who had given Ravyn the blood bags stiffened his neck and back but said nothing as he handed Ravyn yet another bag.

Already her hunger slowed, and she emptied the third bag less frantically as Bash cautiously retraced his steps to stand near her. Not breaking eye contact, the red outlining the black in her eyes quickly faded. Her black pupils pulsated, fluctuating in size, but also grew smaller with each swallow of her throat.

After the third bag left her lips, Bash could feel the change settle over her. No longer ravenous, her hunger couldn't control her now. "I killed him," her raspy voice scratched out.

The vamp medic held another bag out to her and with hesitation, she reached out to accept it without removing her eyes from Bash. "I killed him," she repeated as she brought the bag haltingly to her lips.

Her blood-encrusted nails were broken to the quick, Bash noted. Knuckles bruised and bloody, and still he couldn't tell whose blood covered her.

"Toby is alive. You didn't kill him." Bash gently cleared her of the blame she obviously was laying upon herself.

"No," Ravyn rasped out. "It. I killed *it*."

"Yeah, girl." Delta's whispered voice carried clearly across the trail and even without looking, Bash was certain she'd followed those words with a fist bump to the air.

He wanted to hush her; nothing was a certainty.

"Toby is alive," Bash reassured her gently, in case Ravyn thought that Toby had been lost to them but hoping, as Delta had assumed, that she meant the wendigo. He reached out to offer her comfort but stopped just before he touched her.

Ravyn removed the bag from her lips. With a quick, sharp shake of her head, she hissed out, "The wendigo. It's dead."

Intently watching Bash through green eyes that now just bled red on the edges, she awaited his understanding,

He rewarded her with a pleased nod. "Good. Nothing less than I would expect from you."

"Too quick," she whispered. "It deserved to suffer. It was a monster." Her eyes flashed red at the anger over his too quick death, but it quickly subsided, and once again she brought the bag to her lips, emptying it. She shook her head no as the vamp offered her another.

Clearing her throat, her voice came out shaky at first. "Could I..." she rasped out, and she coughed before continuing. "Could I request a change of clothes? These are no more use to me. And we still need to find what's left of my sister."

Sister? Bash fought the urge to bombard her with questions but knew that despite her words, her sanity and control were still shaky at best.

Within seconds, unfamiliar clothes passed through hands to quickly reach her. Ravyn flipped open the clothes and as the unfamiliar scent wafted through the air, for the first time she dropped her eyes from Bash's to examine the earth-colored set. She sniffed the air, then dropping her nose to the clothes, Ravyn inhaled deeply, trying to determine whose scent marked the borrowed clothes.

The earthy scent hit Bash's nose, filling it with the newly discovered but unmistakable scent of Kai. For a human, he was silent and soft on his feet. *Even for a werewolf*, Bash mentally amended.

The borrowed clothes belonged to Kai. Of course, he would be the only one who had clothes on hand and even close to Ravyn's size. The young man didn't have the stature of a werewolf, and even his smaller human frame was still larger than Ravyn's.

He didn't have a chance to open his mouth to explain to Ravyn that they'd made a new ally before Kai suddenly stood beside him, much closer to Ravyn than any of the others had had a chance to approach.

"My lady," Kai began even as Ravyn ripped away the rest of her ruined clothes, keeping his eyes focused on her face. "I am Kyle Tarkirk." Glancing up at Bash, he continued, "I'm called Kai."

Pulling the shirt on over her head, Ravyn interrupted, "Tarkirk? You're of the moon?" Glancing between the two, she began rolling the long sleeves to her wrists as she took in the young man standing before her. She glanced at the symbol of Fenrir tattooed on his wrist. "You're a friend of the wolves?"

Clearly, the name meant more to Ravyn than it did Bash, but he continued to keep his focus on Ravyn as she now began pulling the well-worn joggers over her hips. His surprise from seeing the two exit the compound was being replaced by the familiar feelings of failure. He hadn't been there for the two of them. Time and time again, he wasn't there for those that he cared about.

"My family name is the moon, yes. And at one time we were one with the moon and wolves, but it's been many years since my people were a friend of the wolves. But I hope that can change now," Kai added diplomatically as Ravyn pulled the string in the waistband tight and knotted it. She folded the band down, looking around, then down at her feet with a strange expression as if for the first time realizing she stood barefoot before them.

"If I may?" offered Kai, gesturing toward her feet.

Nodding, Ravyn stood still as the young man kneeled in front of her.

He reverently picked up each of her small feet and deftly encased them in leather that formed around them as he expertly looped thin straps of it around her feet and ankles. Leaning back on his heels, he examined his work with satisfaction. "These were my mother's," Kai whispered. "She would be honored to share them with you."

Ravyn looked down at her feet before softly placing a bloody, dirty hand on the young man's shoulder.

Kai flinched briefly at the unexpected touch. He'd been out here alone for too long, Bash noted with anger at the torch the boy had picked up with the death of his father.

"I thank you, Kai, friend of the wolves and one who serves the moon." Ravyn's voice came out softly and clearly. "I am in your debt," she added, making it clear that not only was he a friend of the wolves, but hers as well.

Nodding ever so slightly, cheeks flushed, Kai stood back up. "They've got your pup to shift twice. Your medics and the witch have been working on him. He's resting now." Reluctantly he added, "They've stopped the bleeding in his, um, his hand, but the fingers didn't regrow. It sounds like that was a possibility, but the demon's bite did too much damage. Its saliva is poison designed to torture and destroy. I've added what I could to his healing, and he'll live. Someone drew a sigil on his wrist after the bite. That prevented the poison from spreading and causing more damage."

Bash met Kai's eyes. He hadn't known the extent of Toby's injuries, but he trusted his people would do everything possible to heal his nephew. Guilt surged through him even as he tried to reassure himself.

Losing some fingers was better than being dead. Gulping, he asked, "How many fingers?"

"Two. Forefinger and middle finger. There's some damage to his hand, but he'll heal. He's strong. His wolf is strong, and Fenrir has watched over him."

"The demon had a servant whom I doubt served of her own free will. She must have done it when she wrapped his wrist."

"Whatever she did saved him from even more damage," Kai assured them before focusing on Ravyn. "How did you incapacitate the wendigo? No one has ever escaped from his compound."

"Not incapacitate. I killed him. There's no coming back from having your head removed from your shoulders and a spike rammed through it as well." She looked around the makeshift camp sitting outside the gates that just days ago had appeared so welcoming. "Bash, I'm sorry. I'm so sorry. The driver. Mark," she amended, reminding him once again that one of the vamps had accompanied her inside. "They ripped him apart. I'm so sorry, but they ripped him apart. I found the ash."

She trailed off, clearly not wanting Bash to know how she knew Mark had been ripped apart, but he could imagine. He offered a silent prayer to Fenrir to guide the fallen vamp in the afterworld. Smashing down the feeling in his heart, he reminded himself that all of his men knew the risks. They knew what they'd signed up for, and while the pay was good and the danger rare, it was still there.

"My lady," Kai began again, reluctance filling his voice as he attempted to interject.

"Call me Ravyn." The voice that came out sounded more like the Ravyn he knew, and Bash realized with a flash of anger that the dark imprints around her neck weren't dirt or shadows but bruises from where the creature had crushed her vocal cords. If the damn unholy thing wasn't so dangerous, he would have ordered a necromancer to revive it so he could kill it again. Any death was too quick for the damage it had inflicted on Toby and Ravyn, as well as countless other victims who hadn't been so lucky. How long had that creature hunted and preyed on innocent victims? How many unmarked graves were hidden on this property? And how had the thing lived among them undetected for so long?

"Yes, ma'am. Ravyn. I'm sorry to say the wendigo is alive still," Kai reluctantly but confidently informed her as well as the entire group.

The men shifted, refocusing their attention once again to the perimeter of the area. Those who weren't guarding the perimeter snapped their attention to the young man in disbelief. Not many creatures could withstand a beheading, and this youth was claiming a wendigo was one such being.

Sebastian felt his skin ripple at the words as his wolf fought to break free, wanting to bash its body against the magical forcefield until it could break free and rip the wendigo limb from limb. Closing his eyes briefly, he asked the wolf to stand down. *The time will come*, he promised the creature.

"It's more powerful than you can imagine. The body is just a host, ultimately unstoppable with the deal that was struck," Kai explained hesitantly as the tension flared briefly through the group before they each reined in their emotions. "It's the demon that he invited in that keeps the body functioning and pasted together. To truly kill the demon is *impossible*. But with a specific ritual, we can divide the demon into pieces and trap its parts in what are essentially magic jars."

Bash realized that the boy was giving the dumbed down version of events, and he raised an eyebrow, silently asking him to continue.

"The ritual is a part of the process, but there are a lot of moving parts," Kai explained. "Traditionally, my tribe supplied the hunter and the shaman to perform the ritual." He looked down as if embarrassed. "As the last member of my tribe, I took the mantle of both, but doing them both is impossible," he clarified. Looking at Bash, he continued, "We need a wolf to wield the blade to separate the creature, as well as any extra muscle we can find. Teams in the past might have had more wolves, and a witch as well. I've never heard of a vampire being a part of a team, but I would welcome any help."

His words hung heavy in the air, thick with both

promise and hope. The wendigo wasn't dead, and the young man needed help to make it so, and until its demise was certain, Ravyn as well as anyone else who crossed its path wasn't safe.

Holding a hand out toward the youth, Bash promised solemnly, "I will honor the agreement that your ancestors and Fenrir made."

Kai reached his own hand out, relief crossing his face as they grasped forearms, sealing their agreement.

"I, as well, will see this abomination dead or trapped or whatever it is we do. I look forward to killing it again, as it deserves," Ravyn promised with anger flaring in her eyes. "How many times have you preformed this ritual?"

Good question, and one that Bash was afraid he knew the answer to before the boy spoke.

"Never," he admitted, lips tight and eyes flashing as they flitted uncertainly around the group, as if their promise of help depended on his ability to complete the ritual. "I've practiced it since I could walk and talk, and theoretically I could do it in my sleep, but…"

With a solemn if not confident nod, Ravyn accepted the answer as her jaw tightened. "It looks like we're all getting a few firsts here. How do we do this?"

"In a nutshell? With perfect timing. Timing is imperative here. It can burn through magic in minutes, maybe even seconds. We need to reach between its teeth, down its throat, and pull out its fucking, frozen heart and burn it to ash. At the same time, we divide the body into pieces and trap it forever."

Chapter Twenty

Union of the wolf and raven shall bring glory to the battlefield

Although still gray, Toby had regained a bit of his color and his breathing was slow and deep along with a now steady heartbeat. Bash needed to reassure himself with his own eyes that his charge was at the very least stable, before he sent the boy, a medic, and another wolf back to his apartment where treatment could continue without them having to constantly look over their shoulders.

The wave of guilt that washed through him as he watched the teenager breathe in and out nearly brought him to his knees. He was responsible for his nephew, and he knew that since the boy's father died, he'd been taking too many risks, yet he still hadn't discouraged his involvement with the team. His sister-in-law had made a huge mistake entrusting him with Toby's safety. No wonder Fenrir never offered him a mate; he didn't deserve one. If gods had any fairness about them, they would have left James on the earthly side of the veil. Then none of this would have happened. With a low whine, his wolf tentatively reached out to offer praise and reassurance to the boy's wolf.

The wendigo would die, they both promised.

But that was easier said than done. Ordering the witch, Summer, to stay and form a sound barrier from their group and the outside world had been the last simple order Bash had issued. Despite Kai's knowledge of the wendigo, an attack wasn't as simple as a full-frontal assault. The creature had had decades of time to build the compound, and it could simply lie low until they left. Despite Ravyn making her way out of the compound, neither she nor anyone else could make the return trip. The magic trapping them outside still held.

Used to leading the team but clearly not the expert, he allowed Kai and Ravyn to talk possibilities and strategy while he simply listened, soaking in Ravyn's bits of information on the compound's layout and manpower while his mind ticked through any discarded possibilities. His admiration for the both of them grew as he listened. Despite his youth, Kai was confident and knowledgeable about the wendigo, especially this one. Unable to destroy the creature on his own, he'd used the time to gather intel, learning its habits.

As Ravyn listened intently to the shaman, adding her own insights as well, Bash could see the calculating warrior from years gone by staying firmly in the forefront of her actions. This lifetime had allowed Ravyn to pursue acting as a career, but it was easy to forget that even that was an act. First and foremost, she was a shrewd predator and at the least, a battle-hardened warrior. Could he ever learn all the layers she possessed?

Just a few hours before it began its final descent over yet another day, the sun was ticking off the need for timeliness of their attack. The closer they came to the new moon, the stronger the creature became. The night allowed the strength of the vampires to rise and the wolves, just days off the pull of the full moon, were still at almost full strength themselves. There was no chance of successfully waiting the wendigo out, and if it went on the run, they might never find it again. A creature its age hadn't survived without its wits, and the crafty thing surely had other funds as well as hidey holes to sink down into. Cutting off its current funds was simple enough, definitely an easy assignment for Oliver's side of the security business. Tracking down other sources of revenue and accounts wouldn't be as simple, but a team was already working on it. Bertrando Roland would exist no more one way or another.

"We need to focus on its weaknesses," stated Ravyn, much to Kai's frustration. "And we need to bind the demon Ibis's power."

Delta interjected, "I doubt that Ibis is currently a problem. It sounds like by killing the other witches and mage on staff, you've effectively neutered her. At least temporarily. Her magic is utterly useless unless she has someone to channel or boost. At this point, she's a side quest. The living magic that formed and entwined her needs to be unraveled, but despite her hatred of you, Ravyn, she's completely defenseless."

Delta didn't seem to have any qualms about battling the black magic that had kept Ibis alive as well as warding the place against their every attack. In fact, at the news of a powerful witch abomination, she'd nearly shaken with the glee of taking down the creature. Delta was an odd one, but Oliver trusted her with his life as well as the life of his mate, and if he trusted her, then Sebastian could do no less.

Bash hadn't fully understood Ravyn's explanation that perverted demon magic had kept a part of her sister Ibis alive. The sweet Anya he'd met would never have made the choices and decisions that her dark side had, and wrapping his mind around it had been difficult. Unfortunately, the remains of Ibis had fed on and used the connection that she held on Anya to manipulate the woman into seeking out Ravyn and placing a talisman in her home.

Whatever talisman she'd planted had weakened their resolve and given the creature yet another crack back into Ravyn's home. The wards were designed to keep out those who wished to harm Ravyn, but Anya had no such designs. She was simply another tool used by Ibis to get what she wanted.

"Of course we do," Kai hissed out, responding to Ravyn's words as he rubbed a frustrated hand across his eyes. Bash had noticed early on that he was clearly not used to working with others but was trying. "The damn thing just doesn't have any that we can use."

"Wrong," Ravyn insisted, and Bash noticed that despite their disagreements, she didn't attempt to control the youth or squash his thought process. "We do know some." Ticking off on her fingers, she listed, "First, the thing is all ego; it literally thinks we can do nothing to it. That ego is a huge weakness. Second, we know that however it's controlling its minions isn't all that great. Clearly, it doesn't inspire loyalty; its housekeeper or slave wouldn't have given us help. And the damn thing is obsessed. It's so fixated on me it can't see straight. Since it began its stalking of me, it has made more mistakes than it probably has over the entire course of its lifetime."

Since the Donner Party attempted to cross the mountain, Bash mused after Ravyn had shared its origins nearly two hundred years ago. All that time, it had been quietly living in California, killing off its only known enemy as well as countless victims without a hint of it wafting to other parts of the paranormal world. It had grown confident and careless with its hunger for all things.

"I think Ravyn's right…" Bash finally allowed the words to leave his mouth.

The two turned, a surprising and questioning look

passing between them before settling on him.

He continued with a deep breath that caused his wolf to whine as if begging him to not say the words, but they both knew this was their best chance. "Ravyn needs to draw it out. It's obsessed enough to try to recapture her and egoistical enough that it thinks it easily can. And for all we know, it still thinks that we think it's dead. But the longer we hang out here, the more it's going to realize we aren't just considering the best way to destroy the compound. No slash and burn operation takes this long to formulate."

The fake voiceovers that added to their cover could easily be discerned if one listened long enough and if the limited pattern repeated itself enough, even the demon would recognize the illusion for the time-stopper it was.

"Getting out of its lair isn't the problem. We need to be allowed in."

Bash hated himself for saying the words. He, as well as his wolf, wanted to protect the dark-haired woman with their dying breath, but they also knew that Ravyn didn't need protecting. Their team had always been in place to make her life easier and to keep her secrets hidden, but not to protect her; never to protect her—until this wendigo turned it all upside down.

Then, not caring who watched, he did what he'd been wanting to do since the moment Ravyn had emerged from the tree line in all her glory. Looking deep into her eyes, he pulled her close and kissed her while the others watched in surprised silence. At that moment, Bash didn't care who knew or who saw. If he waited until they were alone, the moment might never come.

For a half a second, Ravyn stood frozen against him before she relaxed into his kiss, wrapping her arms around his neck to pull him down closer, melting into him.

Drawing back, he closed his eyes as he leaned his forehead on hers. "I thought I'd lost you," he admitted quietly, knowing that all those around them with enhanced hearing could hear his admission.

"I'm not going anywhere," Ravyn vowed, "and this time won't be the same at all. I don't need to come back; you just need to come with me."

The creature, the wendigo, would pay for maiming his nephew and torturing his mate. *"Mate,"* his wolf growled, ready to spill blood for Ravyn, and Bash wasn't about to argue semantics with himself before going into battle.

At that moment, Sebastian understood the fear and agony Fenrir himself had felt when his own mate was threatened by the other gods. Nothing could stop the flood of vengeance.

Chapter Twenty-One

Their loyalty tied them together as deeply as their love

They spent the remaining daylight arguing the specifics. Well, Bash, Kai and Ravyn did.

After Ravyn again explained how the talisman had been snuck into her home by a work around and subtly weakened her wards, Delta nodded and listened intently.

"Definitely something we can work with," the witch informed the group. "It bypassed the wards by not being intended to cause harm. And then once it was on the inside, it weakened the wards, allowing other items to slip through, creating a larger crack each time."

Anger rolled off Sebastian, who seethed at the supposed negligence of the security team—his team, the one for which he alone was responsible. But there was no point in beating himself up over it. Mistakes had been made by all of them.

Ravyn reminded the group that Anya knew

nothing about the incident and that somehow a connection still lingered between her and the leftover magic from her transformation back to human. If anyone was a complete innocent in this, it was Anya. Anya and Toby anyway. No matter what happened, Ravyn demanded assurances that Anya would remain safe.

Ravyn watched as Delta considered the talisman and how it had merely weakened intent and resolve. "Simple, but effective," Delta admitted with a grudging respect. "And the carrier had no idea she was doing it, effectively hiding it even more. We could do the same. It wouldn't even need to be that elaborate."

Delta paced the small dirt area hidden from view as she thought aloud. "The wards are actively keeping people out, but they don't appear to have alarms or any other sort of deterrent.

"I think we could get this wendigo to carry in a similar item. Something that cracks through the magic even temporarily, but big enough..." Pausing, she looked toward the sky. "Ah, yes, now that I've seen and recognize this magic, I can *see* it. I'll be back for you."

The group looked at each other in confused silence at Delta's promise but didn't interrupt her train of thought.

Her words didn't make sense to the others, but Delta rarely did. She spent several moments quietly but animatedly discussing options and possibilities with Summer, who did seem to understand Delta's words and a possible plan.

No one mentioned the kiss.

Bash and Ravyn had slid back into tactical mode, although she brushed against him more often, and she noticed he didn't stand quite so far away. Ravyn couldn't help but steal glances at her tall guardian as he mapped out the plan in hushed tones despite the fact that they were inside a quiet bubble. To anyone outside of the bubble, the group appeared to be arguing in loud tones with wild gestures, while the rest of the camp seemingly packed up as if to leave within the hour or less.

Delta muttered as she traced the empty space in the air around the compound, seeing things only she could see and talking to things only she could hear. She occasionally barked off an order to Summer, who dutifully wrote down her instructions in a small, spiral-bound notebook.

Ravyn would be the first to admit that Delta was a bit of a strange thing. Something about her birth was apparently off-putting to her coven, but her mother, Hecate, had squashed any opposition to Delta's continued survival. Ravyn had spent enough time with Hecate that she'd spotted the young woman over the years, beginning as a small child poking into the air, muttering and moving bits and pieces of nothing around. Strange, but Ravyn honestly didn't care enough to determine why Delta was such an oddity beginning from birth. She was powerful in ways Ravyn didn't understand and that, she could appreciate and respect.

Finally closing the notebook as Delta turned to walk away, Summer bowed her head toward Delta in respect. "Your words to our Mother Goddess, Maiden."

At those words, Delta's attention snapped back to Summer, harshly whispering, "I'm not the Maiden."

"I apologize, but your mother..." Summer's confidence was once again squashed as she whispered her apology.

"Never mind who my mother is." Delta softened her voice. "My sister is the Maiden. I'm just Delta. Always Delta."

"Put me down, you bastard!" Ravyn screeched as she fought against the vamp who had her casually tossed her bound body over his shoulder, strolling toward the gate. "I demand it of you." She dropped her voice a notch to remind the vampire who and what she was.

Trussed up like a Christmas turkey, her kicks barely registered against his unyielding body. Normally even a spelled rope couldn't have held her, but multiple layers would take her several minutes to get out of. Yet that was all she needed; if they'd really wanted to keep her subdued, silver chains would have been the better choice, just as the wendigo had used.

Tooth and Claw

One of the benefits of getting older was that, while the sun did drain her, silver definitely didn't have the same hold over her body it once had. It burned her and held her, but as she'd done within the creature's prison, she could still break free from it. And since there were so few ancient vampires, even fewer would hold their secrets.

Lifting her head from banging against from the unyielding vampire's back, she pleaded with Bash, who strolled along several feet behind them, his face a line of anger. "Please, it was an accident. You know I would never hurt the pup."

In disgust, Sebastian spat on the ground. "I suppose you never mean it, but nonetheless, it's still what you do. You're careless with our lives, and no money in the world is worth trading on the cost of my nephew's life." Pointing a sharp finger toward her, he reminded her, "It was you who brought him here! He should have never been anywhere near this place—or you."

Her head dropped to the vampire's back before she raised it back up. This time her face kept the view hidden, but she knew Bash still followed. "No, no, it's not like that."

Sebastian had reluctantly admitted to himself that his wolf wouldn't allow him to carelessly hand Ravyn back off to the enemy. Sadly, it was still confused and stubbornly determined that Ravyn was their mate. It was better for all if another vampire subdued and

275

tossed her out of the group, rather than have Bash fight his own wolf for the privilege of doing so.

"It is, though. Your ego is what has us here. You thought you could handle everything, and you took a child into the home of a demon. I'm done with this and I'm done with you."

Closer now, he gathered her hair up with one hand and the hatred in his eyes burned down to her soul—if, in fact, she still had one. She hoped she did. Ravyn tried not to remember that these were the same hands that had touched her so reverently just days ago. The same eyes that had worshiped her. Pulling her head up so they were eye to eye, his next words chilled her.

"This is it; you will pay for what was done to my nephew, but it won't be by my hand. They will be clean—unlike yours."

"Dammit, you're all paid to guard me!" she screeched to Sebastian's chilling face, including the entire group in her reminder. "Oliver will kill you all for this," Ravyn promised the group.

His words twisted a knife in her heart. It was true. She was responsible for Toby's injuries and he was lucky to be alive.

A dry laugh barked out of Sebastian. "As if Oliver will know how anything goes down," he countered. "He'll pat me on the back and thank me for our attempts. Then he'll go back to his lover's bed and forget you ever existed.

"Roland! Ibis! Whoever the fuck is here!" he

bellowed, raising his arms as he turned in circles before looking at the camera. "She's all yours! We want no part of this, and we expect it to remain that way." Silence followed, which he took as acceptance to the offer.

With a sharp nod to the vamp, he carelessly tossed Ravyn to the ground inches from the gate.

Then the gate eased opened.

Ravyn's heart sank. After everything she'd done to escape the creature, here she was, tossed right back into its lair.

"Please," she begged softly, still trussed and struggling against the ropes, but rising to her knees. "Please, you don't understand what he plans to do to me." Looking over her shoulder at the empty gate looming behind her, she offered, "I'll do anything, everything. I'll give you anything. Just don't—"

"It's done." Sebastian spat the words at her, adding in a low voice, "There is nothing you have that I want, except this." Drawing a foot back as if to kick her, he paused, considering, before turning without another word.

Silently, the team moved to their remaining vehicles. Sebastian had instructed the one who had left earlier with his nephew to not bother returning. Dust filled the air as the vehicles spun out back along the road, leaving Ravyn alone as a sacrifice to the creature.

Fighting her restraints, Ravyn managed to free her

hands before frantically attempting to unravel the mass of rope and knots that kept her feet and legs immobile. Looking around, she considered the possibilities of escape, and how much time she had before the creature came to gather its prize.

Not enough.

"Come with me, my love," it beckoned with its long fingers, nails still stained with the blood of its last victim. That blood could be Toby's, she realized as it impatiently picked at its teeth again. Better yet, it was now its own blood staining its nails from trying to hold its head on its neck. It remained inside the gate, just feet from her. Despite its ungainly, oversized body, it moved quietly. Its skeletal deer head turned to the side as it watched her consider the options.

"Burn in Hades!" Ravyn spat at him, not allowing the terror in the pit of her stomach to grow larger than the knot it currently was. What if this was, in fact, the plan? Sacrifice her and the others could move on with their lives? No, Sebastian wouldn't do that to her, and even in the short time she'd spent with Kai, she knew his own personal system wouldn't allow him to leave her behind—or the creature to live. The plan was the plan. No more and no less. Still, she pulled at the ropes binding her legs, knowing that freedom wasn't possible.

"Do you think creatures like us have friends? Loyalty? We have food. You know that, although you deny your true self. In our world, you are either eaten or eat." It hesitated, as if considering its words. "Although you will find that what you are will transcend both. You will be the prey *and* the predator. The meal that will fill me." Its words clipped out without hesitation in a familiar voice, but one she couldn't quite identify. It didn't matter. The creature only had its imitation, and she promised herself that it would die soon enough.

Despite the ropes still tightly binding her, Ravyn attempted to stand, but all she managed to do was scoot across the gravel of the road. The wendigo silently watched her, tapping its fingers against its taunt upper thigh, impatiently waiting for her to accept the inevitable. Gasping for breath as if vervain had once again altered her system, weakening her, Ravyn struggled to begin unwinding the carefully tied knots.

The wendigo had different ideas about that, though. It bounded forward on long, sinewy legs, seeming to lengthen with each step faster than her eye could track. Once again, it backhanded her across the face so hard she would have flown across the drive if the snickering creature hadn't snatched her up in the same moment. Wrapping one arm around her head and neck, its fingers splayed across her mouth and nose, promising to break her neck if necessary. Frozen in place, Ravyn considered the possibilities. Damnation, it was fast.

She could recover from a broken neck, but that would take time; time she might not have. Struggling against him in such a position promised to leave her more vulnerable for the next few hours. Better to wait and watch.

"As enjoyable it is to watch you struggle and pretend there is hope, I would rather leave you in the ropes your lover tied you in." Tilting its head, it asked, "How did that feel? How did it feel for someone to know you intimately and then turn on you?"

Ravyn seethed silently, promising the creature death with her eyes.

"You are alone. You have no one, outside of me. This is your destiny, the reason you were made," the crazed creature gurgled in her ear as it drew her closer against its body. Its rough skin was cold and unforgiving against her own. "And if you fight me, I won't be nearly as forgiving as your wolf," it promised with a hiss, drawing her even closer as it felt the fight leave her body.

It wasn't difficult to feign weakness and hunger in the face of this demon. It moved quickly and efficiently, knocking away her fight as if taking building blocks away from a toddler.

Tossing her carelessly over its shoulder, it knocked the air out of Ravyn. She was unable to catch her breath as, with spinning leaps and bounds, it followed the path back into the bowels of its domain.

Depositing her gently, almost reverently on the floor, this time not bothering to restrain her, the wendigo paced the length of her jail cell. "You let a perfectly good meal go ffffree," it chided as though she were a child who had neglected her vegetables. "And you destroyed many of my people."

At least now she had confirmation that those in the guard house were dead and not coming back. To be honest, unless she saw them transform into wendigos, she couldn't be sure if they were possessed by such creatures or if they were simply evil men. Kai had suggested that wendigos were solitary, greedy creatures that had never been known to share their domain with another, but despite the youth's knowledge of them, she truly only trusted what was right in front of her. Trust had never been her strong suit; for so many years it was her and her alone. Ravyn prayed to the goddess that she hadn't made a mistake in counting on others now.

"You will die," she promised the creature from her place on the floor, testing her limbs to see if any had been broken in its careless handling of her.

The creature smirked, if that was possible, while looking at her. "So I've been told. Perhaps someday, but that day is not soon. But you. You may wish you were dead, but you are immortal flesh." Smacking its lips, it added, "It will fill me; it will satisfy the hunger."

With calculated steps it crept toward her, slowly extending a claw as she shrank back into the unforgiving concrete. Then, with movements quicker than her eyes could follow, it snapped forward to snip the ropes that wrapped her legs from knees to ankle with one precise movement.

"You really believe that? She sold you a line of bull; all she's worried about is herself," Ravyn spat out. "And if you want free of this curse so badly, why don't you drop yourself into the Houska gateway and take that bitch you serve with you."

"Agh, I do not serve her. She is a tool. Nothing more and nothing lesss," it hissed. "You think you know the gateway?" It paced around the room. "You know nothing. My brethren crawl out of there, but we do not return through the gateway. It is a one-way trip. Hell couldn't take back your sissster or me even if it wanted to."

"Not true!" Ravyn shook her head insistently. "Travelers can journey both ways." She thought she saw a flash of movement out of the corner of her eye. Shifting her eyes the opposite direction, she imagined they were still alone and that nothing and no one else dwelled in the darkened room with them.

"You've heard the legends, the lies. The gateway only allows creatures out or separates truth from lies, but those lies are still freed into the world. Once we come to this plane, there is no going back. Going back only ensures we are ripped apart and tossed back into the world. Only those with special access can make the journey both ways, and those routes are not known."

"Did you come from that gateway?" What had started as a measure to delay the creature had inevitably spiked her curiosity. Had the evil taken from her sister been tossed back into the world to continue tormenting it? Anya had seemed so certain that the evil within her had been forced through the gateway back into hell, but never did she hint that it might have escaped to live among them in a different form. Did she know? Had the twins known even then and kept it from her, so they could study and experiment on what remained?

"I came through *a* gateway," the creature hissed enigmatically, as it tossed the blood-stained chains that had held Toby to the side of the room.

"There is more than one gateway?" Despite the fact that Ravyn had only just recently learned of the existence of one such gateway, the probability of more than one left her shocked.

How many doorways to hell does a world need?

Another flash of movement opposite the monster caught her eye, but she refused to acknowledge it and kept focused on the decaying creature in front of her.

Pausing its pacing, the creature hissed with a scoff, "Of courssse. Do you have only one way to exit your home?" Twisting and turning, it looked up at the bar-laden windows high off the ground and small enough that even Ravyn couldn't contort her way through them. The beast was cleaning and securing her cell, Ravyn realized with dread. In some weird way, it was making a home of sorts for her, clearly planning for her to stay here indefinitely. Despite being discovered by the team, it was so certain that they were no threat to it, that it wasn't bothering to move on from this lair.

"Right, but I can get back into my home any time I want."

It didn't fear her either, Ravyn realized as the creature turned its back on her, inspecting the room as if uncertain how she'd escaped from it before, surely not realizing that it had aided her itself when it forced Toby's blood past her lips. She hoped that the woman who had tended to Toby's wounds and traced the healing rune still lived. She couldn't bear to be responsible for another death and was certain that the woman was as much a trapped victim as she was.

Another flash from the other side of the room. Hope bloomed in Ravyn; they certainly weren't alone. Once might have been her hopeful imagination, but three times was a certainty. The plan was still the plan.

For a moment, she allowed herself to imagine the coffee beans, round and brown and scattered across the cool, white granite of her table. In her mind, she began counting them, deliberately and in control. *One, two, three, four, five.* She blocked out the grunts of the creature as it stacked and shuffled items and rambled on about goddesses and queens. When she reached fifty-six, she let out a slow breath. It was time.

Almost immediately, her suspicions were confirmed with a flash so bright it temporarily blinded her. She shut her eyes tightly against it as smoke filled the room. Summer had warned her that both were to be expected, but still Ravyn couldn't help the immediate adrenalin rush that hit her bloodstream. Her fangs dropped, preparing her for whatever was to come next.

Within seconds, a *whoosh* sent her across the room, bashing her into the wall while the smoke cleared out, leaving behind a room well-lit with tall, thick white candle and an enraged, howling beast.

The hit was hard. It took a second to pull air back into her lungs, and for seconds more all she could see were stars. Ravyn could feel her pupils dilate as they quickly adjusted to the room's new lighting.

"Sorry about that." Delta gave a little wave from across the room as Ravyn allowed herself a sigh of relief. Despite the plan, the words and actions as the team had left her had felt so real, and a small part of her recognized that they could leave her and a whole slew of problems behind a whole lot easier. But they hadn't. Bash stood to the side, warily alternating between looking at her and watching the monster beat against the invisible walls of its trap. A smug Delta stood, hands raised, holding it in place.

The cloaking spell had worked. The sigil spell had worked, a temporary means to hold the deadly creature was in place. The team hadn't let her down or left her behind.

Leaving her behind had been a combination of illusion and truth. Kai, Bash, Delta, and Summer had silently followed them to the cell, laying a trap as the demon paced. They'd drawn the five-pointed star on the smooth concrete floor and quickly filled it in with the sigils that Summer had taught the two men. Despite not knowing the magic or what the sigils meant, Summer and Delta assured the group that the intent would still remain, and the witches would do the rest.

Kai placed jars at the points of the star that wavered into view as the spell dropped, careful not to damage the lines while the beast screamed and beat on the unseen walls, shrieking in anger and sputtering promises of a slow, painful death.

Silently, Ravyn easily stood. Once again, the creature's ego had seen her as helpless and less than despite its claiming it desired her due to her power and strength. Her eyes flickered over the unknown sigils on the floor. How the witches remembered what each one meant and did was beyond her despite the fact that magical sigils had shaped her life since the beginning. The five-pointed star's lines were thick and black, carefully shaded in so that not even the tiniest break could allow the demon to slither free. The sigil lines were thick in spots and thinner in others, forming swoops and angles connecting at edges before fading off, again carefully drawn and shaded to keep the creature trapped at least for a few minutes while Summer laid out a more complicated spell designed to hold the wendigo for the ritual.

Tooth and Claw

The ritual was designed to tear the demon apart before containing it indefinitely—assuming Kai's untried spells worked as they should.

Ravyn had to trust that the other wolves who had also crept inside the compound had done their job and were destroying the remaining lesser demons or evil men. Just as Anya's spelled talisman had allowed a small break in her home's wards, the spelled ropes had created an entire pathway through the demon's well placed wards. In single file and under a temporary invisibility spell, they'd silently marched right into the compound, set on destroying the creature's entire lair.

The most difficult part was still before them, and Ravyn blocked the others out of her mind, intent on focusing on the upcoming ritual. Each of them had to have faith that the others could do their own part and, in turn, each of them had a responsibility to focus on their own part. Distraction was all that stood between life and death.

Chapter Twenty-Two

Then death lay its gentle kiss upon her lips

Summer's incantations rose above the clattering and banging coming from the trapped creature. Both witches' hands moved in finite details, quickly flashing through the carefully choreographed movements. Despite not knowing the language, the intent was clear to Sebastian as well as the demon, which struggled even more, vigorously beating against the demon trap.

Already minutes into the operation, the walls around the trap trembled and shook, shimmering under the candlelight as the powerful wendigo, shaking with anger, beat on the invisible walls. All they needed to do was hold for a few more minutes while Delta and Summer secured it and Kai began the ritual.

It paused its momentary beating on the trap to examine the small group within the cell before its evil eyes settled on Kai, who was bent over, laying ancient words on the each of the jars.

"Oh, young Kai Tarkirk, how you've grown. So

handsome, my young nemesis," the creature cooed in a man's voice that Bash didn't recognize, but Kai clearly did.

Kai's dark neck flushed while his jaw tightened, but he continued to do his best to ignore the creature. "You've been busy trying to keep my meals from me. What a merry-go-round that has been, seeing your feeble attempts to save those girls who beg to come visit me. Were you jealous? Did you wish to share the women?" Its voice dropped to a whisper as it taunted him.

The voice shifted to a higher pitch to question the group. "Did the boy not tell you? Yes, I met his father." Its voice once again dropped, deepening before it bellowed, "Aw, yes, I sucked the blood and marrow from his bones after I picked the flesh from his body." Wild laughter surrounded them, echoing off the walls of the cell as it shrieked, picking up speed, whirling around them. "And it was so good, so good, ssso good, but I was still hungry. So hungry."

No one found any need or desire to respond to the creature, and Kai's flinch was barely discernibly. Still, Bash lay what he hoped was a supportive hand on the young man's forearm. Kai tensed under the touch before relaxing; then he nodded, his jaw clenched, as he blinked rapidly and refocused on the task on hand. The painful taunts had hit home but only fortified the youth on what needed to be done.

Delta continued working her magic in the room,

the clean scent of sage battling against the stench of burnt offerings saturating the room, the scent that Ravyn had claimed was Ibis's altered black magic. She zigzagged through the air as sweat built on her forehead, fighting for control of the creature's body even as its taunts filled the air. With the zip of a finger and barely discernible movements of her lips, the beast's arms were wrenched out to its sides with a sharp *snap* and *crack* as the bones were pulled out of place. A slight movement of her other hand brought the monster into the air before slamming it down twice. Salt and dust rose with a puff as the wendigo was planted in the middle of the pentagram, pinning parts of its outstretched limbs on the floor with another snap of the bones. It howled with anger, promising slow retribution to the witch, who ignored it as if it didn't speak at all.

The creature didn't like being ignored, though, and questioned Kai directly, this time straining to lift its head from the floor to look straight at the young man. "Would you like to hear how he sounded as he died? Would you like to hear how he offered me his tender son in exchange for his life?" It clicked its yellow-red teeth sharply, tapping its clawed fingers against the concrete of the cell as it recalled the moment, eagerly awaiting a reaction, a break in their concentration, a chink in the armor.

The masculine voice coming out of the creature was unfamiliar to Bash, and even without looking at the young man, he suspected it to be his father's voice, but not his words. Such cowardly torment reeked of desperation; he would rip its tongue from its vile mouth. But Bash fought the urge to step across the spelled floor and shut the beast up. Delta and Summer combined still only had time to create a spell that would allow one person through the wards. Of all of them, Ravyn had the highest chance of success—fast and strong, as well as having flesh that could heal from the bitter cold of the wendigo's heart.

He'd argued against that.

Knowing that if Ravyn failed someone else would need to step through, he'd insisted on keeping the doorway open wide.

But no. They each had a job, Kai had patiently explained over and over to the group. It was imperative that they each focus on their part in the plan and trust their teammates. The youth had earnestly patted Sebastian's arm as if understanding how badly his wolf fought against his mate entering danger at all, let alone completely unprotected.

"She won't be alone," Kai had reminded him in a low voice.

More desperate laughter bubbled from the wendigo. As it opened its mouth to offer more torments, in movements quicker than Bash's own, Ravyn stepped through and into the demon trap, careful to avoid smudging any of the dark lines on the floor.

Launching herself with one foot onto its hairy thigh, pushing down hard enough to elicit another snap of bone, Ravyn propelled herself into its throat, forcing the creature's head back to the ground with one hand.

Another explosion of motion came as she deftly pried its mouth open even as it struggled against her, snapping its mouthful of teeth at her. She pushed her fingers in through the rows of sharp teeth that cut into her flesh, blackening the edges even as her body instinctively fought to heal itself from the poisonous injury. Thank the gods she'd been well fed before the mission.

Seeming to not even notice her injuries, Ravyn grasped its tongue, readjusting her grip to gain better control before ripping it straight out of its mouth.

The wendigo let out an animalistic howl of indignation mixed with pain.

Wrinkling her face with disgust, Ravyn tossed the appendage onto the floor, where it flopped around, struggling to return to its angry, shocked master. She pushed the now wide-eyed creature back against the floor, where Delta quickly added more magical lashings.

Ravyn wiped its blackened blood on her borrowed clothes, her wounds healing almost instantly in her well satiated state. "I think we can all say we've heard enough from this bastard. Let's get on with this before it can grow back another tongue, although I can't say it would disappoint me to keep ripping body parts off it." She settled for a solid kick to its side that didn't seem to affect the creature, which now stared at her with fire in its eyes as more brackish, foamy blood bubbled from its mouth.

Beautiful.

Damn, she was the most beautiful thing he'd seen in his entire life. Bash's wolf hummed in agreement and pride. The most beautiful, terrifying creature he'd ever seen. Leaving her behind in the dirt after his harsh words had been one of the hardest things he'd ever done. Despite knowing the actress was feigning fear and helplessness, he couldn't help but cringe as his words struck her. His wolf had battered against his mind and control despite his repeated assurances that it was all part of the plan. *"Mate,"* the wolf had growled as the helpless female lay behind them. Bash hadn't dared to look back and possibly lose the tenacious hold he had on his animal.

Now, however, splattered in various fluids, dried or otherwise, her strength had returned. Ever the graceful lady even as she channeled her inner Valkyrie to tear an enemy limb from limb. Despite the fact that she lived every day among humans, keeping in touch with her humanity, underneath that facade simmered the Fury she'd correctly been labeled throughout history. The earthly embodiment of vengeance, Ravyn had been written about in every era throughout history.

Fenrir, he cursed himself, he loved her. Bash's

wolf howled with pleasure and laughter at this sudden realization. Finally. But this wasn't the time to dwell on it. Gathering her up to kiss her senselessly in the death house while the demon spilled its blood on the floor seemed inappropriate, and his wolf hummed in agreement. *Soon,* he promised his wolf.

"It lies," Kai whispered despite the fact that all of the room could hear him easily. In the shadow-filled room he looked even younger than when Bash had first seen him. "All it knows is hunger and lies. I will end this today. Now."

Bash fought the urge to lay his hand on Kai's shoulder again. The boy was strong, stronger than he had a right to be and when this was over, he was going to find a way to return some of what had been lost to him, give him a tribe, a home, or at least a pack.

"We finish this. Get your part ready." The words were unnecessary. Kai had been ready since birth to fulfill this destiny just as his ancestors had been. Despite the torments, he double-checked the alignment of the crude jars around the wendigo, setting them up just out of the creature's reach.

It silently watched him with dark eyes, baring its teeth at Kai as he finished the setup.

Without removing her eyes from the creature, Delta nodded to the small group, already straining from holding it in place but still managing to keep it secured to the floor. Trapped now, nearly immobile, all it could do was stare unblinkingly up into the space above it. It lay on the floor where Ravyn had unceremoniously tossed it; even its tongue had stopped its spasms as it waited for what was to come.

Bash held the still sheathed knife loosely in his hand, enjoying the feel of it, the weight of it. A part of him wondered if yielding the knife would change him. Ancient, ancestral magic tended to do that; the ancestors did what they wanted, everyone else be damned. But he looked at Kai intently dipping his fingers in a mixture of blood, animal fat, and salt to create the runes outside the demon trap that would assist in permanently imprisoning the spirit of the wendigo in the jars—hopefully for eternity, if the ragtime team had their way. There would be no chance of it bouncing back to hell and returning someday. No chance it would sneak back though a gateway to torment humanity ever again.

"Ms. Sinclair, once the heart is ripped out, toss it straight above the monster." Kai took charge, reiterating the plan they'd gone over numerous times. "Summer and Delta, it's important that you freeze it in place and hold it simultaneously above the body. If it returns, then this has all been for naught. We must time this perfectly. It's imperative."

So much was riding on the witches and their power. Delta and Summer would need to divide their attention as well as their magic for the next bit. Bash had complete faith in Delta; he knew her, knew her story. Despite Summer being on Oliver's team,

Sebastion hadn't worked with her before. Bash reminded himself that only the best were on the payroll, but they'd already asked so much from the witch.

Summer had refused a shot of Ravyn's offered blood, admitting that the adrenaline boost might cause her to lose focus or intent. An older witch might have been offended by the offer, but thankfully she hadn't been. Delta had giggled and suggested she might take Ravyn up on the offer afterward. Bash didn't want to think what that might mean.

Each of them settled into place and out of the corner of his eye, Bash was aware that Delta's hands now flashed with movements quicker than even he could follow. Despite its apparent stillness, the wendigo still battled against the temporary five-pointed trap, and as quickly as its magic battered the tenacious structure, Delta fought back, rebuilding the wards on weakened spots, as well as trying to guess where the next magical battle-ax might strike.

The trap was, at best, temporary; they needed to move quickly. Earlier, Delta had admitted her unfamiliarity with the demon's magic. She might be able to hold it off for an hour or less; there was no way of knowing. But looking at the strain on the young red-headed witch's face and the fever to her movements, Bash suspected that they didn't have an hour and might be lucky if they had more than a few minutes.

Tooth and Claw

His hands felt sweaty. He couldn't imagine how Kai sounded so calm as he chanted the incantations to begin. If the heart returned to the wendigo's body, the backlash of the magic would knock the creature free of the already failing trap. Bash dreaded thinking about the others who had learned that unfortunate fact the hard way.

"Focus, Bash. Remember: five pieces as equal as you can." Kai looked at him. "I promise you once the knife is in your hand, it will fit the need." He quoted his father once again. Apparently, neither he nor his father had ever seen the knife in action, but previous users had passed down that it would always fit the need. Bash had to believe him, had to trust him, just as they were all trusting the other members of their haphazard team.

"It's time." Kai's voice sounded clear as the moon reached its zenith, shining over the group. Bash had never taken part in killing something that was as subdued as the wendigo appeared at the moment, but now wasn't the time to hesitate. If the creature had its way, it would feast on all of them, perhaps lingering over Ravyn for years.

Kai began reciting words in a language that Bash didn't understand but once again, he didn't need to for any of it to work. As he intoned the words, his voice grew deeper and heavier and the air grew thick around them. A quick gesture at Ravyn ensured it was her time.

Time to pull the heart from the beast.

With quick efficiency, she once again drove her hand through its mouth and past the rows of tiny, sharp teeth that ripped and tore at her skin despite the vampire armor. With a combination of horror and fascination, Bash watched her drive her hand past the teeth while the beast gagged and fought against the magical bonds holding it. Already its eyes were twitching in panic, its long, clawed fingers tapping in the air as it struggled to free itself from Delta's magical grip.

With a roar, Ravyn pushed and squeezed her hand down its throat up to her elbow, and then to her shoulder straight down its chest. The cracking of its breastbone reverberated through the room as her fingers frantically searched the frozen cavity for its heart while she remained face to face with the unholy creature, determination and perspiration peppering her face.

The wendigo's vocal cords apparently broke free from the magic and it let out a guttural howl around her hand, promising death to all as it increased its struggle to pull away from Ravyn's hand, which dug through its chest in equal determination. Its body pulsated and quivered in its attempt to escape as it burned through the magic holding it at an alarming rate.

Bash could see the struggle on Delta's face as her magic fought to hold it in place. *"Hold,"* reverberated through his mind, a reminder to his wolf that they each had a part to play. Any deviation from that part could mean the entire plan would fall apart, ensuring the death of the entire team by an enraged wendigo. *Hold*, he once again ordered his wolf while sending calming thoughts down their connection.

Summer stood nearby, face frozen in determination and hands raised, bouncing in anticipation of the exact moment to call open her magic, breaking through the magical barrier with which Delta had surrounded the creature. Too soon and the creature would have a shot at freedom; too late and its frozen heart would be drawn back into its body before their shot at destroying it.

The moment Ravyn's hand grasped its heart, Bash could tell. The triumphant look in her eyes was mirrored by the immediate look of panic and anger in the wendigo's expression as its body desperately tightened and twisted.

With a pained look, Ravyn shifted her arm and tightened her fingers around the frozen appendage. She began methodically pulling and twisting her arm back up its path, even as the creature's chest and then throat pulsated around it. Instinctually, it fought to survive, contracting deeply, determined to hold its frozen heart in place.

Her exposed forearm grew frosty with cold as the creature rebelled against the attack. The skin first turned white, then purple as the cold dug in.

Bash couldn't imagine the damage it was doing to the parts of her still inside the creature's body. He fought down the urge to pull her free. Kai had stressed to not become distracted and to trust each other to do his or her part. Bash's wolf growled in distress as Ravyn fought with the gaping, sunk-in chest before finally pulling her hand free from its mouth with a loud *pop* as the body released the suction it had on her arm and its own heart.

At the *pop*, the wendigo's clawed hands broke free from the magic bindings, reaching out to grab Ravyn in the waist. Without reservation, it dug its claws deep into her side as she screamed out in pain. Too late, though; working past the pain, she triumphantly raised her hand in the air even as the creature pressed its claws deeper into her side.

Ravyn's hand and forearm were a deep purple, nearly black now from the unrelenting cold. Cold that Kai had warned could freeze a man through in seconds. Seemingly unbothered by the frostbite that had already settled in, her mouth formed a victorious grin. Without time to celebrate, she launched the heart high above the group with a strong throw.

They all watched as it went up and then started to come down even faster, heavy with the cold that encased it.

In a breath, Delta's hands slashed downward through the air, severing at least one section of the magical pentagram, allowing an opening for magic and, if done incorrectly, also an opening for the wendigo to retrieve its frozen heart.

Holding his breath, Bash waited for the next step of the plan to be executed, the part that still didn't belong to him. *Please, Fenrir.* His lips silently shaped the prayer, hoping the god understood the specifics of his request.

"*Duratus*," Summer commanded, moving her hands to form the hidden magic before tossing it toward the falling heart. She missed!

Sebastian fought the urge to move from the spot Kai had placed him in, clear in his instructions to not move. They had to count on each other to complete their assigned tasks. If they stumbled, it would all fall.

However, Summer recovered as quickly as any battle-worn witch might, repeating the command to freeze.

"*Duratus!*" she summoned, twice in quick succession, tossing both spells toward the heart, both of them catching it and holding it suspended less than a foot above the body. Close, but close didn't matter as long as it remained frozen away from the body with its hands twitching as it strained to move them in the direction of its frozen heart.

"And you're up, Daddy Wolf." The strain on Delta's entire body was beginning to show as she shook.

With a roar, Sebastian pulled the knife free, dropping the sheath at his feet. The hilt grew warm in his hand as the blade pulsated once, twice, three times, glowing as it dragged him toward the motionless monster, compelling him—no, commanding—that he finish the job. How many times the knife had completed its task was anyone's guess, but it seemed to know perfectly its job.

Without hesitation, he stepped through the area of the pentagram that Delta had previously said she would bring down, trusting the witch to do her part; otherwise, the original magical constraint would kill him instantly. But there was no other option. Delta had only been able to spell it for Ravyn to pass through unharmed. A longer, lengthier process would need to occur to open it for any more of them. That was time they didn't have. Dropping it was the quickest, if not the most dangerous option.

The shield of the demon trap was dropped. The heart hovered in place above the wendigo, taunting it with its closeness. This was the most vulnerable time of the entire operation.

As he raised the blade up it pulsated again, harnessing the power of the moon, growing longer, changing its shape to a silver battle-ax that fit perfectly in his hand. He brought it down across the wendigo's legs, slicing them bloodlessly and with ease while an inhuman howl echoed through the room.

Amazement and power coursed through Bash as he continued another arch, removing torso and arms, easily switching the weapon from one hand to the other. The arm deep inside Ravyn's side thrashed violently once, twice, before falling helplessly to the ground.

Bash swung the weapon lightly as he moved, aware that the ax felt made for him, that perhaps the magical weapon was an extension of him. The blade cut and cauterized with each fatal swipe and with the final one, it pulsated one last time before both the glow and the extra length faded away. It turned once again into a simple bone and leather athame, mysteriously clear of blood.

Sweat beading on his brow, Kai continued his chanting as he opened a jar, preparing to drop inside one of the parts. The mouth of the small jar opened wide, forming its own set of tiny, jagged teeth as it wrapped itself around the body part and inexplicably expanded, sucking the section into its base before shrinking back to its smaller size and shape. Kai repeated the procedure four more times, each jar somehow ingesting the large portions of the wendigo's body into it. As each jar sucked in its pound of flesh, the frozen, blue heart flickered and twisted as it struggled to free itself from its magical restraint.

When the last piece of the monster was engulfed by a jar, the heart quit twisting. Within a breath it burst into flames, leaving behind a handful of blackened ash that haphazardly floated to the floor and across the room as Summer released her magic and collapsed to the floor, drained. Delta wavered back and forth on her feet but managed to remain standing even as Ravyn moved with a flash to give her a helping arm despite her own injury.

Lids sucked onto all the jars after they'd swallowed the body pieces as Kai also collapsed, leaving only a shocked Bash and Rayvn standing amid the remains of the monster and the spell. Ravyn held up a pale and shaking Delta.

Bash caught his breath as the sight of the disheveled Ravyn filled his eyes. She dripped in both her blood and that of her enemy. A light dusting of ash from the now destroyed heart of the beast covered her. Her blackened arm already was starting to have bits of color flood into it. She needed to feed—and soon.

Delta grimaced as she pulled her arm out of Ravyn's grasp, determined to put some space between herself and the mess surrounding them.

"Goddess, I may be speechless," she admitted, letting out a deep breath followed by a laugh of relief. "I honestly can't believe that worked."

Leaping across the mess on the floor and his exhausted comrades, Bash caught Ravyn in his arms, lifting her triumphantly to meet him as he lowered his head toward her. Meeting her lips, he could taste the grime and death on them as well as the sweet taste of her underneath. Her tense lips relaxed after a mere second with him, and she pulled him closer. Invited him closer, before pulling away.

Bash reluctantly let her slide down his body before

only half releasing her so that she might stand on her own two feet.

She graced him with a small smile that he hoped promised more to come.

Rubbing the arm with her other hand as feeling returned, a wide, relieved grin crossed her face. "We did it," she whispered, looking around the room, as if not really believing it had worked.

"Go team, go," Delta intoned in a flat tone, rubbing her own arms to bring feeling back to them as the chill remained heavy in the cement room. Letting out yet another deep breath and laugh of shock, she exclaimed, "Wow."

"We did it," Bash agreed softly, then repeated more loudly with a gasped laugh of disbelief as he squeezed Ravyn once again in a half hug. "We did it! Never doubted us."

Still massaging the damaged appendage, Ravyn admitted, "I did."

"Me too, just a smidge," Delta confessed, holding up a small space between her thumb and forefinger. "Your side good? To be honest, I don't think I have an ounce of healing left in me, but—"

"It's good."

Looking around the room at the still exhausted forms of Kai and Summer, Ravyn repeated, "I can't believe it, but I'm really, really glad we did it."

Despite Ravyn's assurances, Delta moved the cloth that remained on Ravyn's bleeding side.

Satisfied, she silently examined Ravyn's arm, pushing into the purpling flesh as Ravyn groaned against the pain.

Bash reluctantly loosened his grip on her, knowing that Delta would offer healing that he couldn't.

Delta waved her hands around the arm, muttering words that Bash couldn't understand and could barely hear. He watched as a bit more color returned to the arm.

"I'm sorry, that's all I can manage at the moment. Once you feed, it should help more," Delta apologized before adding with a smile, "But you two can feel free to get a room if you need to, you know, take care of things."

Both sets of eyes flew to the red-head's hands, which shot up innocently. "You know, to take care of healing and whatever else needs taken care of after a battle."

The look Ravyn gave him when she looked up at him nearly brought him to his knees. Large eyes, framed with sooty lashes and bits of ash had his heart pounding harder, "Bash, I l..."

"I think it's too early to celebrate," Bash declared pulling away, before she could complete her sentence. He kneeled next to Kai, pulling the disoriented youth to a sitting position. "I still need to find Ibis. And I need to get my nephew home to Missouri." A hint of apology crept into his voice and he couldn't bring himself to look directly at Ravyn. Instead, he busied himself checking Kai over. "He needs me to get him home. The rest can wait, but..."

He felt Ravyn go still next to him at the declaration, pausing, waiting for him to continue, but that was it. Honestly, his priority now was getting Toby back to his mom and begging her for forgiveness.

Delta admitted, "Ravyn's sister is long gone. I think she saw the writing on the wall and took off." Slowly walking around the room, shuddering as she examined the sterile, cold killing room, she continued, "Her magic saturates this place. I would guess she ran while we were making plans, by the age of this magic. Not bothering to let this one know…" She gestured with a nod at the small dusting of ash from the remains of the wendigo's frozen heart.

Speaking to Ravyn, she went on. "Her last need of him was a distraction while she covered her tracks. She attempted to burn over her magic in and around this place, but there is too much and she didn't expect me. Now that I've tasted her magic, we can specifically ward you against her." With a spit of distaste, Delta continued solemnly, "This is witch business now. I need to report her to my mother, but I already know what will be happening next. The great mother's will be done."

"Let your mother know I'll help as needed," Bash offered, ready to stab the witch who had taken part in maiming and torturing Toby and Ravyn.

Nodding in acknowledgement, Delta kneeled next to Summer, who also sat up in dazed amazement that they'd survived the night.

"Well heeded, witch," Bash mumbled toward both of them, unable to say more to express how deeply he appreciated their help. Despite being employed with his and Oliver's company, both witches had right of refusal, and neither had hesitated to stand alongside them. They'd destroyed a great evil today and few would know about it.

Delta nodded again as Ravyn kneeled on the other side of Summer. Working together, they carefully brought the witch to her feet. Was it just his imagination, that suddenly she wasn't looking at him? That was what he wanted, right? He had stopped her words spoken off the high of a battle, before she could regret them. His wolf whined and pushed him to release his hold on Kai and approach her, but already despite her own injuries she was half carrying the exhausted witch away from the room. *"Fool,"* his wolf hissed as Sebastian followed with Kai, confused as to what just happened but realizing he'd missed something important and things had shifted within seconds.

Delta shook her head sadly as Bash passed by her with Kai. "Should have just gotten that room, Wolf," she chuffed at him softly, taking a place behind him in leaving the wendigo's house of horrors.

Chapter Twenty-Three

And the gods laughed when the wolf was bound

*B*ash picked up the bags from the entryway that he assumed were Toby's. He'd already taken his own bags downstairs packed with everything he owned to take to Missouri with him. It had been years since he'd had a home base of operation. His job dictated that he travel often and lightly, but somehow in the last few months, he'd acquired more than what fit easily in his bags.

"Tobias Franklin, why are your bags still empty?" Naturally, no answer. His injuries had healed, but Toby didn't hesitate to take advantage of the guilt his uncle felt. He swore he didn't blame anyone but the wendigo for his injuries, but that didn't allay the guilt. So now, he freely manipulated it to his advantage, without repercussions. Not being around when he was supposed to was one way.

"Toby? Toby!" he snapped.

No answer. Hadn't the teenager just been moping around the kitchen complaining there was nothing to eat, apparently forgetting the fact they were emptying out the apartments and were leaving in a few hours to return to the Midwest? Sara was anxiously awaiting the return of her only son and surely ready to chew Bash's ear off in person for letting injury befall him in the first place. She'd apparently forgotten that she was the one who insisted Toby accompany him out of state, despite the fact that he'd stated time and time again that dangerous things could happen on any mission, no matter how much of a cake walk it might seem.

Toby had called it her "mom amnesia" or "momnesia"—the ability to only remember what she wanted to the point that anything else didn't exist. The ability seemed hereditary, Bash had told the teen wryly, and gender didn't appear to be a factor.

Just go. Take him home. Me, this job, it's done now.

Ravyn only heard him say that he needed to take Toby home before she shut down against him. He wanted and planned to come back, but he hadn't been able to form the words. Still, he didn't regret shutting down her words after the heat of battle. Only too soon would she realize that he wasn't deserving of what she might offer. He hadn't been there for her.

His tongue sat paralyzed until he uttered the ugly question, "Do you even need me? Do you need anyone?" Even as the words left his mouth, his wolf cringed away internally and Sebastian immediately wished he could swallow the words back up.

Too late. He would never forget the look of pained hurt that crossed Ravyn's face before she shook it off, pulling her shoulders back and wiping her face clean, and responded just as sharply, "Do you?" Not bothering to wait for his response, she continued working alongside his men in the cleanup operation, determined not to leave until it was finished.

Thank Fenrir, his nephew had mostly recovered; physically anyway. He was still missing two fingers on his hand, as they suspected the shift hadn't been forced fast enough to change that fate. Despite the potential loss of dexterity, he still managed to kick ass in most of his video games, and his wolf definitely hadn't let the loss of a couple toes slow him down. Looking for the bright side of things, his nephew had taken the loss with a casual shrug, declaring that chicks loved scars.

Ravyn had laughed in delight when he stated this and gently told him that women loved men willing to stand up to evil, as well as not being called chicks. After she said this, Toby spent the rest of the day wandering about the apartment with a goofy grin on his face. Bash understood too well; she was easy to love.

It was past time to head out—assuming, of course, he could find his nephew, whose stomach could be leading him halfway across town or, Bash thought with a sigh, up a floor to Ravyn's apartment. Despite the fact that she didn't eat, Ravyn always managed to have a stocked refrigerator and pantry, which also managed to contain a favorite for anyone who visited, friend or employee. Another dramatic sigh left Bash, then he wanted to hit himself in the face. He sounded like a love-struck teenager. All he needed to do was go upstairs, pick up Toby, tell Ravyn goodbye if she was around, and leave.

With Oliver back stateside for a bit, it seemed like an excellent time to take a well-deserved vacation of his own and in this case, Sebastian simply wanted to go home. Home to Missouri, where his sister-in-law could fuss over Toby and him. Assuming, of course, he was forgiven for putting Toby in harm's way in the first place. But Missouri wasn't feeling like home; he only hoped the sentiment would change when he and his wolf got to feel the dirt under their feet and fresh air all around.

He knocked on the door to Ravyn's penthouse, a bit surprised when no one answered. Tentatively, he pushed the door open; despite all the time he'd spent with Ravyn in her apartment these last several months, today he felt like an intruder. Stepping aside from leading the team and back into his office logistics role was the right thing to do. Aside from the vampires being a little too agreeable with Ravyn, the team was solid, and the threat that caused him to join them had been eliminated. As Delta said and her mother firmly reiterated, Ibis was the witches' problem to detain and despite his offer to join them, they insisted he wasn't needed.

A search of Ravyn's apartment building after the rescue had found the talisman, the culprit that allowed magic to whittle away an entrance into her building. The spelled item that Anya had entered the building with had been hidden by her pure intentions. It had been slid into a couch cushion during her visit, spelled to be forgotten once she'd planted it.

A picture of Anya's family. That was the culprit, the item that weakened their intent and magical barriers. The item that finally allowed the manuscript to make its way into Ravyn's home. The item that allowed an insistent voice in Ravyn's mind to determine that she must meet with Bertrando Roland immediately. The magic that may or may not have made the vamps agree to Ravyn attending the party, although Sebastian admitted to himself that they might not have needed a magical item to agree to her plans.

The picture Anya had held so reverently now belonged to Ravyn, who had refused to throw it away and had traced the small image of her sister's face over and over again. It had been spelled to nearly the entire building. Bertrando Roland had been sending his script to her offices for weeks before and after they killed his mage, but he hadn't effectively managed to get it into her hands. The wards in place hadn't allowed the script to make it through the building's doorways, recognizing the ill intend even if the rest of them didn't. Most likely, the script would have been rejected on sight based on a gut feeling or messengers would have "forgotten" to deliver it or a drink would have been spilled on it, destroying it. Magic, oddly enough, worked that way when it deterred harm—a series of forgetfulness and random mishaps.

However, once the script made its way into her hands, the magical photo continued to weaken their intent: Ravyn's intent to follow the rules and remain safe, the guards' intent to keep her within the building's boundaries. A part of Bash wondered if the spell had weakened his resolve to stay away from Ravyn and that letting their inhibitions down was due to the spelled picture. Perhaps this mating bond his wolf was insisting upon was simply a remnant of the attraction he felt for the vampire and the confusion of the spell. Ravyn certainly didn't act as if she had an uncontrollable attraction to him any longer.

Now the picture was simply a picture, one that Ravyn had placed carefully in a small box with a faded blue lotus carved and painted on the outside. The blue lotus was a sign of the afterlife and rebirth. Ironic that the flower Ravyn loved even in her mortal life nearly foretold her future.

And the crack in the window. Oddly enough, it was simply a crack in the window of a settling building. Birds caught up in the odd reflection continued to hit the window at random points of the day. Ill-timed and ill-placed, but nothing nefarious no matter who looked at it.

"Just get it fixed by a window guy or gal," Delta had told them after a cursory examination. "Maybe put up one of those fake owls or whatever."

Duh, building maintenance.

Delta might still be in the city. After returning to Ravyn's apartment, she stayed one night as a guest and then declared she was heading out. No need for a flight, she said, waving the offer off. This emergency took less time than she'd thought it would. While she was on the coast, she needed to look up someone. Not a friend, she answered sharply when Summer had coyly asked her about it. In fact, if Sebastian remembered correctly, she'd called the person a vile piece of shit who had stolen all of her gear on a recent raid in a game he hadn't heard of. Something with dragons, hunters, and battle warriors, maybe.

"Oh yeah, high five!" had been Toby's response. Now Bash wondered if the two played games online as well. Was this the sort of shit he was supposed to be keeping track of the last few months? No wonder he'd failed to keep his nephew safe.

"Off to kick his moronic ass!" Delta responded cheerfully before heading out the door. "Got the company credit card, so I can just spring for first class in a day or two."

"Is 'kicking his ass' code for something?" asked Bash, nearly afraid to hear the answer, but Delta was an adult; she could more than take care of herself.

Tilting her head, Summer considered the question. "No, it's Delta. She probably really means she's going to kick someone's ass."

Ravyn was no longer stuck in the apartment now that the wendigo was gone. She'd been able to immediately step right into her work and social life with a post about being back from a well-deserved extended vacation. It didn't matter the reason; her pubic adored her and were delighted to have her back. Meanwhile, Bash's heart was breaking into a million pieces as he could feel her being pulled away from him despite the fact that he'd done nothing to encourage her to stay near him. She'd seamlessly floated away from him and while the human part of him understood his wolf mourned the loss of the vampire it had decided was his mate.

"Tobias?" he called out softly as he opened the door. The lights were off and the curtains were open, allowing in the filtered sunlight. "Toby?" Bash called again despite knowing that the apartment was empty. "Ravyn?"

Annoyance once again flitted through him. Sure, Ravyn had her own security team to answer to, which technically didn't include him, but Toby was his nephew, his responsibility, and for her to just leave with him… That was, well, just wrong and irritating. Although admittedly he hadn't kept track of him well the last few months, they might try to loop him in occasionally.

TOOTH AND CLAW

No longer bothering to be quiet, he stomped angrily from room to room, looking for any clue that might indicate where they'd gone. Hesitating at her bedroom door, he decided to skip it. No chance they were holed up in that particular room not hearing him. Despite having instructed the team lead that he no longer needed to be notified of her every move, his irritation grew as each room proved to be as darkened as the last. His wolf whined long and low at him, matching his mood, and he resisted the urge to snap back at it. This wasn't the wolf's fault; it wasn't anyone's fault. Ravyn had offered a night to remember, an offer he'd eagerly accepted. Bash had developed feelings and his wolf simply got caught in the crossfires. Understandable that it had confused lust and infatuation with love—or worse, a mating bond.

Distance and time would certainly set things straight, even if the wolf currently didn't believe him. And it wasn't like he wasn't coming right back to work after his quick drop off in Missouri. He planned to return Toby and face his sister-in-law like a man before returning to his office job just a few miles from Ravyn. California was as good as anywhere to set up temporary shop until he was called out again.

Bash sat rigidly on the sofa, arms crossed, facing the doorway he knew they would eventually have to come in through, muttering unhappily to himself at this delay.

His wolf huffed and circled within Bash's mind

before curling up in a corner, choosing to continue ignoring him. It didn't stop Bash from talking to it even if the conversation was currently one-sided. Sighing, he settled a hand on each of his knees. He refused to call or text the team and mentally berated Toby for not telling him his plans despite the fact that the entire duration of his visit—or prison time, as Toby liked to call it—he hadn't kept tabs on the teenager. It was a bit late to be angry about that now.

He didn't have to wait long; not really. The door opened in a swift motion and one of his wolves led the way inside, immediately noticing Sebastian. A laughing Ravyn followed, along with Toby and Kai, all three ladened with shopping bags. The sound of her laughter gripped his heart tightly; it had been days since he'd heard that melody. Another wolf followed close behind, shooting a quick glance both ways down the hall before shutting the door and locking it.

Sebastian grouchily noted that neither security guard weighed themselves down with packages; he was torn between wanting a reason to lash out and snap at the group and pride that they kept themselves at the ready even when he wasn't there to observe. Too often, security found themselves as overpaid shopping companions, carrying too many parcels to stay at the ready or react to any potential dangers—a pet peeve of his that had apparently been driven home to the teams beneath him. Simply put, the clients carried their own bags and left security free to keep things secure.

Ravyn hadn't seen him yet, her entire focus on his nephew and the young shaman. "Are you boys hungry? I can fix you up something."

Bash could see his nephew's face light up immediately with the offer, his appetite voracious even for a young wolf. Irritated, he snapped, "First, you can't cook, and second, we can get something on the way."

Ravyn's face fell at his words as well as his tone, and Bash's wolf snarled at him, driving a stabbing pain between his eyes, both causing regret at his sharp tone.

"I may not be able to whip up a gourmet meal, but I've lived long enough that I can do more than throw a raw steak on a plate," she replied, her tone sadder than sharp. "Beef Wellington, it is kids."

The guilt stabbed into Bash's stomach, twisting and turning to drive the point home.

"You could just give them leftovers," he offered dumbly as his wolf begged him to shut his mouth.

Toby ignored his words and his tone. "There's still plenty of time to get to the airport, like six hours or so. Besides, Uncle Bash, look what we got Kai." He raised a few bags in his hands, clearly pleased with the impromptu shopping trip.

Kai's face remained blank. His arms hung loosely at his sides, clutching his bags while his eyes darted between the two of them, probably questioning his decision to leave the forest for a madhouse.

With another internal groan, Bash wanted to punch

himself in the face and his wolf happily agreed. First time the damn thing had perked up in days, if he was keeping track.

Kai had been living off the land, camping outside the wendigo's estate since the death of his father. Quite possibly that had been what the two of them had done in the years before that as well. Kai remained mum about his past.

He needed clothes, of course. Clothes, shoes, hygiene products, and a sense of normalcy. Kai had eagerly agreed to accompany Sebastian and Toby back to the wolf pack in Missouri. He'd been alone for so long and had only heard the stories of the relationship between his tribe and the wolves from long ago. This was his chance to regroup, set down roots, and form relationships like his ancestors had. All the young man had were the clothes on his back, his second set having been ruined by Ravyn during the raid. Borrowing from Toby only worked for so long; he was swimming in the young wolf's borrowed clothes. Now the outfit he wore looked like it had been tailored to him, just a collared shirt tucked into dark jeans that fit, tapering down to new, hole-free boots.

And he had a haircut; not all cut off but trimmed up and combed straight until it shone black down his back and across his shoulders. With his sharp nose and dark hair, he could be Ravyn's brother apart from eye color.

Softening his tone, Bash felt his eyes mist. When

had he become so emotional? "You look good, Kai," he admitted as the young man visibly relaxed. After all they'd been through, it was too easy to forget that despite the maturity that had been thrust upon him, Kai was barely older than Toby. He still wore the leather necklace and medallion around his neck from his father.

Ravyn had taken the time to meet Kai's needs; she just did what Bash should have done when he offered him a place to stay. Despite his heritage, the young man wouldn't be well received by the pack if he showed up in worn through boots and oversized castoffs. Not that the pack or anyone should judge based on that, but Kai already held his head up higher as confidence in his appearance began to match those of his tracking and hunting abilities.

"Thank you, sir." Kai nodded appreciation with a small half smile and his cheeks pinked just a bit at the compliment, one he wasn't used to hearing.

Bash continued beating himself up, so wrapped up in himself he hadn't thought of the things Kai needed. Kai wanted so badly to stay with them, but Bash knew he struggled with where he fit in among them.

Kai slept outside on his balcony each night with a single blanket on the hard decking but crawled into bed early in the morning to pretend he'd stayed the night in its comfort. Bash piled the youth's plate full at each meal, knowing that the boy stopped himself from gorging on all the food placed before him. Sometimes he would gobble down a few bites with his hands before catching himself and continuing with a fork, taking the time to chew between each bite. The sounds of the city had the former hermit jumpy and uncomfortable; he often flinched as if the sounds outside were striking him physically. Kai needed the healing of the pack and the openness of the forest. He'd taken on a mantle that he'd been too young for and it had aged him. He needed a chance to be young and carefree again. He needed a chance to make mistakes that wouldn't get him or others around him killed.

"Thank you for that," Bash told Ravyn in a low voice. Low enough that Kai couldn't hear; despite his unusual upbringing, he still was human and didn't have the excellent hearing that his supernatural counterparts had.

Ravyn's back stiffened, but she nodded nearly indiscernibly. "It wasn't for you," she hissed back equally as low. "I do things because I want to, not because I need to."

Shame flushed through Sebastian; he didn't know what he was doing. Fenrir had both blessed him and cursed him.

"Guys, go check the closet in my spare room and get those suitcases I told you about, the rolling ones. And you can start packing his things. Just take off the tags. Wash anything you want to as well." With a glance at Sebastian, she added dryly, "You have plenty of time."

They did. The commercial flight wasn't leaving for hours, and technically being partial owner of the security firm with Oliver, Bash could have taken the company plane. Wherever it was. Had Delta taken it back to the Midwest or had she made other arrangements like she'd talked about? Then he reminded himself that none of this was his responsibility anymore. Delta or Oliver could arrange transportation with the company transport. Currently his only responsibility lay in getting the boys home to the pack.

Laden in purchases, the boys left the room more subdued than they'd entered it, and Bash knew that was entirely his fault. Was this what he was to become? Someone who sucked the joy from the room? From life?

"Ravyn," he began softly, "I'm so sorry for snapping. And truly, I thank you for taking care of Kai."

Her back still to him, Ravyn set down the knife she'd been using to chop some vegetables. Despite the fact that most of the team who ate in her apartment were wolves, she insisted that they needed to eat their vegetables and added them to most meals. Her back straightened and her black hair rippling down her back begged him to stroke it.

"Again, I didn't do it for you. It's way less than what Kai deserves after everything he has sacrificed and everything he did. The gods have tested him strongly, and he never faltered. Ever."

The final line hung accusingly in the air between them, heavy with a tinge of bitterness, before she continued, "Clothes that reflect the man he is, is the very least I can do and doesn't even begin to repay him for what he has given.

"And for the goddess's sake or Fenrir's sake"—with her back still to him, she picked the knife up, waving it around a bit as she spoke, before returning to cut up the cucumber—"just take the plane. It's on stand-by, fueled and ready to go whenever you are. The pilot will update the flight plan as soon as you're on your way. Besides, then Ollie could have his plane back in his half of the country."

Dismissed. Bash felt her dismissal. He'd told her he was coming back, hadn't he? This dismissal sounded final, as if he wasn't welcome back. The air reeked of sadness… or was it regret? Sniffing the air cautiously, his ire grew. Who was she to feel regret? Did she regret what they'd shared? In the end she still had everything she wanted, while he had…

He had exactly what he came with in addition to a broken heart. His wolf snorted at this, and Sebastian felt the disdain of his pouting beast. It would feel better when they arrived home in Missouri. Surely it would want to run the old trails with the pack. He cajoled his wolf, which ignored him with another huff, turning circles in his mind before curling up into a tight ball and closing its eyes.

"Ravyn," he whispered, watching her back stiffen at his voice. "You said…"

With her back still toward him, she lowered her chin forward nearly to her chest. "Thor, I know entirely what was said, by the both of us. Words said in the heat of the moment…" This time it was her who trailed off.

In the heat of the moment? The words and promises they'd panted the night before the full moon? Or the words said in anger and frustration? Words could be the truth, a lie, a promise, a pleading. Whatever words that needed to be spoken during that moment would boil out; the emotion would be there and it was up to them to decide which words were truth and which were the result of adrenaline. Which had her words been? And his? He knew what his words meant, but still he was leaving.

"Guys, ready to eat?" Ravyn called out to them before crossing the room with a wave of her hand. "I'm going to rest for a bit," she explained to the young men as they trampled in with the grace of young bisons, their chattering growing silent as they entered the fog of the room.

Frustrated, Sebastian ran a hand over his hair, removing the hair tie before smoothing it back into place and retying.

Toby gave an accusing stare over the counter at Bash, while deliberately cutting into the beef. Kai awkwardly shifted back and forth on his feet before sliding onto a bar stool and focusing intently on his plate, quietly eating and obviously aware of the uncomfortable feelings clouding the air.

Chapter Twenty-Four

Though he chases the moonlight he cannot catch the beams

*T*aking a deep breath, Sebastian inhaled the fresh, clean scent of the Missouri forest. The mixture of crisp pine mixed with a melody of clean grass, fauna, and sunshine enveloped his senses, even extracting a contented sigh from his currently quiet and moody wolf.

Home.

He was home now. Relief as well as trepidation filled him. His sister-in-law, after her initial tears and panic, had been relieved that her son hadn't been more severely injured or worse. Over the phone, she'd assured Bash that she didn't blame him, but that could have been a mother's way of ensuring he let his guard down before ripping his throat out for endangering her pup.

Closing his eyes, he let the sunlight dance on his skin as he inhaled deeply, embracing the scents of home quite possibly for the last time if Sara decided to cut his head off. While it felt and smelled like home, something seemed off. He'd thought when he arrived here he would feel more. Something more. It was home, but not quite home anymore.

"Uncle Bash!" a twin symphony of voices screamed shrilly, breaking the quiet of the moment, accompanied by the sounds of two sets of feet running toward him, kicking the rust-brown and yellow leaves out of their way.

Bash barely got his arms out before their furious launch into the air toward him. The boy shifted in the leap to gain an advantage over his sister, hitting Bash's chest with the force of four paws and a mix of fluff and muscle. Instantly following was the blond head of his slightly smaller sister, whose arms wrapped around Bash's neck, squeezing it tight before peppering the side of his face with tiny kisses. Similarly, her twin's nose butted happily against the other side of his face along with the lapping of a minuscule tongue.

Sebastian's trepidation left him as the twins' joy reflected through him and he carefully returned their exuberant greetings. Surely their mother wouldn't have allowed her eight-year-olds to greet him if she planned his demise?

"Hey," Toby said sharply, "what am I? Roasted vegetables? And here I'm the one that got injured." He waved his healed hand in the air, enticing his siblings with his scars.

Both twins, still in the same form, squirmed to be

let down. Sebastian managed one last squeeze of each of them before they hit the ground running. This time, Penelope crouched down to grab her twin's pants that had been carelessly left on the ground after his shift. Vin had already lunged into his big brother's arms, peppering him with puppy kisses before turning a reproachful eye to his sister, who now was swinging his pants above her head.

"Don't you dare shift on me, Vin," Toby warned his brother.

The pup let out a sharp bark toward his sister, who innocently flipped the pants into the air with a tiny giggle, tossing her blond curls back as she taunted him.

"Pen, leave your brother alone. Our new friend will think you were raised by animals." Sara's soft voice drew the small groups attention once again.

Bash became aware of Kai silently gaping at the display before him, quite possibly wondering what he'd gotten into when he agreed to visit the pack.

Nodding toward the quiet young man taking it all in, she formally added, "Kai, I welcome you to our land, our pack, and my home." With a nod toward Bash, she added less formally, "I'm the big idiot's sister-in-law, Sara. And all these hoodlums belong to me."

"Sara of Missouri, I thank you for your welcome." Kai displayed the same solemn vow to Sara. "I thank you for your family's sacrifice and help."

Toby let a wiggling Vincent hop back to the ground, before slapping Kai on the back and moving toward his mother. "Ma," he began with a laugh before wrapping his arms around her waist, picking her up to twirl her around. "I'm home."

With a laugh, Sara agreed, "I see that! And what have they been feeding you in California? You've grown like a sapling, but you're nearly skin and bones." Patting his broad shoulders, she added, "Thankfully, I have a few things prepared for you all."

Despite her cheerful words, Bash could still hear the tremble of fear in her voice—a fear he'd placed there by his poor choices.

Gently placing his mother back to the ground, Toby urged Kai forward. "That's our sign to eat." The entire trip across the country, Toby had described all the wonderful food his mom was sure to cook for the returning heroes. And while he certainly hadn't missed many meals over the last few months, Kai had, and he absolutely deserved the finest Sara could offer.

"I'm going to run for a bit." As happy as he was to see the rest of his family, Bash had been pent up. Now that they were home, his wolf was eager to take advantage of it, especially after months of only being allowed out during the mandatory full moon runs.

Not letting go of her oldest son's waist, Sara nodded with understanding and sorrow. "Your cabin down by the river has been aired out and freshened up. You're welcome to take meals here in your own time,

Tooth and Claw

but your fridge has a few goodies in it." Sara had prepared for him to come. To stay. Despite her fear and her anger, she still welcomed him and at the same time foresaw his need for quiet and a chance to unwind however he needed to.

Guilt flooded Sebastian. The feeling was constant in his gut now. He'd caused the fear to return to her eyes, and James would hate that they'd caused his mate so much fear and sorrow. Her children were what kept her going after the loss of her mate. It had taken so much to bring her back from the edge after his death, and Bash knew without a doubt that Toby's injuries had caused all the old feelings to resurface. If something happened to one of her children, she might not make it back.

"Let's get you all fed," Sara repeated, drawing Kai forward with her free arm. Bash could see she was fighting the urge to mother her young wolf, but she clearly planned to make certain Kai received some of the mothering he'd missed out on.

Bash carefully untangled Penelope from her battle with her brother's pants and with a yippy howl, she ran back in the direction of the house with her brother on her heels.

Sara hesitated, drawing back from the boys. "Go on, I'll be there in a minute."

"Ma," Toby began warningly.

"Go on, your uncle is safe with me."

Bash stuck his hands in his pockets, steeling

himself for what was to come. Regardless of what she'd told Toby, he deserved whatever punishment she was preparing to dole out. "I'm sorry..."

Sara looked up at him curiously. "Enough of that. I've tried for years to figure you out. To figure out why after James... left... you didn't come home. Why you avoided me and the kids. I thought sending Toby to you might help you find your place again." Shaking her head sadly, she continued, "But you don't think you deserve a place with us. James would never have—"

"James should've lived; Fenrir took the wrong brother," Bash bit off, avoiding her sad scrutiny. "He was needed here."

"That's not how it works and you know it. And to think you know better than the gods? It was time for James to go, whether we wanted him to or not. You can't continue blaming yourself for things outside of your control. You're not responsible for everything that happens." Sara punctuated the last words with repeated sharp fingers to his chest. "The children may not have a father, but they have a mother. They may not have a father, but they have an uncle. A pack. A family."

Bash looked toward the heavens as if they might contain the answers he needed, the words to convince her that he wasn't a good substitute for James.

Shaking her head sadly, she added, "We all loved him, but he would have wanted us to keep living. He would have wanted you to find your mate, find your happiness. No, maybe you don't deserve that, but then none of us do if we're going by your morality code. Don't die before you're dead."

Sebastian had no words and silently watched her retreat back into the house to her family.

It was time to run. Time to forget.

Chapter Twenty-Five

Its cries broke death's heart

Sitting in the dark alone with her wine, how pathetic. The darkness didn't hide anything from her, and what she most wanted to hide was herself.

The time had come to embrace her normal life again. Time to again set the paranormal security team back in the shadows and not at the forefront of her life. The last many months had upended the routine between the guards and herself. She'd grown used to the hustle and bustle of the men coming in and out of her apartment. Used to their low jokes and the clanking of the coffee they all seemed to enjoy so much, the feelings of not being alone, of being a part of something even if from the outside. But it was time to get back to normal. To keep herself separate from them and to step back into her life. Maybe find a party to attend or host one herself to celebrate her return from her holiday.

Maybe later.

The ringing phone interrupted her revere, but she refused to look at it. Was it so hard to believe she was too busy to answer and just leave a message? She stared off into space, emptying her mind, releasing her own desires into the world. Talking to the goddess.

The phone rang shrilly again, hurting her ears. Why didn't she put it on silent? Maybe if she ignored it, it would stop. It was Oliver's ringtone, breaking the stillness once again. Wasn't he on his honeymoon or something like that? Why did he keep calling?

More rings, same tone. She could imagine him getting angry as she ignored the calls. Text chimes, and then another, and another. Shrill ringing once again. Sigh.

Fine.

"Hello, Ollie." Fake cheerful voice. "Is there a reason you're not taking the hint? I'm currently busy." At one point she'd been surrounded by scripts; she looked around guiltily, trying to locate them. Hadn't they just been right there in front of her?

"No, you're not." Flat, dry, definitely her Ollie on the other end. "You're currently pouting and wallowing." Muffled sounds and he cleared his throat. "I mean, Eva and I wanted to call and check on you. We're back stateside and thought you might like some company."

As if the two madly in love lovebirds even gave her a passing thought. And why did the men in her life always accuse her of wallowing? A pang twinged through her heart at the memory of Bash's dry accusation.

"Fine, I'm fine." More forced cheerfulness. "I'm just reading over scripts. Really no time for visitors, I have a party later." A guilty memory had her eyes glance to the stack of unopened scripts she'd haphazardly kicked off her low coffee table onto the floor.

Oh, yes, that's where they went.

After an electrical fire had raged through Roland Bertrando's compound, he'd been declared missing and possibly dead, and all current projects had been put on hold. In response, her agency had bombarded her with numerous other scripts to fill the void, knowing that she didn't like to go too long without working or having something in the works.

How the last few weeks had changed her.

Ollie needed to let her go, cut himself free from the sinking ship called Ravyn. He had Eva now. For years after his transformation, Oliver had followed her around the world, and even after they decided to go separate ways, he'd created a company that could focus on watching over her. He deserved a break and happiness. Goddess, Oliver was lucky to be alive. Lucky he'd survived the transition she'd offered him while he was at death's door. If he hadn't had demon blood in him... She couldn't imagine the what-ifs.

More harsh whispering and shuffling. Should she just hang up? Even when she finally answered, the two were more involved with one another than with her. They probably wouldn't even notice. But they would.

Ravyn sighed, realizing that if she hung up that they would just keep calling.

"Ravyn?" Eva's soft voice came over the receiver, questioning, her voice portraying love and calmness to Rayvn. Either her succubus powers had evolved since her relationship with Ollie or there was still a connection, however tenuous, between the two. One that the magic had been unable to break for either of them. "Are you still there?"

Holding her breath briefly, considering, Ravyn's heart twinged at the sound of Eva's voice. Funny how she'd never known of their connection, but once the connection was severed, she felt the loss deeply even in its possibly altered state.

"Ravyn?" Eva's voice was soft and hesitant, with the sound of shuffling in the background. "Stop it." Clearly whispered over the line to Oliver, Ravyn let out a half gasp and cry at the comfortableness of the two. They were so lucky, although it went well beyond luck. They were so perfect together that Ravyn imagined that Hathor, the Goddess of Love herself, had ordained their union. Written it upon the stars, and so it was.

Clearing her throat, Ravyn swallowed the last dregs of her wine. "Yes, of course, I'm here." She watched the remaining thick red droplet ooze down the inside of the glass. She wasn't even hungry; she'd poured and mixed the glass out of habit. With Sebastian no longer feeding her regularly, she was trying to find her own hunger cues once again.

With a pained sharpness in her chest, she realized that, in fact, she rarely had missed her meals since early spring. Bash had mixed up the wine and blood or the wine and black coffee daily, casually handing it to her when it was meal time. Always he took care of her. She didn't deserve him.

"Yes, Eva." This time Ravyn spoke a little more loudly, hating how her voice cracked a bit. "I would think the two of you would have better things to do than call me during your... travels."

"Well, yes. And no. It's just I was sleeping. And I know that our connection has been severed, but..." Eva hesitated and clearly, she didn't really want to say the words that came next. "Only it's not always, completely that is, it's not one hundred percent gone. Sometimes you bleed over, I guess. No pun intended."

Eva never intended the puns; they just happened. The only sound for several seconds was Eva's low, hesitant breath as Ravyn considered the words. The bond she'd unknowingly formed with Eva when she saved her life years ago had been violently cut by the crazed warlock who had served the wendigo. For years, the two had unknowingly been connected due to Ravyn's blood and Eva's partial succubus heritage. But knowing about a possible bond made it more intimate than previously. No one should have to feel what she was feeling. An apology began to form in her head.

Eva quickly continued after a beat, reassuring Ravyn. "It's not dreams like before, not complete scenes, more like feelings and images. It could be that my bond with Oliver reinforced a bond with you or altered it or something."

Ravyn imagined that it might be. Delta would find the possibility fascinating and would jump at the chance to study the situation. "Well, I apologize if I disturbed you. I could"—with a gulp and another weak lie—"try to not read such emotional scripts." Staring at the border on the ceiling, she counted, *One, two, three, four, five.*

"No, no, it's not that at all. I don't mind. I—we—called because we wanted to check on you."

"I'm fine." Ravyn could hear Oliver's puff of exasperation over the line. Who was he to judge? He was halfway around the world with the woman he loved. Where had she left off? *Six, seven, eight, nine, ten, eleven.* The points of the border blurred together a bit as she struggled to focus on them. *Twelve, thirteen, fourteen, fifteen.*

"Ravyn, it's okay not to be," Eva encouraged softly. "Can we..." Clearing her throat, she asked, "Can I video call? I want to see your face."

Opening her mouth to argue, then closing it again, Ravyn wondered, *Do you care for anyone? Do you need anyone?* The words echoed through her mind, mocking her. "Have Ollie leave," she ordered before softening her tone. "Please."

Her vamp hearing could pick up the whispers between the two even though Eva covered the phone, followed by the soft click of a door as Ollie left the room. Immediately Eva's face filled the phone screen.

"Ravyn? He's gone now. It's just you and me. What's going on? Is it Bash?"

Ravyn hiccupped as she tried to hold in a sob.

"I'm going to kill him," Eva threatened. "I don't care that he's Oliver's friend. He's a dead dog!"

"Thanks for that, but he doesn't deserve it. He only did what I told him to do."

"And what did you tell him to do?"

"Leave. Go home to his family." Biting back the sob that threatened to escape, Ravyn pushed a hand in her mouth to keep from saying more.

"But that's not what you wanted."

Damn, since Eva had embraced her succubus side, she'd become blunt. Being fed regularly by an endless font had strengthened her.

"It's what I said, but he said it first."

"Why did you say it, then? Clearly, it's not what you want or I wouldn't be feeling your sorrow every time I close my eyes."

"I'm sorry," Ravyn began. Eva had been through so much and deserved happiness as much as Oliver did.

"No, no, it's not like you're going to call Oliver or me and spill your feelings. Think of it like opening up without the hassle of opening up. We can skip the 'I'm okay' song and dance because I know you're not being truthful. And I'll ask again. Why did you tell him to leave if you didn't want him to?"

"Why didn't he ask to stay? He was making plans to leave at soon as the wendigo hit the ground," Ravyn whispered. "He wouldn't give me a chance to even speak."

"You also told him to go. How much can a wolf take? He's not impenetrable. You told him to go, but you wanted him to stay. If he'd asked to stay, you would have insisted he leave." Eva hesitated before continuing, "Ravyn, I don't believe you've ever asked anyone to stay or to come back."

It was true. Years ago, after decades of travel, she and Oliver had separated, and like every companion she'd known, she wished him well and traveled onward without looking back. But to her surprise, Oliver had continued reaching out for her over the years, and she found herself reaching back as well. Even though they weren't together, their friendship still connected them, but if Oliver hadn't tried so hard, she would have been completely alone.

"You have to sometimes be the one to look back and to ask someone to stay. It's raw and it's vulnerable, but that's the real stuff of life, of living." Eva explained to Ravyn, "It's okay to follow your heart. You don't have to always be alone; you're the person most deserving of love I know."

"I'm barely more than a monster," Ravyn admitted

softly. "I was made to be a monster and everyone leaves me because of that."

"Oh, sweetie, your sisters didn't leave because they had to. I've seen your dreams; you all were so young and just trying to survive in a world that you were unprepared for. The monsters were those who did that to you and made you think you're not capable or deserving of love. You did everything you could during those years to find your sisters. And even without seeing that, I would know that the woman who saved a random young girl nearly dead at the side of the road is no monster."

Silence for another breath. Ravyn wanted to deny it, wanted to hang up the phone, but found she could do neither in the hope that perhaps Eva was right. "I don't know if I can believe you. In the heat of passion many things are said. People don't come back and I don't go after them. It's sort of my thing."

"How can you be frustratingly the bravest woman I know, but simultaneously the biggest coward? Hiding away. And I know about hiding away—like recognizes like," Eva reminded her. "You're as deserving as me, as Oliver, as anyone. You're capable of great love and you're just as deserving to be greatly loved. Oliver says you hide away in your movies, your acting, just so you don't have to face being alone. Pretending to be seen and loved isn't the same as the real thing." Eva fell silent, waiting and listening.

Ravyn had made a horrible mistake, and

Tooth and Claw

immediately the self-doubt set in. Had she? Had he asked to stay? Had he assumed he was coming back before she made her horrible declaration? She hadn't asked him to stay; she'd told him to go. She didn't give him a chance to say he was coming back. Her immediate reaction had been to push him away.

How could she expect him to fight for her—for them—if she didn't? If her heart was breaking into a million pieces, his could be breaking into two million. Maybe? Even if he said no, then she wasn't any worse off. Either way, her heart would break. But if he said yes? If he said yes, the possibilities were endless. What was an eternity alive if you were alone? Even her sister Anya had recognized that a life worth living was one not spent alone. She'd sacrificed everything to be with the man she loved, and Ravyn was too prideful to even admit to the man she loved that... Wait... the man she loved?

"Eva, thank you. I need to go."

Eva sighed over the phone. "The plane isn't back yet, and Oliver says he doubts that you would fly commercial even to chase down the man you love."

More shuffling. Dammit, had Oliver never left the room?

"It will be there in about an hour or so and then it needs to refuel and set up the flight plan. We have another pilot and crew on standby as well. Take a shower," Eva ordered. "And Ravyn?"

"Yes?"

"Good luck," she offered before squealing, "Go get your man! And I'm here for you. You can count on it."

Ravyn gasped as the sound of Eva's own hand slapping over her mouth covered her words. "I mean…"

Oliver can't keep a secret for anything, Ravyn thought irritatingly. "Yeah, I got it, no pun intended there either." Damn him, she couldn't help that she needed to count things any more than he needed to watch television.

"He didn't tell me," Eva rushed out quickly, eyes widening in panic. "He didn't…"

Ravyn punched the off button on the phone before muttering, "I totally would have flown commercial." And damn them for sending the plane back to her yet again. It was Ollie's plane and it seemed to constantly end up on her coast.

But it didn't have to stay on her coast.

Chapter Twenty-Six

The wolf shall heed the raven's call

Ravyn hesitantly followed the small path that Sebastian's sister-in-law had pointed out to her.

Halfway over the Rockies, Ravyn's old fears returned. What if Toby's mother blamed her for what had happened? She didn't have a lot of experience with female wolves, but the ones she'd met over the years were fiercely protective of their young. And with the loss of her mate, the protectiveness would be exponential.

However, instead of being met by anger, she was met by the swift, firm hug of the taller woman. The boys had gone into town to watch a movie with some older members of the pack as well as her younger twins, while Sara was catching up on some needed household chores. And, Ravyn suspected, enjoying a bit of quiet time.

"Those boys sure can eat," she told Ravyn, sounding rather proud, "but surely, you know that." She led Ravyn into the homey kitchen where they sat at a well-worn, oversized wooden table which bespoke decades of meals shared among wolves. Ravyn held the warm teacup in hand, only accepting it to appease Sara's desire to extend hospitality when what she really wanted was to see Bash.

Looking at her cup, Ravyn began, "I owe you an—"

Placing a warmer hand onto Ravyn's, Sara gently shook her head. "No, you don't. Our men aren't like regular men. As much as we try to protect and coddle them, they're not like human men. You treated Toby—Tobias," she corrected herself. "You treated him right, and you treated him well. I sent him away because I was afraid of what happened to his father, and I was afraid of the path he was on. I couldn't talk to him or say the right thing. But you and Bash gave him what he needed. I can see the man he's becoming."

Blinking back tears, Sara smiled at Ravyn. "Plus you sent me another son. Kai is friend to the wolves, but he's also family now."

Choosing her words carefully after subtly tasting and testing the air in the home, Ravyn asked, "You're a witch? Not a wolf?"

Smiling in her kind and gentle way, the woman responded almost sadly, "Is that a question or an observation? But yes, I am. I grew up in the town instead of the forest, but I knew James and Sebastian for as long as I can remember. With so few paranormals, we tend to sort of gravitate toward each other regardless of our affiliation."

"Was it a problem… being different? I guess that's a stupid question. Obviously you're here, living with the pack and having his pups." Ravyn tried to wave off the need to know the answer. "I apologize. I overstepped and, well, I apologize for my nosiness."

Shaking her head, Sara considered her question, this time choosing her own words carefully. "As with any mating or marriage, some will be unhappy with it even if there are no differences. But for James, there was never any doubt and he never questioned Fenrir when he chose me as his mate. Sebastian, as well as most of the pack, welcomed me with open arms. For wolves, they're a progressive group." She laughed. "My family had a few more complaints for sure."

"Why would they? Are they prejudiced?" To be accepted by a wolf pack, any pack, was a great honor and surely even a coven would see it that way.

"No, not really prejudiced." Hesitating, she once again considered her words. "I don't want you to see my family in a bad light; they truly aren't bad people. They absolutely adored James and were nearly as heartbroken as us when we lost him. But to mate with a wolf changes your world. Our children were destined to only be wolves. If I had children with a witch or even a human, they would be witches or at least more likely to be. But a wolf? Our children would only be wolves. Both of our people's numbers have dwindled over the centuries, so it hurt my family knowing that my children would never add to the number of witches in the world."

"But they accepted it and the children?"

"Oh, yes. They were saddened by the loss of a future generation, the image they had held in their minds and hearts, but at the same time, who can argue against a god- or goddess-ordained pairing?" She laughed roughly as Ravyn watched her heart break over the loss of her mate.

"I'm so sorry. I didn't mean to bring up—"

"Oh no"—Sara sniffed—"it's wise to question such things. Losing James was the most difficult chapter of my life." After a moment's pause, she added, "Well, Toby's attack is a close second. But the children are what keep me going each and every day. James would want that. Wolves follow one another quickly to the afterlife, and although I look for the day I can meet him there, right now I'm needed more here."

Interesting. Ravyn's mind whirled. She'd always thought that mates' lives were entwined together and if one went, they both went. But Sara made it sound like it was, in fact, a choice rather than a destiny.

Apparently recognizing the realization that crossed Ravyn's face, Sara explained further. "A mating deemed by Fenrir does tie the lifespans together. Fenrir and the goddess chose wisely by our mating. If James had mated with a wolf, she would have joined him in the afterlife quite quickly. There would have been no chance of her living out a natural life without turning feral. But me being me… a witch…" She trailed off, considering. "That means I can be here for the children he left behind. Because the gods chose our pairing, our children still have a parent walking the earth with them. I'm here as long as my children need me or until my natural lifetime takes me."

Standing up, Sara gently removed the still full cup of now cool tea from Ravyn's hands. "Now, I don't want to keep you. I know it isn't me you're here to see. And to be honest, I'm thankful you're here. He's been out running as a wolf since he arrived. He's hurting, and I suspect you are too." Bustling around the kitchen, Sara fanned her face with a small tea towel while Ravyn watched her.

"Does it bother you? That I'm, well, me and he's a wolf?" After their conversation, Ravyn was hopeful that pack relations extended beyond witches and into other species.

"Oh, goodness, no!" Shock crossed Sara's face. "I hope he didn't tell you that?"

At the shake of Ravyn's head, she continued, "Ms. Sinclair, in our pack we grab a hold of any bit of happiness we can find for however long we find it. There can be so little happiness in the world, so grab it with both hands and hang on tight when Fenrir grants it to you. Our lifespan might not be as long as yours but, gods willing, Bash and you should have centuries to hold that happiness. The gods have a plan even if we can't see it. They wouldn't have made you mates if you weren't made for one another."

Mates? Ravyn questioned the word, rolling it over and over in her mind. When Sebastian looked at her, did he see a mate? Ravyn wished she'd taken the time to ask Sara more questions about being a mate. She was inexplicably drawn to Bash and hated for him to be out of the room. The last few days had been torture.

Was this why her heart felt like it was breaking into a million pieces after he'd flown halfway across the country? If he felt the same way, how could he have left?

Ravyn silently walked the shadowed path toward the cabin that Sara had directed her down, her eyes flitting about, searching for any sign that Bash had been that way recently. Sara had brought in the two-person security team who had accompanied Ravyn so that she could feed them a good meal, claiming that California cuisine had nothing on good old-fashioned home cooking. The men had hesitated, clearly torn between the promise of food and the necessity of protecting Ravyn. It hadn't taken much convincing from both women for them to accept that it was fine for Ravyn to walk the secure area of the pack's nearly-empty compound.

It didn't take long to find him. Or truthfully, for his wolf to find her. One moment she strolled along a quiet bend in the path and the next, his wolf stood in front of her before sitting on his haunches with a whine and what looked like a toothy smile.

"Hey you," she whispered, going closer to the shaggy, nearly white animal whose clear yellow eyes watched her intently before laying down, sitting his chin between his paws with an inviting whine and yawn. Stepping closer, she marveled at his beauty, before setting a tentative hand on his head and stroking the soft fur down his neck. Like his counterpart, the fur was pale, and slightly curly, but not nearly as long as how Bash wore his hair. "So handsome," she cooed, stroking the white-and-silver wolf who preened under her touch and words.

Before today, she'd only seen flashes of his animal. Bash had transformed when they left the wendigo's lair. One moment he was a man, then in the blink of an eye, he'd slid into wolf form, leaving behind a pile of clothes and shoes. In another blink, he quickly loped off to circle Bertrando's compound for others—survivors or minions.

There had been no chance to simply appreciate the beauty and the strength of the animal who seemed to preen under her touch. Nuzzling his muzzle against her, he leaned into her lap, soaking up the moment.

Too soon, the wolf stood up with a huff circling around as he backed up a few steps. Hunching over, the transformation began, and the wolf's form crackled and snapped into the familiar shape of the man who unfurled to stand up to his full height.

Naked.

Of course, his clothes didn't shift with him. Ravyn blinked slowly as her eyes adjusted, before belatedly remembering the pack of clothes Sara had sent off with her. She stood wide-eyed and, without a word, shoved the pack toward him.

Keeping his eyes on the pack, he sighed and then let out a sardonic chuckle as he pulled out the clothes. "Sara sent these?"

Ravyn nodded, keeping her eyes up on his face as he held up the pair of joggers Sara had packed.

With a grunt, he pulled them on, wiggling them up past his hips as Ravyn bravely kept her eyes on his face.

"She sent Toby's pants," he announced with his hands out to his sides. "And no shirt at all."

While Toby nearly had his uncle's height, there were at least two sizes separating the two. Allowing her gaze to drop, she snorted out a burst of laughter at the skin-tight black joggers hugging his legs, ending at his mid calves and sitting low and tight on his hips as far up as they could be pulled. "It could be worse. She could have sent Kai's." His shorter stature would have made wearing his pants impossible.

Nodding in agreement, Bash picked up a long strand of grass from the side of the trail and twirled it in one hand between two fingers. "Did you fly commercial out here or something?"

"Why does everyone keep acting like that's such a

big deal? I'm a two-thousand-year-old creature created by black magic and hell-bound demons. I literally kill people," Ravyn grumbled good-naturedly. For the first time in days, she felt the tightness in her chest release just a hint. "No, I did not, in fact, fly commercial. Apparently, Oliver likes sending his plane back to the west coast at every opportunity, just in case," she mocked, using finger quotes but softening her words with a smile.

Silence lay heavy between them as Ravyn struggled to find her next words, her chest once again drawing slightly tighter. Dammit, she had hours to figure out what to say on the flight over as well as the drive down. Others wrote words for her; she could always find the emotion to deliver the words, but they weren't her own. Yet another thing she'd grown lazy about.

"What are you..." Bash began just as Ravyn opened her mouth to say something, anything. "Go ahead," he offered generously

Ravyn groaned inwardly. "Your sister-in-law says you've been out here running in the wolf form since you came back," she offered weakly, still using someone else's words.

Bash didn't break eye contact but continued to twirl the long stem of prairie grass between his fingers. "I suppose I have been. My wolf hasn't been able to run completely free for a while. And it's only been a few days."

Ravyn knew it was partially her fault, or maybe completely. He hadn't cycled out any down time since he'd arrived on the mission. The wolf was only allowed free during the full moon and even then, it couldn't relax completely, running on borrowed land. It went against their instincts, no matter how much they trusted one another.

"I'm sorry for that. I'm glad he's got the chance now." The words sounded weak even as she said them and she nearly grimaced but was determined to keep an impassive face.

"Ravyn…" Bash sighed gently, looking more defeated than he had even in the face of Toby's injuries. Determination and revenge had filled his face then; now it was just sadness. "Why did you come here?"

"Why didn't you ask to stay?" The words shot out of her mouth before she could stop them. But once they were out, she didn't wish them back.

"Stay?" With a huff, Bash looked up at the sky as if begging Fenrir himself to give him the answer. "Why didn't you ask to come? Why didn't you ask me to stay? You told me to go," he reminded her with a frank look.

"I tell everyone to go," she whispered back, admitting it for the first time. "I tell everyone to go, and they go. Even you went." Swallowing the urge to remain silent and bolt, she pushed on, "Would you have stayed if I asked?"

"You didn't ask," he reminded her, tossing the frayed grass strand aside before crossing his arms across his chest. For the first time, his hair wasn't smoothed back into a bun or pony tail. Instead, the curls hung freely down his shoulders, slightly matted in places as well as decorated with twigs and forest debris.

"When you kissed me after… I got scared," Ravyn admitted. "I got scared and I pushed you away. I had words I wanted to say, but couldn't. And it seemed like you immediately were making plans to go. Plans to take Toby home. Plans to hunt down Ibis. None of those plans included me."

"After a battle isn't always the time to profess...things. Things said after the high of battle, aren't always sincere. I wanted to save you from that. Then you didn't give me a chance to include you in those plans. You immediately assumed the worst of me. And after that night together, I thought maybe we were more than that. I thought maybe you would want to be included in my plans or that you would include me in yours."

"It seemed safer not to assume," Ravyn confessed. "And we never had a chance to talk after that night. You were gone. I was gone..."

"Why are you here now? Are you finished being scared, Princess?"

A small smile broke through her trembling lips and she shook her head. "No, Thor. I'm terrified now."

"Why are you here?" he repeated, lowering his arms and taking a step closer.

The forest seemed to grow quieter around them as if awaiting her answer as well.

"I don't want to be alone," Ravyn began softly.

"So, you just want a warm body? You can pay for that! Hell, people—anyone—would pay *you* to be that warm body," he scoffed, folding his arms across his chest.

Ravyn felt her face warm as the first flash of anger flowed through her. This time it was her taking a step closer. Couldn't he just shut up and listen for once? Why was he so difficult all the time?

"No, you big dumb wolf," she began before a soft growl emanated from Bash's chest. Apparently, the wolf took offense to those words. "Not literally, of course," she quickly amended. "I want you, Bash. Only you and your wolf if he'll have me. I want to wake up next to you. I want to go to sleep next to you. I want to be where you are. Whether it be here in the Ozarks, somewhere in California, or anywhere in the world. I want to explore the world with you or stay at home with you. You and only you. When I'm close to you, I can imagine I have a soul and it soars when I look at you. When I'm not with you, my heart feels like it's stopped beating and is attempting to break into a thousand pieces."

Emboldened now, the words flew out as easily as if someone had written them for the two of them. "I don't know how you see us or if it's possible, but I would like to try. What good is eternity if we do it alone?"

The same question her sister had whispered to her when they'd hugged good bye. What good was it?

"Even if we only have your lifetime, I'd rather have that than nothing. I'm tired. I'm tired of being alone and tired of being afraid of losing."

Step by step, she moved closer and closer until she could reach up and gently pull a twig from a massive curl. "I was scared. I *am* scared, but I can't keep living in that state. You asked me before why I acted, why it was so important to me. It's because it's the one place I can safely let all my emotions play out. It's safe," Ravyn stressed, watching his face intently.

Does he understand?

"I can't suppress all my emotions, but when I get in front of the camera and become someone else, I can let it all out and then once the camera is off shut it all off again. And yes, yes, hide away from reality."

Sebastian's eyes flickered over her face, examining her for the truth in her words.

They were truthful. The most truthful she'd been in centuries.

Roughly, he admitted, "I'm not the easiest either."

"We can practice together; we can learn together," Ravyn volunteered, refusing to plead and refusing to let her pounding heart feel relief at his words. Was he going to let her down gently? Or what? A flicker of hope took hold in her heart despite her attempt to await his declaration.

"I'm not perfect." Another low growl emanated from his chest, as if his wolf agreed with his words.

"Neither am I," Ravyn promptly agreed, placing a gentle hand on his chest, where his wolf hummed in approval from her words and touch, flooding her with comfort and love.

If only the man would agree.

"You are so beautiful. The first time I saw you, you took my breath away." Sebastian pulled away, looking her earnestly in the eyes.

Strong, rough hands circled her waist, lifting her up to his nodding face.

Wrapping her arms around his neck, she lifted her chin to look him in the eyes. "Are we doing this?" she questioned softly, ready to say the words.

His low laugh reverberated through him as he nodded. "Yes, I think we're doing this." He hitched her up closer.

"Wait," holding his face in her hands to forced him to look straight into her eyes. "With no battle adrenaline or off the high of feeling you on my body, I need you to know. I. Love. You. Now and forever. I go where you go."

She wrapped her legs around him as he lowered his mouth to hers, and his wolf rumbled contently against her chest. "Princess, I love you with all my heart and soul. I will spend the rest of my days showing you all the ways I love you."

CHAPTER TWENTY-SEVEN

Under the light of the moon the wolf and the raven shall dance

With twigs and leaves enmeshed in both of their hair, Bash and Ravyn, feeling much more content and well loved, returned to the Moldover home.

The previously quiet house now bustled with life as Toby and Kai greeted the two of them, pushing each other out of the way to give Ravyn a hug in greeting. Already the stay had done wonders for Kai. No longer did he hang back in the shadows and Ravyn gave him an extra tight, careful squeeze.

The twins grew quiet when they entered. Frozen in place, they watched Ravyn with large, solemn eyes, not at all how Toby had described the little terrors. Bash had introduced the two solemnly: Penelope and Vincent. Kneeling to their height and a safe arm's length away from them, Ravyn offered a quiet, friendly greeting, careful not to show too much tooth. A tiny bit of her was saddened that Bash's niece and nephew were frightened of her. Family was Bash's reason for living and he needed his family to accept her. Ravyn was determined to show them that vampires might be different, but that didn't mean they were bad.

The little girl broke first, her tiny, high-pitched voice shaking in awe. "You were in our movie." Her little hand reached out toward Ravyn's hair, too shiny and enticing to ignore even with the added forest debris.

Not to be shown up by the bravery of his sister, Vincent added in a louder voice, but just as shrill, "You're much prettier in real life," before turning toward his brother and attempting to tackle him with a running leap.

Relief flooded Ravyn. They weren't scared of Ravyn the vampire; they were in awe of Ravyn the actress. She could work with that.

"Did you play hide-and-seek with Uncle Bash? When we play, my hair gets stuck in the bushes too." Pen innocently worked free a dead leaf from Ravyn's less-than-perfect hair. "Mama says if I braided it first it wouldn't turn into a rat's nest."

"And that's enough questions for our guest," Sara interjected, drying her hands on a kitchen towel as she examined the two, before nodding. "Food will be on soon," Looking toward Ravyn, she added lowly, "I don't know when you late ate, but some subsistence for you is being sent over from the pack house. Or you're free to wrestle the boys for a rare steak."

Ravyn smiled her thanks; Bash had told her that his pack were progressive in the ways some weren't. They were prepared and welcomed any visitors who came through their doors. That's why they'd known that bringing Kai here was a good idea. Kai's people at one time had worked side by side with a pack. They were returning him to his roots and giving him a family, a pack, at the same time.

"Are you guys moving back out here then or staying in California?" Looking between the two, Toby asked the question on everyone's mind as he bit into an apple. Apparently, the fact that they'd made up was clear to all. "Ma said Bash needed some roots somewhere. I hope you guys pick somewhere cool."

Sara perked up at the question but also managed to flush as her children outed her gossip.

"I don't…" Ravyn began before looking at Bash.

Bash waved a hand. "Maybe? Maybe both, maybe neither... We both have our work, but we're committed to figuring it out."

"I only have a few more years left in Hollywood this go around," Ravyn admitted. "Claims of plastic surgery and Botox only work so long. And as of late, other things have begun to look more enticing."

Bash gave her waist a tiny squeeze.

"Nothing has to be decided right away," he told the nosy group. "We have our entire lives. If she wants to stay in California, I'll be beside her. If she wants to live or travel elsewhere, I'll join her."

"Maybe a combination of both," Ravyn suggested to Bash as the group's faces volleyed between the two. "I'm open to cutting back before retirement. I'd wondered if my last offer might be my grand finale, so to speak, and I know Oliver doesn't require you to be so hands-on with every security job," she teased, knowing she would kill the next client if that were true.

"Sounds perfect." Bash kissed her head before adding, "Nothing has to be decided right this moment. Where we live and sleep doesn't matter as long as we're together."

Vincent let out a groan while Penelope giggled at her uncle's softer side. "Are they always like that?" Vincent demanded answers from Toby while he squeezed his brother's face tightly between his hands.

With a howl, Toby tickled his little brother. "Oh no," he whooped, "sometimes they're much, much worse."

"We've got this, Thor," Ravyn promised. "We still need to find my sister. She may be helpless for now, but I doubt she's going to give up hope that I can change her. If she regroups and gains a few witches, she'll be a danger to our family."

Our family. That sounded nice. *Our pack.*

The parts remaining of her sister were still out there. Despite the assurances by the witches that they would find her, Ravyn still felt responsible. Ibis might be powerless on her own, but she'd proven that wouldn't stop her. The conniving magic user would surely regroup and find other magic users to manipulate but for now, Ravyn could breathe easier.

"Together a pack is strong," Bash promised her, "and I swear to the Creator himself, that she will not ever get close to my mate again."

Mate.

Tooth and Claw

AMY NEVILLS